NOW PLAYING
Taking Back Mary Ellen Black

Starring

Mary Ellen Black...in the role of a spunky single mom determined to reclaim her identity after losing it (and everything else) in her recent divorce

Supporting characters

Jenna O'Brien...in the recurring role of brutally honest best friend

Amber Nowicki...as Mary Ellen's preteen daughter who's just beginning to understand what it means to have an identity

Shelby Nowicki...as Amber's pesky, attention-grabbing younger sister

Frank Black...as Daddy, Mary Ellen's first and most enduring love

Grandma Czerwinski...as a woman, wise *despite* her years

Mrs. Jacques...as friend, neighbor, cheerleader and benefactor

Nonsupporting characters

Eddie Nowicki...as a man whose broken dreams break him financially and emotionally

Louise Black...as Mary Ellen's hypercritical mother who is threatened by her daughter's strength and determination

Special guest star

Ryan "Rye" O'Brien...as the young, studly love interest

Lisa Childs

Award-winning author Lisa Childs has been writing since she could first form sentences. She grew up not far from the west side of Grand Rapids, Michigan, which was *her* dress rehearsal for creating Mary Ellen. At eleven she won her first writing award and was interviewed by the local newspaper. Now, with a wonderful husband and two young daughters, she is a veteran player in the trials, tribulations and joys of motherhood and marriage.

Readers can write to Lisa at P.O. Box 139, Marne, MI 49435 or visit her at her Web site, www.lisachilds.com.

LISA CHILDS

Taking Back Mary Ellen Black

TAKING BACK MARY ELLEN BLACK

copyright © 2005 Lisa Childs-Theeuwes

i s b n   0 3 7 3 8 8 0 5 7 X

This edition published by arrangement with Harlequin Books S.A.

® and TM are trademarks of the publisher. Trademarks indicated with
® are registered in the United States Patent and Trademark Office, the
Canadian Trade Marks Office and in other countries.

TheNextNovel.com

 HARLEQUIN®

PRINTED IN U.S.A.

With special thanks to my editor, Stacy Boyd,
for your help and support with all my books
but most especially for understanding how important
Mary Ellen is to me!

And for three of the strongest women I know, love
and admire—my sisters, Helen, Phyllis and Jackie.
With extra thanks to Jackie for providing the
mortgage brokerage information.

CHAPTER D-DAY
Divorce

Usually, the A, B, Cs start it all, the beginning of the alphabet, of words, sounds, books. In this case, the first chapter of my life will start with D, for divorce, which, in some ways, is really when my life began—when I first took back Mary Ellen Black.

My husband, ex-husband as of today, hadn't wanted her, hadn't even bothered to turn up at the courthouse to contest my asking the judge for my name back, the name I'd been born with but couldn't use again until I was told it was legal. Eddie hadn't contested my full custody of the girls, either; he knew pushover Mary Ellen would let him see them whenever he wanted. But he hadn't wanted, not since he'd walked out on us for the twenty-year-old waitress at the restaurant he owned—or barely owned. If what he'd convinced the Friend of the Court was true, the restaurant was losing so much money that he couldn't pay child support.

And so I was stuck where I sat, in my grandmother's car, in the alley behind my parents' house in the old West Side Grand Rapids neighborhood where I'd grown up and where I'd had to return after the bank had foreclosed on my gorgeous six-year-old house in Cascade. The repo man had taken my SUV, so I had Grandma's Bonneville to use since her cataracts prevented her from driving anymore. Of course, she could still keep track of ten bingo cards every Saturday morning at Saint Adalbert's.

Sitting in the car behind my parents' house wasn't going to help me figure out how everything had gone so wrong. I knew that, but still I couldn't summon the energy necessary to open the car door and crawl out. I'd done enough crawling when I'd begged Eddie to come back, to work things out, and then when I'd lost the house, I'd crawled home to Mom, Daddy and Grandma.

No, Mary Ellen Nowicki had done all the crawling; Mary Ellen Black was stronger than that. I didn't know much else about her anymore, but I knew that. Yet still I slumped on the bench seat of Grandma's old Bonneville. No wonder her blue-haired head didn't show above the steering wheel. This seat was low, really low.

I glanced over the wheel and around the alley. No yard. Just the big, square two-story house where I'd grown up, the alley and the detached garage. Inside the dark shadows of the garage, the tip of a cigarette glowed. Dad had knocked off early from the butcher shop and was checking his oil. That's what he told Mom he was doing when he was really out getting a smoke. Nobody checked his oil as often as Dad did.

If he wanted to talk to me, he would have stepped out. Despite living in the same house since the foreclosure on mine a few months ago, we'd managed pretty well to avoid each other. I was his little princess, and he had always sworn to protect me from all the bad things in the world. He couldn't protect me from this. And that hurt him more than it did me. I had grown up; I was responsible for my own happiness or lack thereof.

I pushed away the fleeting thought of turning the key in the ignition and backing out of the alley. Three blocks farther down was a bar, a strip club now. I could get a drink there. The fact that I didn't drink didn't erase the temptation. Hell, maybe I could even get a job there. Divorce was the only successful diet I'd ever gone on. My clothes hung on me.

A glance in the rearview mirror revealed lank, brown hair and a washed-out face. Yeah, like I could get a job in a strip club. I probably wouldn't make as much as I did waiting tables at the VFW, and the biggest tips the vets gave were quarters. That was the only job I'd been able to get since being out of the workforce so long, as a stay-at-home mom. Before dropping out of design school to marry Eddie, the only job I'd ever had was waiting tables. But the job at the VFW was only temporary while the regular waitress was healing from a broken hip.

With a heavy sigh, I threw open the creaky door. Dad couldn't ignore that sound. Nothing moved in the garage but the glowing tip of the cigarette. "Daddy?"

He eased out of the shadows toward the gravel driveway. "Mary Ellen?" He never lifted his gaze from the tip of his contraband.

"Yeah, Dad." *It's me. Look at me!* But we weren't that kind of family. We didn't face our problems. We ignored them until they walked out on us. We both turned our heads, scanning the alley and the little ribbon of grass between the garage and the house. "So, Mom's gone?" I asked.

"Yeah, she took the girls and her mother to the store. Thought you might want to be alone after…"

But I wasn't alone, not if he would look at me and talk to me, really talk to me. But that wasn't happening. And Mom, fearing that I might fall apart in front of my children, had taken them away. I wasn't allowed to fall apart with anyone. I had to do it in private, crying into the lumpy mattress of the foldout bed of the couch in the den. Maybe I didn't want to wait until I was alone in the dark to fall apart. Not that I *wanted* to fall apart. "That was nice of her," I said.

He nodded. "Yeah, your mother's really worried about you. So are the girls."

They'd had to leave their home and their school. Next week they'd start at a new school where they knew only a handful of neighborhood kids they'd met over the summer. Their world had fallen apart, and they were scared that I couldn't fix it. They weren't the only ones.

"I'll be fine, Daddy." Maybe if I repeated the lie enough, I'd believe it, like I had believed Eddie and I had had the perfect marriage, the perfect life…until debt and infidelity had eaten it away.

"Yeah, you've always been a smart girl, Mary Ellen. A real smart girl."

The laugh slipped out. Daddy was the only one who ever complimented me, but he didn't have a clue. "Thanks, Dad."

"I mean it, Mary." I detected a slight slur and eased closer to him. Beer breath almost covered the scent of blood and garlic that clung to his clothes. So he still had another stash from Mom; I'd thought he'd given up drinking years ago. With his high blood pressure and his high cholesterol, cigarettes and alcohol weren't just forbidden, they were suicidal. If only I'd had an ounce of my father's strong, stubborn will…

"Got another one, Dad?"

"Smoke?"

Since my eyes were already tearing up, I doubt I could adopt that vice of his. And I'd die if my girls ever saw me smoking. "A beer."

"You don't drink."

"I just started."

He hesitated a moment before easing into the shadows of the garage. His beefy hand wrenched open the rusty door of an old refrigerator, and he snagged the last two cans clinging to the plastic rings of a six-pack. "You sure?"

I wasn't sure about anything. "Is it cold?"

"Damn thing may be old, but this fridge could freeze a man's—" His round face flushed. "Let's just say it's got a lot in common with your grandmother."

Another laugh slipped out. Grandma Czerwinski was only cold to Daddy. She had never believed he was good enough for her daughter, her precious only child. And Daddy had been a hell-raiser in his day.

The cold can shocked me back to the important issues. I popped the top, breaking a nail. Icy foam fizzed over the rim and across my fingers. I slurped at it, ignoring the sour taste.

How low had I sunk if I had to get drunk with my dad? Lower than the bench seat in Grandma's old Bonneville.

Not an especially outgoing person, I'd only had one really good friend and a few friendly acquaintances when I'd married Eddie eleven years ago. The friend had hated Eddie and vice versa. And then I'd become too busy for the acquaintances and lost touch. I'd been a wife and mother, throwing myself into doing the roles until I performed them to perfection.

"So, did Morty the lawyer get you the money?" Dad asked after we'd slurped some more of our slushy beers.

Another laugh bubbled out, this one edging toward hysteria. "Money? What money?"

"The money, Mary. The child support and mortgage money that jerk owes you!" Getting Daddy worked up was never a good idea. Too much of the scrapper remained despite his gray hair and potbelly.

"There is no money, Daddy, nothing but a mountain of debt. Besides the house and the car, he's on the verge of losing the restaurant, too." And that would upset Eddie far more than losing me. He'd had to know his dreams were crashing down around him. Why not turn to his wife instead of some girl?

Dad slammed his fist down on the hood of his pickup truck, which he'd backed into the garage. "Son of a bitch!"

"Daddy—"

"I'll get you some money, Mary Ellen. We'll get your house back."

I shook my head. "I can't afford it. Not the taxes, not the utilities. It's too much for me."

"We got some money saved, your mother and I. I can borrow against this place. We'll help you!"

I smiled over the oft-repeated offer. I knew he meant it; that he'd mortgage away his life in a minute if he thought he could get mine back for me. But he couldn't. The house didn't matter anymore. Sure, losing it hurt, but I'd grabbed a few more things, what I could fit in the trunk of Grandma's car, and a Volkswagen would fit in that trunk. I had a twinge in my back from getting in an antique chest and a couple of oak end tables. I'd left the wedding portrait hanging on the wall, and the answering machine on the gleaming granite counter, the tape full of threats from creditors for Eddie to pay up.

I gulped a mouthful of frosty foam. "I'm better off without Eddie." I'd been saying it for the last six months, but I think this was the first time I believed it, that I *knew* it. I would be better off without the lying, cheating snake. The man who'd left me for the twenty-year-old was not the man I'd married. Something or someone, maybe even me, had changed him over the years.

"I'm sorry, Mary Ellen." The anger had left Daddy, and he sagged against the truck. His broad shoulders slumped, and his head bowed. "I shouldn't have made the marriage happen…"

"I could have said no, Daddy. I could have raised Amber alone. I know Mom and Grandma and you were worried about what people would think, about the neighbors…" I glanced toward Mrs. Wieczorek's house where curtains swished at a back window overlooking the alley.

"You think I care what people think?" He laughed. "I

leave your mother and grandma to that craziness. I wanted you to be happy. I wanted you to have what you wanted. I thought you wanted Eddie."

So had I. I'd loved the man he'd been *then*. "What are you saying, Daddy?"

"He told you. I'm sure he told you. A man like him—he'd like throwing it in your face—"

My stomach pitched more with dread than from the beer. "What?"

"I threatened him. I told him I was going to grind him up for hamburger, if he didn't marry you."

A shiver rippled down my spine. "You threatened Eddie into marrying me?"

Daddy glanced up, meeting my eyes for the first time. "He didn't tell you?"

"No." Now it made sense that Eddie hadn't been able to look at raw hamburger without gagging and why he'd never gone to Daddy's butcher shop. "But when he left, he said he'd never loved me. That's probably the only time he told me the truth." Because he certainly hadn't told me about the growing debt. I set down the beer can on the hood of the pickup truck.

"I'm sorry, Mary. I never meant to hurt you…"

I flung my arms around my father's protruding stomach, hugging him close. "You were just trying to get me what you thought I wanted, Daddy. And I did love him then." As much as I'd like to, I couldn't lie about that.

He patted my head. "I'll make this right, Mary Ellen. I can get you the money you need."

I imagined him, wearing his bloodiest apron and waving a meat cleaver, storming into Eddie's restaurant. Though I enjoyed the look I imagined on Eddie's face, I couldn't risk Daddy winding up in jail for a little payback. "No, Daddy, it's time I figure out what I want now and get it for myself."

A small smile played across his broad face. I'd like to think it was pride, but I knew it was pity. He didn't think I could do it—either figure out what I wanted or get it if I did happen to figure it out. But Daddy was the only one who ever complimented me, so I waited for some words of encouragement. And I waited while he swilled down the rest of his beer and then the rest of the one I'd left on the hood of his truck.

When the engine of a car rumbled in the alley, he still hadn't said anything. He just passed me a piece of jerky from a bag he carried in his pocket. "Your mother's back. Eat this, Mary, it covers up anything."

I bit into the spicy, dried meat. Garlic and cayenne pepper exploded on my tongue, warming it. No wonder Daddy always smelled like garlic.

Mom's minivan crunched over the gravel driveway as she pulled it next to Grandma's Bonneville. The side door slid open, and my six-year-old Shelby, vaulted out, blond pigtails flying. "Mommy!"

I caught the little bundle of energy in my arms and pulled her tight. "Hi, baby. Did you have fun with your grandmas?"

She nodded. "We got Happy Meals. Grandma Mary likes the nuggets."

I looked over Shelby's head and into the interior of the van. Ten-and-a-half-year-old Amber sat in the back seat, hunched over a book, her glasses slipping to the end of her little nose. My oldest was always buried in a book. Better, I thought than the sand where I'd had my head buried lately.

"Did you eat yet?" my mother asked as she slid out from behind the wheel. My mother's cure for every ailment: *feed it*. Her expanding waistline proved she took her own advice. But I couldn't eat her greasy cooking or listen to her well-meaning advice. She'd been doling out a lot of both since I'd come home, the way she had the first nineteen years of my life. She leaned close to me and sniffed. "Oh, you got into the jerky with your father."

That wasn't all I'd gotten into with Dad. More than the beer and the secondhand smoke, I'd gotten perspective. I was better off without Eddie, and I could take care of my daughters and myself. I wouldn't be trapped in this house another nineteen years.

The biggest part of taking care of the girls and myself would be obtaining gainful employment. Waitressing two nights a week at the VFW was hardly gainful, and the woman I was replacing, Florence, was a fast healer. With her new hip, she'd be back to work soon, and I'd be out of a job.

I'd gone on some interviews, but my résumé for the last decade hadn't impressed anyone enough to hire me, not when the job market was flooded with more qualified individuals than there were positions to fill.

Bleary-eyed, I stumbled down the steep back stairs to the kitchen. The house showed its age in design as much as decor. The main floor had no bathroom, so I had to climb upstairs from the den anytime I wanted to use it. But with Shelby's tendency to wait until the last minute, it was better that the girls be in the bedroom across the hall from it. In our house in Cascade, we'd each had our own bathroom. That was a luxury I doubted I'd be able to afford again.

Mom was already up, and she'd brewed the coffee. I needed caffeine and the classifieds. Today I was determined to get another job, no matter what it paid or what I had to do.

In her ratty robe and slippers, Mom was watching TV, sitting at the old, metal table; the one at which she'd sat since she'd been a kid. Even after marrying Dad, she'd never left home; her new groom had just moved in. Grandpa Czerwinski had died by that time, and the house had been too big for Grandma alone. Dad had also taken over the butcher shop where he'd worked since coming home from the navy. But neither Mom nor Dad had ever made their mark on the house or the store.

The kitchen counter was still the same worn yellow Formica it had always been. The walls bore the same lime paint and coordinating wallpaper with yellow and lime teapots. My last visit to the store had revealed the same worn vinyl flooring, the same setup; the only change there had been inflation. But Dad hadn't gone overboard. His meat prices were still the cheapest around.

Hadn't either of them ever wanted anything else, a life away from the West Side? I'd worked up the nerve to ask my mother once, when Eddie and I had moved to Cascade despite her protests that seventeen miles was too far away to move her grandchildren. She hadn't cared that I was *moving*, in fact she'd called me a snob for being ashamed of where I grew up. I wasn't ashamed; I'd just wanted more. She'd denied ever wanting anything else, had claimed she was happy, even though she never acted like it.

Back in high school, I had known I hadn't wanted this life. After graduation I'd enrolled at the local art college, and instead of working at the store, I'd waited tables at a restaurant in the city where I'd fallen for Eddie, the night manager. His dream to buy the restaurant had become mine. He'd painted a bright future for us far from the West Side, a future full of wealth and happiness. Whatever dreams I'd had of my own I'd abandoned for him. And now Eddie had abandoned me.

Time to move on. Time to move out again. But I couldn't manage that on my quarter tips. "Morning, Mom."

Mom turned from her fascination with the early-morning news. The years had taken their toll on her hearing as well. "I didn't see you there, Mary Ellen. Up long? Do you want some coffee?"

I'd already grabbed a mug, sloshed some thick brew into it and settled at the table across from her. Instead of turning on the furnace this early in September (in Michigan late summer was fall) she'd turned on the oven and propped the door open a little…just enough to take off the chill. I edged my chair closer to the heat. A glance at the teapot clock above the sink confirmed I had a little while before I had to wake the girls, so they'd get in the habit of waking up early for school. "Where's the paper, Mom?"

She lifted last night's edition from the vinyl chair next to her, but she never turned from the TV set. She had a thing for Matt Lauer.

"Thanks."

She nodded, her tight curls refusing to bounce. She'd overdone the home perm again, frying her dyed-black hair to frizz. Her purple robe was threadbare, but she refused to give it up for all the new ones my brother and I had given her over the years. She was a creature of habit, of routine, from her extra thirty pounds to her frizzed-out perm. Maybe she'd stayed on the West Side, in the same house, all these years, because she was *scared* of change.

After all the changes in my life the last six months, I could understand her fear. But then during a commercial break, she began the lecture I'd heard repeatedly since moving home. And I knew we'd never really understand each other.

"It's just too bad you couldn't have given Eddie a boy. I'm sure he would have stayed then. A man needs to have a boy."

I nearly dropped my head to the table. "Mom…"

"If only you would have drunk that tea. I did when I was pregnant with your brother, and look how that turned out…"

Despite the times I'd called Bart a retard while we were growing up, I couldn't slight him. He'd turned out well, but he and Daddy were not close and had never been. "He lives in another state, Mom. He and Dad never talk, never did."

"Your brother didn't want anything to do with the store." She sighed. "Your dad can't understand that. He took it over from my father, and carried on the legacy."

Bart had hated the store, hated the smell of blood, hated being called the butcher's boy, the taunt that had followed him through every year of school. "Bart had other obligations." To himself.

Mom nodded. "A wife and baby *boy* now." Her smug smile told me that once again, in her personal scorebook, Bart had won.

"And I'm happy for him, Mom. He has everything he's ev-

er wanted. His dream job in the city, and his dream girl."
Who had actually grown up right next door. Neither of them
had wanted to stay on the West Side.

Despite not knowing what my dream had become, I knew
it wasn't a fast-food job, which was all that the classifieds con-
tained.

Even though Matt Lauer had lured Mom's attention back
to the television, she made another remark. "I still think a
boy would have saved your marriage."

I crinkled the newspaper in my fist, but couldn't contain
my temper. "Mom, if Eddie had wanted a boy after having
Shelby, he wouldn't have gotten a vasectomy. He didn't want
a boy. That's not why he left. He left because he didn't want
me anymore."

Maybe he never had. If Daddy hadn't threatened to grind
him into hamburger, would he have married me? Back then,
he'd assured me that he wasn't proposing just because I'd been
pregnant. Back then, he'd told me that he loved me. But that
was a lifetime ago.

Mom's gaze stayed steady on Matt Lauer's smiling face.
"Maybe if you'd kept yourself up more."

My hand relaxed on the paper. I was too tired and too
scared about my future to fight with her. Even though Eddie
had gained weight and lost hair, I was expected to maintain
the face and figure of a supermodel? I'd never had one to begin with. "Mom…"

"Instead of working at the VFW, you should have gone
back to work with Eddie," she went on. "When you two
worked together, you were close."

That was the one thing she'd said that I couldn't argue with. Even after Amber had come, I'd still found time to hostess at the restaurant and to help with the menu and redecorating. But after Shelby had come along, I'd wanted to spend more time with my children, and then we'd bought the new house.

"While Jesus is out of town helping his brother on their family farm, I'm going to be working with your dad," she said. But for Daddy that would be more of a punishment than a privilege. He wouldn't be able to sneak as many smokes.

Despite how much I'd hated working there as a kid—the blood and garlic seeped into your pores, bled into your hands until it stained. I found myself volunteering, "Mom, let me do it."

"But Mary Ellen, it's already been decided..."

I owed my father for putting a roof over our heads. "Come on, Mom, let me. I need to pay you back for everything you're doing for me and the girls."

She waved a hand in dismissal. "You're our daughter. You've fallen on hard times..."

Obligation and charity. I fought the urge to cringe and gulped coffee instead. The back stairs creaked, and from the scent of garlic, blood and tobacco, I knew it was my father.

"I'd pay you to work with me, Mary Ellen," Dad said, not even bothering to hide the fact he'd eavesdropped.

"But—" Mom began her protest.

"Come on, Louie." My mother's name was Louise, but Dad always called her Louie. "You could only spare me a few hours a day in between carting your mother around town.

And I'm short-staffed right now. Jesus—" Dad pronounced his helper's name the biblical way instead of the Spanish way "—is gonna be gone at least a couple of weeks. I need the help."

Mom nodded, accepting what my father said as she always did, as I'd accepted all Eddie's lies. But Daddy didn't lie about anything other than beer and cigarettes.

From the earnest, pitying expressions on both their faces, I heard what had been left unsaid. *And Mary Ellen needs the money.* I couldn't argue with that even though I really didn't want to take his money. I'd only intended to help him out. "If you're sure…"

Dad nodded, his gray, sleep-rumpled hair standing straight up. "I don't expect anyone to work for free."

But I wish I could. I hated taking money from my parents, hated relying on their generosity to put a roof over my family's head. But it was either Grandma's outdated house with the oven heating the kitchen, or a box on the street.

My first week on the job I thought Dad was running a special. But the business didn't let up during the couple of weeks following that. Then it occurred to me that all the neighbors weren't patronizing the store for the kielbasa and kishka. *I* was the fresh meat, the fodder for their gossip mill. Everybody wanted to know how badly little Mary Ellen Black had failed. Standing behind the meat counter in a bloodstained apron, I didn't have to say a word. They tsked. They commiserated. They told me how I was better off without the SOB. And most of all, they rubbed it in. Maybe they didn't mean to. Or maybe they did. Maybe it was just human nature to feel better about oneself when someone else was doing badly.

For instance, after her commiserations, Mrs. Klansky flashed pictures of her grandchildren, who are enrolled in private schools because her son-in-law is such a good provider. She also pointed out that her daughter wouldn't have to work, but reminded me of how ambitious Natalie, the prominent lawyer, has always been. Now, maybe I should have been happy that Natalie has done so well, that Natalie doesn't have to move back home with her mother even if her old man was screwing a twenty-year-old cocktail waitress. But my humiliation was still too fresh. And I felt a little bit like Mrs. Klansky had kicked me while I was down. So I wished that Natalie would leave her prestigious job and her perfect family and run off to live in poverty with her pool boy.

But I figured Natalie and her family were pretty safe. None of my wishes had been coming true lately, or Eddie would have been written up in medical journals for a part of his body inexplicably shriveling up and falling off. And that hadn't happened. Where was the justice? Not that I'd actually seen Eddie lately to know my wish hadn't come true. Despite his inability to support them, I had agreed that he could see his children. I couldn't deprive the girls of a father, although he could.

But as Amber had pointed out, in one of her rare moments of openness, Eddie had never been around much, at least not the last few years. The restaurant had been his child much more than his flesh-and-blood daughters. Once, I'd admired his dedication to support us. Like my father, Eddie had called me his princess and had wanted me to live in a castle. That had been his excuse for working so hard to provide his wife and daughters with everything we deserved. The truth was, the restaurant had been his whole existence. Despite his twenty-year-old waitress, it probably still was. The risk of losing it had to be killing him. Like my marriage, this was another thing I had to thank my father for. For our wedding he'd given Eddie the money for the down payment to buy the restaurant from his employers. But I couldn't be mad at Daddy. Unlike Eddie, he'd been involved in his daughter's life. Granted, too involved, but he'd had the best of intentions.

As polka music filled the store, vibrating around the scent of raw pork and garlic, I reminded myself of that. "Daddy, when is Jesus coming back?" I pronounced it the correct way.

"Jesus?" Daddy asked, in the biblical way. With a sigh, I swallowed a Spanish lesson. If after years of working with Jesus, Daddy hadn't learned, I wasn't going to be able to teach him. Jesus had inspired other additions to the store, though. Chorizo and farmer's cheese and fresh tortillas. Daddy's store met the needs of a blending neighborhood, and his business thrived. Probably even when I wasn't around for the neighborhood to wallow in my humiliation. Too bad my presence hadn't attracted this kind of business to the VFW. I might have made more than a handful of quarters a night.

"His cousin Enrico just stopped by. I was talking to him out back." And here I'd thought he'd just been sneaking a smoke. "Jesus should be back in three days."

Sounded a lot like the homily I'd just heard the Sunday

before. Going to mass was a requirement when living at home. To add to my humiliation, the girls had told Mom how rarely we'd gone before, only on Easter and Christmas. But the restaurant had been closed on Sundays, and between sleeping late and watching football, it was the only time that Eddie had actually been with his family. My time would have been better spent lighting candles to secure my future, as Grandma said. Figuring that at her age the end was near, she lit a lot of candles. Good thing Saint Adalbert's didn't have a sprinkler system, just a leaky roof.

"Don't worry, Mary Ellen."

I pulled myself from my maudlin thoughts. "What?"

"Don't worry. As you can see, business is good. I'll have enough work for you and Jesus." Knowing Jesus worked circles around me, I doubted it. And I didn't want it. The apron, the false sympathy of neighbors, the polka music, the raw meat and garlic smell of fresh kielbasa. I enjoyed the VFW more. Too bad Florence was coming back this weekend.

"Dad…" I was tempted. A job I disliked was better than no job at all.

"It's fine, Mary Ellen. You'll earn enough money here for your girls' clothes and lessons and stuff. You don't need any more than that."

"What?"

"You've got a roof over your heads—"

As all the neighbors had chortled, little Mary Ellen Black was living with her parents. Yeah, it was better than a box. But it wasn't my home. Heck, it wasn't even Dad's home, not when he had to smoke and drink in the garage. "I want my own house, Dad."

"You said you couldn't afford it, honey."

"Not that house." That house had never been mine, either. It had been Eddie's. I had decorated it. I had filled it with the smells of home cooking and fresh potpourri, but it hadn't been my dream house. Like the restaurant, that new multilevel house in the suburbs had been Eddie's dream. I'd always preferred the character of older houses. But would I ever be able to afford one?

"Then what? You want another house?"

"I don't know." Maybe I didn't need a house; a condo, an apartment, anything away from the West Side and my mother.

"Mary Ellen..." The bell dinged above the door, announcing the arrival of another customer. And so my employment from hell continued.

I hadn't told Dad or Mom yet, but I intended the day before Jesus came back to be my last. I was passing over working at the butcher shop in favor of something, anything else. Not that I'd figured out my dreams...

They say a girl can dream? Not this girl. I can bake cookies, drive daughters to gymnastics and Girl Scouts and decorate a house like nobody else. Now that I had current experience waiting tables and providing customer service in a shop, I'd find another job. I had an interview down at Charlie's Tavern, and if they didn't hire me, I could always make Eddie give me back my old job at the restaurant. That was the least support he could provide; I'd certainly make better tips than at the VFW.

Mrs. Klansky returned for more pork chops and to kick me again. She brought photos of Natalie's six-bedroom contemporary to flaunt in my face. The stark white color scheme inspired nothing in me but a need to grab up a paintbrush.

"So she doesn't have time to decorate, huh?" I asked as I wrapped the chops, purposely picking out the fattiest ones.

"Well, she's really busy..." Mrs. Klansky peered at her own photos.

"Can't afford a decorator then?" What about a pool boy?

Dad snorted beside me, but amusement, not reproach, glittered in his green eyes. He might like the extra sales, but he didn't like people kicking his little girl.

"All that white is the thing, you know," she argued, all bluster.

I snorted now. "Ten years ago, maybe."

"Well, at least she has a—" She stopped herself, not out of sensitivity, but because Dad had lifted his cleaver and sliced neatly through a rack of a lamb. He was the best butcher in town.

"I'm sure she's much too busy to worry about a house, anyhow," I said in a sweet tone. The same one she'd used when telling me that I'd surely find another husband, someday... Like I wanted another husband! Not!

I wanted a job, where people didn't come in for raw meat with a side of gossip. After I rung up her purchase and she'd left, Dad patted my shoulder with a bloodstained hand. Although the health department now required them, Dad hated plastic gloves and refused to wear them. And as I could attest, the blood seemed to seep through them, anyhow.

"Why don't you knock off early? Things are slowing down, and your mother mentioned this morning that she could use an extra for her weekly bridge game."

More old ladies wallowing in gossip? I shuddered.

He laughed. "Mrs. Klansky won't be there. And they really do seem to have fun."

I couldn't remember the last time I'd had fun on my own. I had fun with my children. Although Amber spent most of her time in a book, she could be relied on for an occasion amusing comment, and little Shelby was a regular comedienne. But I needed my children to rely on me, not me on them. "Yeah, maybe you're right."

And that night I would tell both my parents that I wasn't coming back to the butcher shop to work. After what I'd seen in my few weeks of employment, I probably wasn't coming back to purchase anything from it any time soon, either.

The bell dinged again. "Take care of this last person and take off. I'm slipping out back a minute..."

"To check your oil," I finished for him as he reached for his cigarettes.

"Don't tell your—"

"Mother," I finished again with a giggle.

"You two still do that," said a familiar voice.

Any fleeting amusement fled. I could handle playing bridge with Mrs. Klansky better than I could handle this. Having my oldest, closest friend from school see me down and out. Jenna O'Brien. Jenna wouldn't fantasize about Eddie's dick falling off if he'd cheated on her. She would have grabbed up Daddy's meat cleaver and taken care of that problem herself. Despite being petite and gorgeous, Jenna had balls and if her husband had cheated on her, she'd have his in a glass jar to warn anyone else from making the same mistake. God, I'd missed her.

"Still do what?" I asked like it hadn't been nearly eleven years since I'd talked to her last…shortly after my wedding, in which she'd been my maid of honor, when she'd helped me into my dress and told me point blank that I was making the biggest mistake of my life. Was she back in my life now to say *I told you so*? Should I have listened to her? Should I have had her help me back out of that hypocritical white dress and out of the church? She'd offered, and I'd turned her down.

"That thing you and your dad always do…" I caught the wistfulness in her voice. Jenna's dad had died when she was eight.

I shrugged, still not meeting her eyes. "Yeah, some things never change. Guess it's just a bad habit."

"Heard you kicked your other bad habit." Like on my wedding day, she was offering me the gracious way out.

Waddling down the aisle five months pregnant, I'd displayed little grace then. Why start now? And since I'd chosen Eddie over her, Jenna deserved to gloat. "Kicked him? I wish I had. But hell, no, I packed his bags so he could kick me aside for a twenty-year-old cocktail waitress. I actually packed his bags for him."

And then, bracing myself for pity or triumph, I met her gaze. I didn't have to guess what was in her big brown eyes, the amusement bubbled out with her laughter. "You packed his bags?"

"I thought he was going on a golf trip. Never saw it coming."

She shook her head, brown curls dancing around her shoulders. "You saw it coming on your wedding day. You just didn't want to face it."

"So you've come to say I told ya so?" I got up the nerve to ask.

A trace of bitterness passed through her dark eyes. I'd hurt her all those years ago, and she hadn't deserved it for just being a friend. She sighed. "Where's the fun in that?"

"Fun?" There was that word again.

"Naw, that's not why I came."

Enviously I eyed her tiny figure. Obviously she hadn't come for the fatty pork chops. "So why did you come?"

"I was playing bridge at your house—"

"You were?" I had imagined a group of women closer to Grandma's age.

She sighed. "Yeah, Mom suckered me in, and I had a minute. Anyway they sent me to get you." No doubt she wouldn't have come for me on her own. Unlike the other old neighbors who had wanted to rub my nose in my misfortune, Jenna hadn't even cared that much…not after all these years. "We could use another person or two."

"For bridge?"

She glanced toward the back door and lowered her voice. "For poker. You in? I heard you could use the money."

Following suit, I lowered my voice. "They play for money?"

She laughed. "Hell, yes!"

Damn. Did I know Mom and Grandma at all? Apparently not. "Well…"

"Or would you rather stay here for all the neighbors to wallow in your misery?"

"You know about that?"

"I grew up only a few doors down from here. I know about that." She'd had her own misery for the neighborhood to wallow in. Her old man hadn't exactly died from natural causes, unless it was natural for a man to drunkenly fall down his own basement stairs and bust his head open. And then there were the skeptics who had always wondered if Jenna's mom hadn't gotten sick of being knocked around and knocked him for once…right down those basement stairs to the unforgiving surface of the concrete floor.

"So you coming? Or you love working here too much to lose the apron for a couple of hours?" Jenna. Eleven years hadn't smoothed her sharp edges any, edges she'd no doubt developed to fend off the pitying pats of the neighborhood, for the poor little O'Brien girl.

Even after all this time, I could be more honest with her than I could be with my family…or sometimes, myself. I lowered my voice more. "I hate working here."

"Figured as much. You try to get something else yet?"

I nodded. "I've got an interview at Charlie's Tavern."

"So you like waiting tables? Is that what you want to be when you grow up?"

"I don't know what the hell I am now, let alone what I want to be."

The amusement left, and concern flooded her eyes. "Ah, Mary Ellen…"

"Don't feel sorry for me. I feel sorry enough for myself," I admitted.

"And working here isn't going to help that." She blew out a breath. "And if you think it's bad here, Charlie's is the neighborhood bar. It'll be worse there. I have a job opening. Mom said I should mention it to you."

Jenna had always been close to her mom, even more so after her dad's death. She was fiercely protective of the woman who'd been through so much. And she never disappointed her. If Mrs. O'Brien hadn't told her to, Jenna wouldn't have brought up the job to me. Probably wouldn't have come to see me at all.

She hurried to add, "It's only temporary. My processor— I'm a mortgage loan officer, by the way—"

Like I didn't know it. Mom bragged about Jenna as if she was one of her own children. And with the amount of time she'd spent at our house growing up, she very nearly was.

"Yeah, I know. You're doing very well." And I wasn't jealous, not like I was of Natalie. I'd never begrudge Jenna any of her success because I knew how hard she'd worked for it. She'd always been ambitious, like Eddie. Maybe that was why they'd hated each other; they'd been too much alike. Then. Not now. Because Eddie hadn't ever achieved what he'd hungered for. Whereas even Jenna's tailored business suit, a rich burgundy suede, shouted out her success as loudly as my mother did. She looked great, but she shrugged off my compliment.

"Well, interest rates are good right now, so we're busy. And my processor, the person who handles all my paperwork to make sure the loan closes, is pregnant. She wants to take it easy. She'll come back after she has the kid. But she's as big as a house now and needs to kick back. You in?"

I blinked. "What? The poker game?"

"The job, you interested?"

"Working for you?"

"It's crazy, demanding work. But you don't have to wear that apron."

I dragged the offensive garment over my head and tossed it on the counter. Yeah, it was temporary. I was becoming my own temp agency. Someone off with a hip replacement or a maternity leave, send in Mary Ellen Black. But I wouldn't be handling raw meat. And hopefully I'd make more than quarters and hear a lot less pity over my divorce.

And maybe while her processor kicked back, I could figure out just exactly what I did want to be when I grew up. Hopefully, she'd be off a long time with this pregnancy and baby, because if I hadn't figured it out in almost thirty-one years, I didn't like my chances of figuring it out in six weeks. "Yeah, I'm interested."

Jenna nodded as I came around the counter. "And what about the poker game? You in?"

"Since they're playing for money, I guess that depends on what you're paying me," I hedged.

She glanced around the small store; we were the only two inside. "Cash, or that creep might sue you for alimony."

Just like Jenna, always thinking, even when I wasn't. Just what the heck did go on inside my head? Only the orchestra of crickets singing?

"And he would," Jenna continued. "Creep never deserved you."

That was why Jenna and I had stopped being friends. Because of her and Eddie's mutual animosity, I had had to choose between them, a choice I shouldn't have had to make. Now it was clear that I shouldn't have dropped her friendship. "I'm sorry."

She shrugged, too proud to admit if I'd hurt her. But pain showed in her dark eyes. "You were knocked up, scared, and pressured by your parents."

And she would know that because she'd always known everything about me. "Yeah. And in love. I really loved him. How stupid was that?"

"Cut yourself a break. It happens to the best of us."

"Not you."

She lifted her ringless left hand, but a faint indent marred the third finger. "I was."

"Was not!" I ignored the pang of hurt over not being invited to her wedding. Why should she have invited me? We hadn't been talking after my wedding day.

"Your mom never told you that?"

"She mentioned something once, but it was around the holidays and she was making rum balls. Mom's never completely lucid when she's making rum balls."

Jenna chuckled and grabbed my arm, tugging me toward the door. "Mr. Black, we're leaving for the bridge game."

"Have fun!" my dad called from the back, a puff of smoke drifting in through the open door.

Jenna's car waited at the curb, a black Cadillac. She clicked a switch to unlock the door, and I stepped over the leaves in the gutter to crawl inside. "God, I stink like the store. You sure you want me in here? I can walk."

"Shut up and buckle up," Jenna said as she slid behind the wheel. "You're fine."

No, I wasn't. But talking to Jenna again after all these years gave me hope that I might be. After all, I wasn't the only one with a newly ringless hand. I'd pawned mine to pay the cheap, neighborhood lawyer. "So tell me about your marriage."

She laughed with no amusement. "I fell for a pretty face, a very pretty face."

"That makes more sense than falling for Eddie. Nobody could ever call him pretty." Thank God the girls didn't look a bit like him. When we'd first met, I had thought he looked like Andy Garcia. Now he looked more like Danny DeVito.

She laughed again, in agreement, but no resentment flared in me. How could I resent the truth? "So he was pretty. Tell me more," I urged.

"You know, Mom was right. Pretty is as pretty does. Never could figure out what that meant until it was too late. He was in construction. So picture the big, hard bod. Strong, silent type. Mom also says beware of the quiet ones, still waters run deep. I don't know about deep, but he ran all around."

"On you?"

She snorted. "Yeah, go figure. Guess I worked too much for him." She'd always been so driven. Growing up poor had given her ambition.

"But he worked a lot, too. Out of town. Building houses." She snorted again as she maneuvered the Cadillac through the back alley to my parents' house. "Playing house was more like it."

"So how'd you find out? Did he finally tell you?"

"Stupid ass had my little brother working with him—remember Rye?"

As a thirteen-year-old too small for his age. "Yes."

"Well, Rye picked up on it. Told him to come clean. So he did…on Christmas Eve. Merry freakin' Christmas, huh?"

"So you killed him, right?"

She laughed again as she jerked the Caddy to a halt behind my mom's minivan. "I'll never tell."

"It's me, Jenna. You'll tell me." It was my way of saying I hoped we could be close again, as close as we'd been when we'd told each other everything.

She stared at me for a minute, dark eyes cautious, reminding me that I'd betrayed her trust as much as her ex had. Then she sighed. "Yeah, I probably will. But right now, I'm feeling lucky. They were playing five-card stud when I left, and your granny was kicking ass."

"Grandma?"

She nodded. "Yeah, she's a shark."

Did I know any of the women in my life? Grandma and Mom played poker. And Jenna had gotten cheated on, too, just as I had. I would definitely have to pay more attention to my daughters, make sure I knew them completely. Then maybe, someday, I'd find the time to work on knowing myself.

"You in?" Mom asked as she expertly shuffled the deck of playing cards and dealt them out to the women sitting around our dining-room table. No, this wasn't a bridge game. The dainty teacups and little cakes and cookies were a bit deceiving. But a pile of brightly colored chips in the center of the lace tablecloth gave away the real game. And so did the bland poker faces of the women sitting around the table.

Bluffing. I knew the look. I'd seen it on Eddie's face often enough these last couple of years. "Sure, deal me in." Patting my purse that bulged with quarter tips, I slid onto a chair between Grandma and Jenna.

And memories filtered through my mind. Grandma had taught me how to play this game with my dolls during teatime. How well could I remember her lessons? Apparently pretty well. A couple of hours later, I pushed back from the table, my pot sliding toward the edge. I'd done well. Real well.

Or they'd let me win out of pity. But I was getting as good at spotting pity as I was at recognizing bluffing. And their resentful faces, flushed from the tea and the game, told me they didn't pity me now. I stood, swaying a bit. After the first sip, I'd discovered this tea wasn't simply brewed. It was laced heavily with rum.

"Are you okay?" Jenna asked. "She always got sick whenever we used to drink," she shared with our mothers.

I wasn't so drunk that I couldn't remember and realize she was right. And here I thought I'd stopped drinking because I'd lost my virginity to Eddie the last time I'd gotten drunk. And like a good, God-fearing Catholic girl I had intended to wait for marriage. I really had. But I think it's kinda like that chicken-and-egg thing, because I probably wouldn't have married Eddie if I hadn't had premarital sex with him and gotten pregnant. Love aside, I'd been too young.

"Are you getting sick?" Mom asked, her blue eyes narrowing as she studied me.

"No, I'm fine." If I kept repeating it, I'd believe it. "I got another job today and won the pot." And maybe I could rebuild my friendship with Jenna, too. Life really was good.

"The girls'll be home soon from school," Mom reminded me. The public-school bus dropped them right in front of the house.

They couldn't see me like this. They wouldn't understand their mother being drunk. *I* didn't understand their mother being drunk. Once I'd known it wasn't just tea, I should have stopped drinking. I should have been the responsible one…as I'd been for the last eleven years.

I'd lapsed. And even while the rum and almond cookies roiled through my stomach, I didn't really regret joining the game. And I really didn't want it to end.

Since they'd started their new school a couple of weeks ago, if I wasn't working at the VFW, I'd made a point of being home when Amber and Shelby got off the bus. I wanted to make sure they settled in, made friends and that nothing had gone wrong during their day. I hated the days I wasn't there; they'd already lost the attention of one parent as he wallowed in debt and his affair. They couldn't afford to lose me. Guilt settled heavily on my shoulders.

Mrs. O'Brien, voice soft, spoke close to her daughter's ear. After a second, Jenna sighed and nodded. "If you promise not to puke in the car, you can come along to an appointment with me," she offered, no doubt at her mother's urging, "that'll give you an idea of what I do, so you understand what you'll have to do when you start working for me Monday morning."

"I really should…"

"Heck, go along," Grandma urged. "This morning I promised to show the girls a few card tricks when they got home. Obviously I taught you well." Behind her cat's-eye glasses, her left eye closed in a wink. Had she let me win? She was so good to me, to my girls, too.

I wasn't the only adult in my children's lives. Grandma, Daddy, and even my mother were great with them, loved and lavished attention on them. Wasn't the saying that it took a village? I winked back. "Thanks, Gram. You sure did teach me well."

Swaying on my feet, I turned toward Jenna, not too proud to accept her offer. "You're going to work?"

"Doing a re-fi for Lorraine. She runs the beauty shop around the corner from your pop's store. Come along."

I could savor my little buzz a while longer. And talk to Jenna some more. Eleven years was too long without her, without her brutal honesty. "Gram, you really don't mind watching the girls?"

She shook her head, jostling her blue curls. "Go, have fun."

"We won't be long," Jenna offered as she vaulted to her feet. I envied her balance and energy.

"Bring along your winnings," Mom chimed in. "Maybe Lorraine can do something with your hair." Leave it to Mom to sober me up. Just like having a boy, I bet she thought that having nicer hair might have kept Eddie from straying.

"Thanks, Mom."

Jenna tugged me toward the door. "She still gets to you."

I sighed. "Yup, sad but true, and now she has even more ammunition."

We climbed into the Cadillac and peeled out of the alley just as the bus was arriving at the front of the house. "I'll come in—meet the girls when we get back," Jenna said. She'd never seen them before. How could we have gone from such good friends to no communication whatsoever?

Shame at letting Eddie take over my life had me glancing out the window, and I caught a blurry reflection of myself in the side-view mirror. I looked washed out, old. And I wouldn't be thirty-one until January, the new year. Would I find Mary Ellen Black by then?

I turned back to Jenna, who, despite her several cups of tea, handled the car with expert skill. It was neighborhood legend how well the O'Briens held their liquor... until Mr. O'Brien had fallen down the basement stairs. Before then, drinking had never made him clumsy, just mean. Jenna's hair curled around her face in shiny, chocolate-colored waves. Despite her divorce, her clothes didn't hang on her. I didn't want to be Jenna. I knew I didn't possess an ounce of her drive or ambition. But looking at her now, I knew I wanted to be better than me.

"I have no office skills," I warned her, worried how much I'd disappoint her, especially since she'd only made the offer because of her mother. I was more capable of waiting tables at Charlie's Tavern or Eddie's restaurant.

"Can you dial a phone?" she asked.

"Well, yeah."

"And you took typing classes with me and were a helluva lot better at it. You'll be fine, Mary Ellen."

I wanted to believe her. I shifted my purse on my lap, the weight of my winnings lying heavy against my thighs. "So you think Lorraine can do something with my hair?"

She laughed. "Don't let your mother get to you."

The years rolled away. We were carefree teenagers again...or as carefree as teenagers ever were. At least, we had been more carefree then than the two divorced women we were now. "Easier said than done. I've gotta get out of that house."

"How did you lose the house? You have Morty the lawyer represent you?"

Heat rose to my face. "Morty was all I could afford. And the bank got my house. The bank got my car, too."

"So you have nothing." Her voice held none of the morbid fascination of the other people from my past who had pointed that out to me over the last few weeks.

"Just my name. I took that back. Most people—" especially Mom "—didn't think I should, that I should have left mine the same as the girls'. But I wanted it back." And for once I'd gotten what I wanted.

"I never took Todd's," Jenna said. "I'd already crossed over from real estate to the mortgage company, had name recognition."

"Morty did make sure that I wasn't responsible for any of the debts Eddie had racked up during our marriage. You were right about him." Even though it had taken years for him to become the loser she'd always thought he was.

She lifted a hand. "Wish I'd been right about Todd. It's hard to see when you're too close."

"You owe Rye for making him tell you."

"I gave him a black eye."

"Your ex or Rye?"

"Rye." She'd always had a bad temper. A rueful smile lifted her mouth as she slammed the Caddy to a stop outside the pink stucco building that housed Lorraine's Hair Salon.

From that name, I concluded that maybe I wasn't the only person lacking imagination around here. Lorraine, a heavyset, bleached blonde, settled the pink phone back on her counter as we walked in the door. A few heads lifted from magazines as a handful of women sat under droning dryers. A couple of the neighborhood women waved.

"Hey, Jenna," Lorraine said, then turned on me. "Mary Ellen, your mama was right. That hair needs some serious help. Have a seat!" She spun a chair toward me and pointed to the cracked vinyl seat. "Sit. I won't take all your winnings. But we gotta do something about that hair. Gotta liven up your look."

"We have an appointment, Lorraine," Jenna reminded the beautician. Despite the prosaic name of her shop, a gleam in Lorraine's eyes suggested she had an imagination, all right. She was probably imagining me in some big-hair Dolly-do close to her own style.

"I just came along on Jenna's appointment to understand what she does. But thanks, Lorraine." *For insulting my lank, uninspired hair that is, of course, the sole reason my husband left me for another woman.*

"Sit!" she said again, hands on her hips.

"Lorraine, come on," Jenna interrupted on my behalf again. "The re-fi. I'm going to save you millions or less."

Lorraine snorted. "A lot less since I don't have any millions to save. The papers you wanted are all ready and in that folder on the counter. So stop being a businesswoman for a minute and be a friend, Jenna O'Brien. Tell Mary Ellen that hair needs help if she wants to land another man."

Panic pressed down on my chest, leaving me just enough breath to exclaim, "I don't want another man!"

"Still pining for the old one?" Lorraine goaded.

I snorted now. A sound I hadn't thought I could make. "God no, I just don't want another husband."

"A new do won't get you a marriage proposal," Lorraine began.

"But it might help you find some young stud for hot sex," Jenna chimed in distractedly as she flipped through the folder of Lorraine's financial records.

Hot sex sounded good. But maybe that was just the allure of the unknown. It had been good with Eddie for all but the last couple of years. But I don't think I'd ever had *hot* sex. The possibility of getting some lured me to the chair. That and the rum still humming through my veins. I'd hardly settled back against the vinyl seat when Lorraine whipped a plastic cape around my shoulders. "So a new haircut can get me hot sex?"

Lorraine and Jenna laughed in unison, the husky harmony hinting that they'd both had hot sex at least once. "It'll take more than a cut," Lorraine said, walking in a circle around my chair.

I was glad she did that rather than spinning me. I don't know what had me more worked up, the idea of changing my hair—or the idea of hot sex. But apparently Lorraine didn't think redoing my hair would be enough to get it. No doubt I needed exercise, new clothes, new makeup, new attitude…

"A dye," Lorraine said, bobbing her double chin in agreement with her own wisdom.

"Red," Jenna said with the firmness of conviction.

"Red?" I gasped.

"You always wanted red hair."

News to me. I'd had wants back then besides getting out of the West Side? "I did?"

"You wanted to be Julia Roberts in *Pretty Woman*."

"I wanted to be a prostitute?"

Jenna laughed. "You never said you did, but we watched that movie a million times."

"So, *Pretty Woman* it is!" Lorraine declared, slapping her pudgy palms together in gleeful anticipation of making me look like a prostitute.

I gulped, but I didn't argue. Heck, who would be brainless enough to fight looking like Julia Roberts? The only drawback I could foresee if Lorraine actually succeeded was that I'd have to admit Mom was right. Eddie never would have left me if I'd looked like Julia when we were married.

Lorraine fingered through my hair with one hand while grabbing up a plastic cap with the other. "So, was he a cheater or a beater?"

I choked. "What?"

"Cheater or beater?" she repeated her question. "Like Jenna's Todd was a cheater. So where'd you hide his body, Jenna?"

Obviously the O'Briens had spawned another neighborhood legend. But like the famous mob boss Jimmy Hoffa, Jenna's ex would probably never be found. A smirk slid across Jenna's mouth, but she didn't look up from her paperwork. "I'll never tell."

"Cheater," I admitted. The second I made the confession the drone of the dryers died, and a bunch of permed heads swiveled toward me.

"Who cheated, dear?" Mrs. Milanowski asked. "Your grandmother? Nobody's that lucky at cards."

"Her Eddie," Lorraine explained. I guess there was no such thing as discretion in a beauty shop.

"He's not my Eddie."

"I heard about your divorce, Mary Ellen," another perm-head piped up. "That's too bad. It's so hard on the kids."

What about me?

"He was the cheater," Lorraine supplied, in case anyone had missed it. She clicked her tongue in disgust. "With all the diseases out there now, it's almost better if they're beaters. Safer."

Without lifting her head from her study of Lorraine's business records, Jenna snorted. "You're sniffing too much perm solution, Lorraine."

"My figures can't be off—I have a real good accountant," she defended.

Jenna shook her head. "The math is fine. Some of your ideas aren't. Getting knocked around is not safer."

Lorraine crossed herself. "Forgive me. Your poor mama…"

"Is back at Mary Ellen's house playing cards." Jenna waved a hand in dismissal of Lorraine's concern. "She's fine."

"What she put up with from your father…"

Jenna shrugged. "It's over now."

I shivered despite the warmth of the plastic cape. I'd grown up in this neighborhood. How come I wasn't as strong and resilient as these women? I hadn't pushed Eddie down the stairs or dismembered him. How come I just wanted to pull my lank, drab hair around my face and hide?

But Lorraine had my hair, yanking, clipping and spreading goo on it. An hour later, when she whipped off the plastic cape and whirled me toward the mirror, I concluded that I didn't look like Julia Roberts at all. Probably the baggy jeans and Czerwinski Butcher Shop sweatshirt ruined that image.

But I wasn't bad. The red was deep and rich, and it had conditioned my hair so that it flowed around my shoulders in thick, soft waves.

"That other woman. The one from the cannibal movies…" Mrs. Rewerts lifted her hand and shook it in the air. "You know the one. She has that color hair and Mary Ellen's same green eyes." The other women nodded in agreement and stroked my fragile ego with oohs and aahs.

"Julianne Moore?" I looked like Julianne Moore? She'd do. And maybe, so would I. I turned toward Jenna, who had put down her paperwork to study me. "What do you think?"

"What do *you* think?" she countered.

I shrugged and watched the rich waves dance around the shoulders of my bloodstained sweatshirt. "I like it."

She nodded. "Yeah, me, too."

And I knew she wasn't just stroking my ego. Jenna wouldn't do that, not the Jenna I'd known eleven years ago and not the one I was getting to know again. Maybe we would never regain the friendship we had once shared, but I hoped we could forge a new relationship. I really needed a friend.

CHAPTER G
The Girls

"Mommy, you look like a movie star!" Shelby shrieked before vaulting into my arms. Although Amber had come to the kitchen, too, when Jenna and I walked in, she hung back. A book clutched in her hand, she studied me from behind the glasses that had slipped to the end of her cute little nose.

"So what do you think?" I asked. Although only ten and a half, Amber was wise beyond her years. Maybe it came from all the reading, or from some recessive gene that had skipped Eddie and me. But she was one smart kid, and I valued her opinion.

A slow smile spread across her bow-shaped lips, and she nodded, her perpetual ponytail bobbing at the back of her head. "It's smokin'!"

"Who's smoking?" Mom asked as she lumbered up from the cellar with a jar of stewed tomatoes in her hand. She set it on the counter without taking her gaze from my new hair-do. "Lorraine is a little too wild for the West Side."

Translation: In Mom's eyes, I did look like a prostitute. *Good.*

"It's pretty," Shelby insisted, fingering a strand. "And soft."

Mom sniffed. "Anything's better than it was. Did you see

your father when you came in? He went out to check his oil, and dinner's ready. You're staying, Jenna?"

"Thanks, but I'm supposed to meet some Realtors at Charlie's, Mrs. Black." She winked at me. "They give me referrals for free drinks."

"You need to eat. You're too skinny. It's all ready to go on the table. Goulash." Mom routinely fed the neighborhood, sending dishes to ailing neighbors, cooking for funerals and open houses.

Jenna's stomach rumbled. "One plate, and I'll get Mr. Black."

"Wait, Jenna. You didn't meet the girls." I slid an arm around Amber's thin shoulders. "This is Amber. And this little monkey is Shelby. Girls, this is—" *Was.* But I was hoping. "My oldest and closest friend, Jenna O'Brien."

"Nice to meet you," Amber mumbled, shyly but politely.

"How come you never came to our old house?" Shelby asked with a child's inquisitiveness. "Weren't you friends there?"

"I was really busy," Jenna hedged. "But that's no excuse to let a friend slip away." Jenna caught my eye before she went outside to get my dad.

Dinner was a wild affair. Grandma was still suffering the effects of too much tea. And Dad and Jenna had taken a while and a few beers before they'd made their way into the house. Shelby was *on*, entertaining Jenna with all her considerable charm, while Amber sat back and watched everyone with amusement shining in her eyes.

"So you come into my store and steal my help away, Jenna O'Brien, and then you have the nerve to sit at my table and eat my food!" Daddy shouted, lifting his hand as if to cuff her, but just squeezing her neck with affection.

"If I don't, you'll keep shoveling it in until you explode," she sassed back with a wink at the girls, who giggled at her bravery. Despite their having lived with him for a while, Daddy still intimidated them with his booming voice and gruff teasing.

But Daddy was the only grandfather they had; Eddie's parents had died when he was in his teens. I'd always felt sorry for him because of that. Even as crazy as my parents sometimes made me, I couldn't imagine life without either of them.

"Jenna's right. You need to watch your weight. You know what the doctor said—" Mom began.

Daddy lifted his hand, waving away medical advice. "What does he know with that fancy education?" Obviously Daddy thought the eight years of schooling that he'd had before the nuns had kicked him out for brawling gave him more sense than a doctor who'd gone to college and medical school.

"Daddy, Mom's right. You need to take better care of yourself." Mom shot me a smile for my support. She really did worry about Daddy, loved him even after all their years together. Maybe that was why she nagged him; she was scared of losing him the way she'd lost her father. Could it be why she nagged me? Because she cared? No, nobody could care that much.

"Strong like bear!" Daddy growled, flexing his burly arms.

The girls squealed. He pounded on the table, making the plates dance. Grandma choked on an overcooked noodle. I thumped her back with one hand while I handed Amber a napkin for the milk she'd squirted out her nose.

"I've forgotten how much fun dinner at the Black house always was." Jenna sighed with a satisfied smile, covering her empty plate with a protective hand before Mom could ladle another helping on it.

"You work too hard," Mom tsked, nagging Jenna, too. "You need to come around more."

Daddy spoke to Jenna, but he was staring at me. "Yeah, you do. You're good for this girl."

"That's not what you said when you caught us drinking—" Jenna halted when the girls displayed wide-eyed interest. "Drinking all your chocolate milk."

I leaned in close. "Smooth. Good save."

She flipped me off under the lace edge of Mom's treasured tablecloth. Growing up with three brothers had given Jenna some of her rough edges.

"Grandpa doesn't care if we drink all his chocolate milk," Shelby said.

"Of course not, he always has more in the garage," Jenna teased.

"Stay away from my garage," Daddy growled.

She laughed as she rose to her feet. "Well, I'm late. The meal was wonderful, Mrs. Black. Thanks for…checking the oil in my car, Mr. Black."

I got up to walk her to the door. "So where do I report for work? And what time?"

"You can wait until after you get the kids on the bus. Then meet me at the office. I'm on Walker between the bakery and insurance office. First Choice Mortgage."

"Your own place?"

"Satellite office. The broker's downtown. You'll have to run down there occasionally. Do you have a car?"

"Grandma's Bonneville."

"Is that the same one you used for your driver's license road test?"

"Yes, the car and I know each other well."

"So do we, Mary Ellen Black. You're going to be okay."

I nodded, emotion choking my throat. Standing on the gravel driveway next to her car, an overwhelming desire to hug her compelled me to throw my arms around her despite all the years we'd not had any contact.

She held herself stiffly in my arms, then squeezed back for just a second before pulling away. Had she sought me out only at her mother's urging? Or, as a divorced woman herself, had she understood how alone I felt, how much I needed a friend now? And did she need one, too? I wanted to be that friend again.

"I missed you," I admitted. "And I'm sorry."

"Eddie's your past, Mary Ellen. Forget him."

I shook my head, tumbling my new hairdo. "I can't. I have to think of the girls. He's their father."

"They're great girls. If they came out that big, I might have considered it. But raising babies, having someone completely helpless, completely dependent on me…" She shrugged, obviously uncomfortable with the topic. "You'll figure things out, Mary Ellen. And if you don't, you'll get by. That's what most of us do." I watched her get into her shiny black Cadillac. If she were just getting by, I could handle that.

"How come we never see Daddy anymore?" Shelby asked as I pulled the blanket to her chin. Amber, lying next to her in the old double bed that had been mine, turned from the light to face me. She wanted an answer, too, but from the sorrow in her eyes, I guessed that she already knew.

"We don't all live together anymore, Shelby…"

"I know. We're divorced—"

"No, sweetie, just your father and I are divorced."

"A divorce affects the whole family," Amber said with her usual sobering wisdom.

"Our family got divorced?" Shelby asked.

Before I could think of a response, Amber answered. "Yeah, but Dad was gone before that. He's always cared about his restaurant more than us, Shelby."

Could I argue with the truth? The resentful ex-wife in me wanted to wholeheartedly agree, but the mother in me wouldn't allow it. "Your father loves you both very much, Amber." And I truly believed he did, as much as Eddie could love anyone.

"He loves the restaurant more, Mom. I heard you say that to him a bunch of times."

Waiting until the girls had gone to bed to have our fights hadn't worked, apparently, not even in a house the size of the one we'd lost. Not that we'd fought all that often. I hadn't wanted to nag Eddie, not the way Mom nagged Daddy. But

I had to face the fact that I'd had a lot of resentment, even before the divorce, more directed toward the restaurant than the twenty-year-old waitress—and apparently so did my girls.

"I was mad when I said that, Amber. You know how when you're mad you say things you don't mean." Liar. "Like when you call Shelby names…"

Amber's lips quirked up in a smile. "Well, sometimes I mean those. I hate sharing a bed with her. She's a hog, and she snores!"

"Do not!" Shelby protested vehemently.

"How would you know? You're sleeping when you're snoring. You can't know what you're doing when you're sleeping!"

Heck, I didn't know what I was doing when I was awake. There was no guidebook for how to handle divorce, nothing that applied to every situation and every child. My girls were smart. They deserved honesty. But they also deserved a father.

"Okay, girls, how about we visit your dad?"

"Where?" Amber asked, her eyes narrowed with suspicion.

Since I didn't know where he was living, I had no choice. "We'll go to the restaurant. Tomorrow's Saturday. We'll have a girls' day out. We'll have lunch and go to the mall. I'm starting my new job on Monday. I need a few clothes. You both need some new shoes."

"Shoes…" Shelby sighed, her eyelids drooping as she drifted off to sleep to dream of new shoes. She was definitely my child.

Amber studied me a while longer; I knew the cadence of

crickets never echoed inside her head. "Do you want to show Dad your new hair, Mom? Do you think it'll make him change his mind about the divorce?"

Had she been listening to my mother? I had to find a place of our own. Of course, a reconciliation was what she wanted. Until I'd come to my senses in the form of the foreclosure notice, it had been what I wanted, too, to salvage my family. But Eddie wasn't my family any longer; my girls were.

"Honey, are you hoping…"

"I'm not, Mom, okay?" She reached out to flip off the light, but I caught her hand and held it back. Then after slipping off Amber's glasses, I stared into her eyes, swimming with unshed tears.

"It's okay to hope, Amber. It's okay to dream. But dream about things you can get with your brains and your ambition. Don't hope for your father and me to get back together. It's not going to happen."

"Because of that 'ho?"

My mother wasn't the only one she'd been listening to; evidently Grandma had shared a new word with the girls. I bit my tongue to hold in a laugh. "Amber!"

"Mom, once he sees you looking like that—"

I touched a lock of the soft hair. "I didn't do this for your father, Amber. I did it for me."

And it felt good. It felt *damn* good to do something for me.

"We'll go see your father tomorrow, and we'll talk about setting something up so that you can see him more. That's all we're doing. Okay?" And a visit was long overdue. Eddie didn't deserve them, wouldn't support them, but they needed him.

She nodded.

"I love you, Amber." I kissed her forehead and stood up to head for the door and the couch in my father's den.

"Mom?" I stopped and grasped the door frame, my stomach clenching. What now? "Don't forget about shoe shopping, okay?"

Oh, yeah…despite her brains, this one was mine, too.

Although I didn't want to raise any hopes in my children or my mother, I took extra time with my makeup and clothes. I had some pride; it was about time that I showed it. And showed Eddie what he'd given up… The girls. I wanted him to want them back, to want to spend some time with them. I didn't want him to want me. Okay, maybe I did, but I didn't want him back.

"Going to the restaurant today is a really good idea, Mary Ellen," Mom said, nodding at my hair and makeup, the highest praise she'd ever given me.

Even staggered by her compliment, I had to clarify, "For the girls, Mom. Yes, it is."

"Maybe for you, too, honey." She really did care, did love me. "Good luck." But she would never understand me.

"Good luck with what?" Dad asked on his way out the door to open the store. Jesus was back to help him with the Saturday-morning crowd, and I didn't know who was more relieved—me or Dad. He bussed my cheek on the way out the door. "You look good, honey. I'll miss you today. It was great having you at the shop."

"It was fun being with you, Dad." And despite the neighborhood gossips, I had enjoyed spending time with my dad. While I knew Eddie would never have the kind of relationship with Amber and Shelby that I had with Daddy, I wanted him to have some relationship with them, any relationship.

As I pulled the Bonneville into the restaurant lot later that morning, I realized I should have accepted my mom's wish for luck. Luck that Eddie would be happy to see his girls, that he would show them that they're important to him.

But as I parked in the shadow of the concrete building on the east side of Grand Rapids, I didn't feel lucky. I should have called him, should have warned him. But then, wouldn't it be just like the little weasel to have refused? He'd done it while we were waiting for the divorce. In fact, I could scarcely remember the last time he'd seen his children. And while I hated him for that, I hated myself, too. I should have done this for the girls sooner.

"Is Dad here, Mommy?" Shelby asked.

"God, you're stupid," Amber snarled. "Dad's always here."

The shadow of the building grew, swallowing me in the darkness. This, not some twenty-year-old cocktail waitress, had been my husband's mistress and not just for the last couple of years, but for all eleven years of our marriage. A new hairdo wouldn't make him want me, wouldn't make him regret what he'd thrown away. I couldn't compete with bricks, a brass bar and jovial customers.

I threw open the door of the restaurant and stepped out of the shadow. As the light washed over me, I realized something else D-day had done for me. I didn't want to compete anymore. I didn't want Eddie to act like a husband or a lover, ex or jealous. I wanted him to be a father, nothing else.

The Saturday lunch crowd wasn't what it used to be. But then not much was. I wasn't. I wasn't sure who I was yet, but I wasn't Mrs. Edward Nowicki. Still, the staff glanced up with trepidation when we walked in. Perhaps they expected a repeat of my hysterics on the day the bank had slapped the foreclosure notice on the house. The hostess, standing behind her podium in the foyer, smiled politely, looked at the girls and then back at me. Her pouty mouth fell open. "Mrs. Nowi—"

"Ms. Black. Mary Ellen's fine," I corrected her. "Trina, isn't it?"

Her head bobbed, her fine blond hair bobbing with it. "Yes."

"Is Eddie in?"

Amber snorted at my rhetorical question.

"He's in the office, Mrs.—Mary Ellen." Trina's heavily mascaraed eyes widened with a hint of panic.

"I'll go back and let him know he has visitors," I offered. "Would you mind seating the girls for me? They can order, too. They know what they want." A father. And I intended to make him act like one, if only for a few minutes.

"Mrs.—" The confusion over my name stopped her protest, and I slipped past her and down the hall, past the rest rooms to Eddie's office.

The door was ajar, so I pushed it open the rest of the way. Well, so much for my hopes and dreams. Obviously Eddie's dick hadn't shriveled up and fallen off. All three and three-quarters inches of it jutted out of his pants then disappeared between the lips of the girl kneeling in front of him.

"Excuse me—" Both of them jumped.

"Don't look guilty," I said at their stricken expressions. Good thing I'd come back alone.

"Mary Ellen—"

"It's okay, really," I insisted as Eddie dragged the blond girl in the tight, black waitress uniform to her feet with one hand, while he struggled to zip up his pants with his other hand.

Obviously he still had the same reaction to me, new hairdo and all, that he'd developed the last couple of years. I could deflate him faster than anyone. "We're divorced. It's okay now."

Now. Before it hadn't been. When he'd first told me about this young woman in his life, I'd been devastated, hysterically heartbroken. Now I was just quietly bitter. The divorce decree made a difference. This wasn't my husband getting a blow job in his office. This was my ex. I honestly didn't care. In fact, I was amused by the blush on both their faces.

"Why are you here? I told you there's no money." He finally lifted his chin to face me, and I noticed a yellowing bruise around one of his eyes.

"Money would be nice," I admitted. "You should help support your daughters—"

"I told you—"

The young girl shrank away, probably wishing in her embarrassment that she could disappear. Maybe she wasn't a 'ho, to borrow Grandma's new word. Maybe she was just young and stupid the way I'd once been. But I was older now...

"Eddie, there's other support than monetary. The girls

need your attention. You've hardly seen them since you left—"

"You're staying with your dad, and I can guess how he feels about—"

"I'm going to leave now," the girl said as she awkwardly tried to slip past me and into the hall. I sidestepped, allowing her to escape what she was probably sure would be an ugly scene. She'd been present the day I'd gotten the foreclosure notice.

"He feels like a father should," I went on. "He wants his daughter to be happy. He resents whoever makes her unhappy."

Did Daddy resent Eddie enough to have given him that black eye? Despite his age, Daddy could still be a brawler. And it wouldn't take much to beat Eddie. Although his driver's license said five-eight, Eddie stood only five-six in his stocking feet. I could tower over him with heels, and for some reason, I'd worn platform tennis shoes today. I could take him. And if he hurt my girls, he'd be sporting another black eye. "You should feel that way, Eddie—"

"About you?" he asked, his thin lips twisting into a sneer. "Is this for me, Mary Ellen? The hair? Wearing some makeup for once? You think that's going to make me change my mind? You should have thought of something before you got the dye job. Blondes are more fun!"

A laugh sputtered out. I couldn't help it. "You're such an ass, Eddie. The saying is that blondes *have* more fun, but since that poor girl hooked up with you, she won't know fun anymore."

His face reddened again. Despite the bleached highlights in his hair, he showed his age. Forty, prime time for a mid-life crisis. He hadn't realized all those big dreams he'd had, only owning this restaurant, and he was on the verge of losing that. "You were never any fun, Mary Ellen," he accused.

I shrugged. "Not since I met you, no. I don't want you back, Eddie." I wanted *me* back, wherever I'd been hiding the last eleven years. I wanted fun, but before I could satisfy my desires, I had to make sure my girls were happy. And they needed a relationship with their father.

"Then why—"

"For the girls. I brought them. They—" *Miss him?* How? He hadn't been around much before the divorce. He'd been busy trying to save this sinking ship "—wanted to see you."

"They did?" His flush deepened, and I remembered that middle age was prime time for a heart attack, too.

"You okay, Eddie?"

"There's a lot going on right now, Mary Ellen. Now's not a good time—"

My hand clenched into a fist, but before I could swing, I took a deep breath, exhaled, closed my eyes. I had to keep it together. For the girls. "Just a few minutes, Eddie. Talk to them. Ask them about school, gymnastics…show some interest in them, okay? Fake it!"

He didn't try to lie to me for once; he didn't claim to have any interest in them now, as he was obviously preoccupied with something else. And I knew what a mistake I'd made. Without seeing him, they could weave the fantasy that he might actually care about them, but seeing him, seeing the blank, bored expression on his weaselly face, they would know the truth. Even Shelby who was usually so blissfully oblivious…

As he walked up to the table where the hostess was serving them chocolate milk, the girls didn't meet him with bright smiles. And he didn't wrap his arms around them, torn apart from missing them. I missed them while they were at school. He hadn't seen them in several weeks and displayed no joy in seeing them now. Instead, he looked embarrassed, face flushed, and for a man who usually oozed charm, he didn't look as if he had a clue what to say to them.

"I'm sorry…"

I turned at the meek voice near my shoulder as I held back from the table. "What?"

"I'm sorry…about…"

I waved a hand at the little blonde's anxiety. "I said it was okay. Really." And for me, it would be since I was free of Eddie. But it wouldn't be for her, not unless she ran like hell. I thought about warning her, but I wasn't that benevolent. After all, she had known he was a married man even if he'd forgotten.

"But you were probably expecting…"

I followed her gaze to the table where Eddie stood above the girls, and they carried on a brief, stilted conversation. My heart ached for the disappointment on their little faces. They wanted what I had with my father; that's what had inspired last night's questions. But Eddie would never satisfy their longing. He would never be half the man my father was. "What? A big family reunion?" I shook my head. "No, I wasn't." Too much had changed over the last couple of years.

"Eddie feels bad, really he does." God, she wasn't just young; she was stupid, too. "About losing the house and not having any money. It's killing him that he can't support them. He feels so guilty that he can't stand to see them." Her voice cracked. "There really isn't any money, you know…"

A commotion drew my attention away from the stammering blonde to the foyer. Two broad-shouldered guys strode in, knocking aside some of the ferns I'd potted in brass urns. I winced as dirt scattered across the thick burgundy carpet. Eddie backed away from the table, turning toward the hall to his office without even a goodbye to his daughters.

"Eddie!" the guys shouted and stopped his retreat.

The blonde clutched my arm. "Oh, God!"

I refrained from shaking her off and peered closer at the new customers. "Dougie?"

The guy with the most muscles and least neck turned toward me, staring intently from beneath a bushy unibrow. "Mary Ellen? Mary Ellen Black?"

"Dougie. I haven't seen you in years." Not since high school. Dougie hadn't graduated with Jenna and me, though. Instead, he'd been doing time for some offense or other.

"Great to see you. You're looking great." From the appreciative gleam in his eyes, I figured he meant it.

"So you got married?" he asked.

I nodded. "I'm divorced now. There're my girls—" I gestured toward where the girls sat, wide-eyed at all the goings-on. Plates of pancakes growing cold in front of them.

"Cute kids," he murmured.

Even a hoodlum's compliments swelled my mother's pride. "Yeah, they are."

"I've got a couple of boys," he said. "I married Sue. Remember Sue?"

There had been about ten girls named Sue in every class I'd attended, but I nodded. "Give her my best."

"Mary Ellen!" Eddie's voice rose with impatience. Not that he seemed particularly eager to talk to his visitors, but I guess he didn't want me talking to them, either.

"I'm sorry. You all have business. The girls and I will leave now. Say goodbye to Daddy."

I hustled them out the door, not worrying about paying the bill or leaving a tip. Except I did stop near the 'ho. "You can do better," I told her. That was probably the best tip she'd ever gotten, no matter how long she'd been waitressing.

The girls and I walked past a Lincoln Navigator parked too close to the doors, and headed toward the Bonneville.

"I didn't like the food there," Amber said. "Can we get something to eat at the mall?"

As they climbed into the back seat, I fought the urge to drag them into my arms for reassuring hugs. "Sure we can. Shoe shopping always makes me hungry." And so I'd blow the rest of my poker winnings and leftover VFW tips.

"I don't want to eat here anymore," Shelby declared, her bottom lip jutting out in a pout.

"That's up to you two. Whatever you want." And it was. Eddie hadn't requested any scheduled visitation.

"I used to want to go home," Amber admitted. "Back to our old house. Back to my old school, too. But there're some neat people at the new one. They don't care what you wear or where you live…" Not like the wannabe high-class neighborhood where we'd lived. "Some don't even speak English," Amber said, probably impressed someone talked less than she did; with her shyness, she usually spoke very little.

Shelby nodded. "Yeah, it's okay." And maybe it was. But they deserved more. And somehow I had to get it for them… for all of us.

"Remember that I warned you how crazy it gets around here," Jenna said Monday morning, before I had even swung my purse from my shoulder. No laced tea had mellowed her this morning. "People will yell at you. I will yell at you. Tell her, Vicki."

The woman sitting as close to the desk as her swollen belly would allow nodded. "She can be a miserable bitch, worse than me with these raging pregnancy hormones."

"You regretting the job offer?" I asked. My gut clenched with nerves. I'd been a lot more comfortable at the VFW.

Jenna, in a crisp, burnt sienna–colored pantsuit, shrugged as if it didn't matter to her. But her dark eyes wouldn't meet my gaze, wouldn't let me see if she cared if we resumed our friendship, and that gave me hope that she did care. Maybe she was scared to let me know it. "You regretting taking the job?"

"No, not yet." Because I wanted this opportunity for employment and friendship.

"You might."

I shrugged, too, but my shoulders retained all the tension

I was feeling. "You might regret it more. I don't have any experience."

She nodded, but her hair stayed in the perfect knot on the back of her head. "Well, hell, it's worth a try, huh?"

I hoped she was talking about the job *and* the friendship. "Sure."

"Vicki will show you the ropes. I've got a breakfast appointment." She was gone before I'd yet to swing my purse from my shoulder.

"Here, I lock mine in the desk," Vicki said, grabbing the bag from me. Since the front of the building housing the mortgage office was a wall of windows looking onto a street that had seen better economic days, locking up one's valuables seemed like a wise decision. But maybe a cheap lock on a metal desk wouldn't be enough. And the computers that topped each of the two desks in the outer office were openly on display. Those windows needed blinds.

And the plain beige walls needed some color, maybe some paintings with vivid hues. The soft gray, metal desks could use some vases of flowers to spruce them up and relieve the commercial look of the office. But it was an office, not a house. I couldn't decorate it. I had to work in it…if Jenna still wanted me to. "Was she trying to scare me off?" I asked.

"No, just warning you. It gets hectic around here. Jenna's at it around the clock. She'll work you."

I dragged in a quick breath. Would I be able to handle the job? But that didn't bother me as much as Jenna's hours. Why did she work so much? So that she wouldn't miss Todd?

So that she wouldn't feel so alone? I had the girls. Did she have anyone?

"She'll pay you well. That's why I keep coming back after the babies." Vicki fixed me with an intense, blue-eyed stare.

I smiled at her, hoping to relieve the tension. "So you're warning me, too?"

She laughed but didn't deny it. "It's *my* job."

"Understood. I just need to make some money right now." Enough to get me out of my mother's house, to get away from the West Side again. To make a life for myself and my daughters... And after my brief stint at the VFW and the butcher shop, I was used to temp jobs.

She nodded. "Biding some time until you find another husband?"

Despite the darker hair, she reminded me a lot of Lorraine. "I don't want another husband."

"Not yet, but you will. Look at Connie Snyder. She's been married five times already." She clicked her tongue in disgust.

The ringing of the phone saved me from listening to more gossip but didn't let up enough to give me much training time. So I just waded in. Those weeks at the butcher shop and slow hours at the VFW didn't count. This was my true initiation into the workforce again. And as far as initiations went, I think I would have preferred the one my brother Bart had told me about. Streaking across a college campus naked would be better than this. People screamed about postponed closing dates on their houses. They vented about the interest rates. They griped about how twenty-five thousand in credit-card debt limited how high a mortgage for which they could qualify. And because I was answering the phone, they took all their frustrations out on me.

Somehow, although I'd only been on the job a few minutes, I was to blame. But I remembered the golden rule. *The customer is always right.* I acknowledged their complaints with a smile in my voice and promised to see what I could do. Not a damn thing. Then I called them names after I hung up the phone.

Vicki laughed and rubbed her palms over her belly. Yearning stirred inside me. I had loved being pregnant. And when Eddie had gotten his vasectomy without consulting me, I'd been furious. Resentment had eaten at me. About that, among other things. I should have given him a vasectomy myself and in the same manner in which bulls were made into steers.

The phone rang again. "First Choice Mortgage, may I help you?" As I suspected, just someone else who wanted to rant in my ear about their poor credit and the overinflated price of homes in the area. Keeping my voice neutral, I commiserated and hung up after their thank-you for my promise to look into the matter.

Vicki groaned.

"What is it? Contraction?"

"No, I wish. This kid is already a week overdue."

That part of pregnancy I didn't miss, the waiting for the arrival of a perfect, sweet baby…who persisted in kicking your ribs and sitting on your shrinking bladder. "Are you feeling all right? Anything I can get you?"

She shook her head. "Just promise me that you won't steal my job."

I suppressed a shudder. "You don't have a thing to worry about. I don't have a clue what I'm doing."

"You've said you're welcome to every single caller." Her plump face distorted with disgust.

"Yeah, I guess I have."

"Because they've *thanked* you."

I nodded, not understanding her logic. But pregnant women, at the mercy of those raging hormones, were rarely logical. After all, I'd married Eddie when I was pregnant with Amber.

"I don't get thank-yous. I get cussed out." And she cussed back. I'd eavesdropped on a few of her calls, listening for proper protocol. I hadn't heard it.

"A lot of these people aren't very happy," I admitted.

"No, they're not. But you've made them thank you. You're really good at this. A natural."

Pride lifted my mouth into a smile.

"So you're going to steal my job!" she accused, her blue eyes narrowing with anger and suspicion.

"I'm just filling in like I did for Florence at the VFW—"

"Sure, that's what you say, but you're Jenna's friend."

I didn't want her getting too worked up, not in her condition. "A friend I haven't seen in eleven years. You've worked for her for…"

With a sniff, she relented to reply, "Five years."

"You know this job. You even know Jenna better than I do." And I needed to have her teach me about both if I wanted to fulfill my promises to the grumpy callers and if I wanted to renew my old friendship with Jenna.

"That's true," she admitted. "I do."

I relaxed a bit, sure I was gaining ground, so I pushed my advantage. "I need your help—"

"Sure, to take over my job—"

Was there any way to reason with a woman in this condition? "I don't want your job!"

"Giving up already?" Jenna asked as she blew through the door, swinging her briefcase.

"No—"

"If you're not interested, I can find someone else," she offered quickly. But something about her tone hinted at disappointment. In me, or the world in general? "Just wanted to help you out…"

Charity. I cringed. I didn't want charity. I wanted to make my own way. I should have taken the job at Charlie's. "And you are. I appreciate the opportunity—"

"Sure you do…"

Vicki sighed, a gusty one that pushed her belly against the buttons of her maternity top, straining them almost to the point of popping. "She's doing great, damn it!" the pregnant woman declared.

Jenna glanced from one of us to the other. "So what's wrong?"

"You know how I am when I'm pregnant. I thought she'd steal my job."

Jenna nodded and offered me a smile, one of the first. Then she reached around to squeeze Vicki's slumping shoulder. "You know no one else can put up with me, Vicki. Mary Ellen will be begging you to come back, I guarantee it."

When the phone rang again, I breathed deeply before answering the next barrage of complaints. I believed I would be begging Vicki to come back.

"See," Vicki griped to Jenna as I hung up the phone after another "You're welcome." "She's good, and I haven't taught her a damn thing yet."

Jenna nodded. "The thing you don't know about Mary Ellen, Vicki, is that she's good at everything she does. That's just her."

I laughed off her compliment. "Yeah, right. That's why my husband left me."

"Your husband was an ass."

I nodded my agreement. "True, so I'm not good at choosing husbands."

"You said that's not something you want to do again, so don't worry about it." Jenna's dark eyes gleamed. "Concentrate on choosing lovers instead."

If only... Lorraine's do hadn't gotten me any hot sex yet. I sighed.

"My husband's brother is pretty good-looking," Vicki offered. "And single again."

Again. Probably divorced. But then, so was half the population.

"Matchmake on your own time. Get to work. You have a temp to train." Jenna stressed *temp* with a wink at both of us. "See, Vicki, I'm such a bitch, she'll never last."

"God help us if you ever get pregnant," Vicki teased.

Jenna's face blanched, and she headed abruptly for her back office. "I'll get you this paperwork later."

Later, I'd get an explanation for her reaction to Vicki's innocent remark. First, I had to begin my training for my position as temporary mortgage processor. Then I'd work on being a friend. And if Jenna was right, I could be very good at it. I had a feeling she needed a good friend as much as I did.

Over the next week I discovered why Jenna needed me. She ran herself ragged, leaving no time for friends, food or sleep. Vicki and I couldn't keep up with her. No wonder plaques lined the walls of Jenna's private office proclaiming her top loan originator, but nothing else. No pictures of kids, no flowers, no cards, nothing personal—except me, and I was only temporary.

"You need more, Jenna," I told her, beginning what I considered my own type of intervention. The woman was addicted to work. And like any addiction, it could only hurt her.

She sighed, but didn't look up from her overflowing desk. "I know. I'm so close to beating my own production record. I need just a few more loans. Did you find time last night after the girls were in bed to call those old clients about refinancing? I can save them money and get credit toward my production. They'd thank you for sure. And so would I...with a bonus. A big bonus."

"Big enough to get me out of that house?" I allowed myself a minute to remember some of Mom's more critical comments. She hated my cooking, especially my low-fat cooking. No wonder I hadn't been able to keep a husband, she said, I couldn't provide him with a son or a decent meal.

Of course, if she kept cooking with lard, she'd be losing a husband, too. Not with a nice healthy divorce, either, but from a heart attack. Poor Daddy, but I figured all the years he'd eaten raw hamburger at the butcher shop had probably petrified his arteries. And he loved her cooking, had nothing but praise for it, while Mom did nothing but nag. I had to get out of there.

"I bet I'll have enough work to keep you on even after Vicki comes back from having that baby—if she ever has it. I could keep you both busy, at least while the interest rates are low."

"The cash is great, but it won't qualify me for a mortgage." Once Vicki had finally trusted me enough to train me, I'd caught on quickly. I even understood now how Eddie had lost the house and what that had done to my credit, since my name had been on the mortgage, too. Even though the court said I didn't have to pay back the debts, Eddie had ruined my credit as effectively as he'd ruined his own.

"You want to buy a house?"

"I'd like to, but it's not possible. With my credit, I probably couldn't even rent an apartment." I was trapped on the West Side, with my mother.

"Yeah, you probably couldn't rent," Jenna agreed. "At least not from an apartment complex. But I know some people who own rental properties around the neighborhood. Someone might be willing to help you out."

Pride swelled, lifting my chin. "I don't want someone helping me out. I want to help *myself* out. If all I can expect is charity, I'll stay where I am." I grimaced even as I made the declaration. Stay home with Mom? There had to be another way.

"It's not like a handout. You'd pay rent... Hell, maybe someone would even let you rent to own. But that's up to you. Suit yourself. I never knew you were so stupid proud."

"Neither did I!" And wasn't that the truth? I smiled, then guilt flashed through me as I remembered my mission; Jenna and what her ambition was doing to her.

"Aren't you supposed to be leaving now to get the girls to gymnastics?" she asked.

I glanced at my watch. I had a few minutes yet. It probably wouldn't be enough, not to get through her thick head. "I've got a little time yet." I'd already activated the voice mail. Vicki was at the doctor's office, probably threatening that if he didn't induce her labor, she'd induce his.

"So how many calls did you make last night?" Jenna asked.

"A few. I set a couple of appointments for you."

"Great. I'm telling you that bonus will be big!"

"Still won't be worth it."

"What? They give you a hard time? Thought you'd like that since you never got it from Eddie."

"Sure, mock my sex life—"

"I would if you had one."

"Funny. But at least I have a life. I have my family, my daughters. All you do is work, Jenna. You should ease up."

"What?" She waved her hands over the pile of papers and folders on her desk. "How?"

"Stop taking so many appointments, so many loans. Take

some time for you. Just you, not for schmoozing with Realtors for referrals."

"The poker game—"

"Was the first one you'd made in a year. Your mother told me. And I know you did it for me. I appreciate that, Jenna. I'm so glad we're talking again. And because of that, I'm being selfish. I don't want to lose you."

"As long as you stay away from that dickhead Eddie, we'll be fine."

"No, I don't mean over a man. That won't happen again." The only one that had showed any interest in me lately had been married. "You know, I saw Dougie Arnold. Do you remember him from school?"

"Sure, he married Sue. I did a loan for them six months ago. They needed more room."

"Which Sue? No, forget it. We're talking about you."

"No, you are, Mary Ellen. I'm trying to work. And your girls'll be late for gymnastics. Get going!"

"Jenna—"

"I know what you're trying to say, Mary Ellen. And I would spend more time with my family, but when I do, they harp on me for working too much. I really hate getting harped on." She glared, but her eyes, though narrowed, weren't hard. She didn't resent my concern. And I doubted her family's harping was what kept her away; somehow she felt as if she'd failed because of her divorce. I understood that, and I wanted to help.

"They harp because they care," I insisted.

"Still ticks me off."

"Jenna…"

"Give it up, Mary Ellen."

I glanced at my watch. I had to get the girls to class. The sigh I blew out stirred the lock of hair falling into my face. "All right."

"And make the rest of those calls tonight."

She was my friend or so I hoped, but she was also my boss. "Sure." I turned from her office, but she called me back.

"Mary Ellen, when you're setting appointments…"

"Yeah?"

"Don't go too far in advance." She flipped through the date book on her desk. "Make sure you don't book anything on the Friday two weeks from now."

"Are you taking a vacation?"

She flashed a smile that reached her eyes. "Rye's getting out. We'll be celebrating that whole weekend."

Out? Of what? Had Jenna's little brother gone to prison, and if so, for what? I didn't have time, or the guts, to ask. I was already late.

CHAPTER J
Jackasses
(apparently not all men are)

"That doctor's a jackass I'm telling you," Vicki vented the
following Monday. "Says the dates must have been wrong.
I'm really not overdue. Not overdue my numb ass. Let him
carry this baby around for a year. I've been pregnant a year,
I'm telling you, Mary Ellen."

I nodded while I sat on hold, the phone in the crook of
my shoulder and neck. Hopefully, I could place this loan. The
interest rate would be higher because of their poor credit. But
this was a young couple from the neighborhood. They really needed this house, needed to make a home for the family
they were about to start. But I had to explain a sudden deposit in their bank account, the sizable one that would cov-
er their down payment. I knew little Jimmy wasn't a drug
dealer, so where had the money come from?

Jenna paused behind my chair, so I pointed to the entry
on the bank statement, the one the lender was questioning.
"A gift," she said.

"From who? Neither of their parents have a pot to piss in
or a window to throw it out of." Living with Grandma was

really adding color to my speech. A lot of loans that Jenna originated on the West Side had gifts involved. "Are you loaning them the money?"

"Not me," she said, hand to chest.

"Siggy," Vicki interrupted her pregnancy rant to divulge.

"Siggy?"

"Uncle Siggy. You know him."

Everyone knew Siggy. But I didn't see him as the philanthropist type. I saw him more as a... "He's a loan shark?"

"Excuse me," said the voice in my ear.

"Is the loan approved?" I asked.

"The gift is questionable, but not unreasonable. It's approved," the bank official relented with a disapproving sniff.

I lifted a fist in victory. "Thank you. We'll schedule the closing." After I hung up, I expelled a sigh of pure relief.

"You can call and tell Jimmy and Sheryl. You worked overtime on that one," Jenna said, high praise indeed from her.

"She works overtime on every one of them," Vicki groused, "just like you. No wonder you're friends."

"I don't work like Jenna. No one does." I straightened my spine, not giving up my quest to save Jenna from herself. "And no one should."

"Get over it. And just to prove you wrong, we're going out to lunch. Grab your coat. We're going to the Coppertop to celebrate. Come on, Vicki! You're coming, too."

Vicki patted her belly. "I can't eat that Polish sausage, not now. And if I go there and smell it, I'll eat it. I'm staying here. Maybe I'll call my doctor and jerk his chain again. He's gotta induce."

I was tempted to talk to him myself. Vicki's misery was catching. I caught Jenna's eye and smothered a laugh, realizing we'd had the same thought, just the way we had in school. The years fell away, and I felt as carefree as a teenager again, with the world full of possibilities. Maybe with Eddie out of my life, it was.

"You're sure you'll be okay here alone, Vicki?" I had to ask, hoping she'd wave us off.

She nodded. "I'll turn on the voice mail and put my feet up. I'm fine."

"Sheryl waits tables at the Coppertop. We can tell her about the approval in person," I said, bubbling over with excitement. For those kids, with that cute bungalow they'd own within a week, the world was full of opportunities. Like it had been when I'd started married life. Now I needed a place to start divorced life. Maybe it was time I talked to some of the people Jenna knew who had rental properties around the West Side. Staying in the neighborhood wouldn't be so bad, as long as I wasn't living with my mother. The girls liked their school, they had friends…and I'd discovered I did, too.

The Coppertop had already been decorated for Halloween, which reminded me that I hadn't sewn the girls' costumes yet. Not that Amber wanted to trick-or-treat. That wasn't something she had ever enjoyed, and now she considered herself too old for it. But Shelby lived to dress up and for the attention she received. Eddie had once had that kind of charisma and charm in the spotlight. And if I wasn't so bitter, I'd admit more often that Shelby was like him. I'd prefer to think Shelby had inherited Grandma's love of Halloween.

All around the bar/restaurant, lights shone from the faces of goofy jack-o'-lanterns and spiders hung from fake webs.

"They overdecorate like this for all the holidays," Jenna said as we slid into a booth.

Every available inch of wall space, ledge and counter was covered with something: spider, skeleton, cackling witch or steaming cauldron. "I have to bring the girls here." Maybe Saturday, if I didn't work for Jenna that morning. The girls would definitely prefer eating here to Eddie's restaurant. And they wouldn't have to listen to Mom and me bicker over my low-fat oil spray versus a pound of animal fat to stop the eggs from sticking.

"You always do that," Jenna remarked.

I glanced up from my perusal of the menu. Had she read my mind? "What? Let my mother drive me nuts?"

"That, too, but I was talking about how you always think of the girls first. The minute you walked in the door you were thinking of their reaction to this place, of showing it to them."

I shrugged. "That and dusting all this stuff." I shuddered over that mammoth task. "And taking it back down and packing it away. I love to decorate, but this is a little over-done even for me."

She laughed. "You still think like a housewife, and you always think like a mother."

"I *am* a mother." Hopefully a less critical one than mine.

Her smile faded, and her voice softened as she added, "It's more than that, Mary Ellen."

But the arrival of Sheryl, waitressing our booth, stopped her from explaining that remark. "Jenna, Mary Ellen, I'm so glad you guys came in for lunch. Any news?"

Jenna winked at me. On the way over, we had joked about dragging out the news and making her anxious. Under her lace-edged apron, her belly protruded. Not like Vicki's— Sheryl was only four-and-a-half months along; she had a ways to go yet. And she'd spend those on her feet, waiting tables. I knew how hard that was, but she had to. She would have a mortgage to pay. And Siggy.

"You're approved for the loan."

She threw her arms around my neck, sniffing back tears as she buried her face in my new hair. "Thank you, thank you—"

Even as I hugged back, I protested, "It wasn't me. Thank Jenna. She did all the work."

"Shut up and use your line," Jenna snapped back.

"What?" I smiled at Sheryl as she eased out of my arms. "Oh, you're welcome."

"Lunch is on me—what do you want?" Sheryl said.

"The special," Jenna and I said together, probably both thinking it would be cheapest.

As Sheryl rushed off to get our order, I leaned over the scarred tabletop. "I hope it's not kishka."

We both shuddered at the thought of the traditional Polish dish of blood sausage and barley. Barley and blood. Yum. I'd had that for too many Sunday dinners while growing up.

"And I hope she brings us beers."

I shuddered at that thought, too. Sheryl was behind the bar, working the taps of the kegs. "I'm worried about them."

"Why?" Jenna asked, checking the caller ID on her cell phone. The thing never stopped beeping as people left voice mails. Thankfully, she'd shut off the ringer. I'd made her do that while riding with her to the Coppertop. She'd nearly killed us twice in a quarter block while juggling her phone, a notepad and the steering wheel.

Before I could answer, Sheryl slapped two beers on the table in front of us, then darted from table to table, handling the lunch crowd pretty much single-handedly. "Can she keep working like this with the baby on the way? Can she and Jimmy keep up the mortgage payments, not to mention the payments to Siggy?"

"Jimmy's a good kid. He's not like Eddie, Mary Ellen. Most men aren't."

Was I projecting? Would I look at every man and suspect he lied and cheated like Eddie? Had he broken my faith in the world, smashed my trust into pieces so small I'd never glue it back together again?

"What about Todd?"

Jenna chugged half of her frosty mug of beer. "We're not talking about Todd. Hell, we're not talking about Eddie. I've been trying to talk about you, not Mary Ellen the mother and not Mary Ellen the housekeeper—"

"Who didn't keep the house—"

"Stop it!" Heads turned at nearby tables. Gazes met mine, commiserating, and slid away from Jenna in fear. She was one tough lady.

"What?" I asked.

"Stop putting yourself down."

"I've got my mother for that."

"And your mother talks out her ass. Hair, clothes, a son, meals full of fat, none of that would have kept Eddie."

God, how much whining did I do to Jenna?

"You did nothing wrong but marry that loser when I told you not to!" She finished her statement and her beer.

"You waited a while to say I told you so," I mused aloud. "I guess I should appreciate that."

"Appreciate the rest of what I said. Forget the negative for once."

When had I become this self-deprecating person? Had I become my mother? "I have to get out of that house."

And not just to save myself. The girls overheard too much, picked up on too much. I didn't want to raise negative children. I didn't want to be negative.

"Start dating again," Jenna said, totally misunderstanding. I didn't mean "out" for a night, I meant for life. "Vicki said she's tried to set you up with her brother-in-law a few times," she continued.

The thought of dating soured the beer in my stomach. I hadn't liked dating when I was a teenager. I figured I'd like it a lot less now. "You're single, too. Why don't you go out with him?" I asked.

She grimaced. "He's got kids. I'm not good with kids. And Vicki knows it. She likes you."

That was news. "So she never offered him up to you?"

"No. He's all yours. Go out with him."

"But when I said I had to get out of the house, I didn't mean—"

The special of the day turned out to be beef tips and noodles. Sheryl slid two plates next to our beers from her overloaded tray. "Enjoy, ladies. I'll get you a couple more beers, too—"

"No!" At her startled look, I smiled reassuringly. "Tea, please." I needed it to settle my stomach over the beer and the horrifying thought of dating again.

"You need to do something just for you, Mary Ellen," Jenna went on. "Not something as a mother, or a daughter or even a busybody well-meaning friend. You need sex."

Good thing I didn't have the tea yet; I would have spurted it all over the table if I'd taken a sip. "What?"

"You heard me loud and clear." And if not for the "Monster Mash" playing in the background, the entire restaurant probably would have, too.

"I'm not ready yet..."

"Bullshit!" That brought a few heads around again.

"Jenna." I lowered my voice and leaned over our plates. "The ink is hardly dry on my divorce decree."

"So? Some people—" both our erstwhile spouses "—don't even wait for the divorce. Hell, they don't wait until the ink is dry on the marriage license before they start cheating." Despite her flip words, pain darkened her eyes. She must have loved Todd a lot for him to have hurt her so badly. But she shook it off and focused on me again. "How long since you've taken a ride, Mary Ellen?"

"You know I've been taken for a ride." Straight to the

poorhouse. And I wouldn't trust a man to not do that again. I probably wouldn't trust a man again. Period.

"I know you got screwed, Mary Ellen." And thanks to the volume of her voice, most of the restaurant knew, too. Good thing it was a small restaurant. But it didn't matter. Everybody on the West Side already knew how stupid I'd been. Despite the tantalizing aroma of beef and noodles, I couldn't reach for my fork yet.

"But how long has it been since you had sex?"

Sheryl laughed as she put another beer in front of Jenna and a cup of tea near my untouched plate. "Don't you like the special, Mary Ellen? I can get you something else."

So she wouldn't go running off for me, I forced a bite into my mouth, the warm, peppery beef sliding down the back of my dry throat. I nodded. "Good. Thanks."

"Jimmy's got a cousin who's still single. He lives with his mama yet," Sheryl said. "She's kinda bossy, but George is nice. Want me to set something up?"

"No—"

"Yes!" Jenna's louder answer overrode my refusal. "Have him call her!"

With a nod, Sheryl darted off to another table.

"What about Vicki's brother-in-law?"

"You date 'em both. Little Mary Ellen Black dating two men!" She pressed a hand to her chest and widened her eyes over the scandal.

With a laugh, she returned to her lunch and her second beer. "But if you're going to be this wild swinger, you need a new wardrobe. Baggy pants and sweaters are fine for the office, but for dating, you need new clothes." Day after day, Jenna showed up to work in tailor-made suits of every style and texture. Today she wore a platinum suit in rayon that glittered like metal under the jack-o'-lantern lights.

"I can't afford to shop where you do," I pointed out. Although she'd been paying me well and in cash, I was putting that money aside for the girls and for the house I hoped to someday rent or buy. The same desire that had sparked this conversation still burned in my soul. I had to get out of my parents' house. My mother was only part of it; the neighborhood wouldn't feel sorry for me if I hadn't given them something to feel sorry about. I needed independence.

"You can shop where I shop," Jenna insisted.

I shook my head. "I don't want to blow my money on clothes." Especially clothes for dates that I didn't want to go on.

"I can't believe you said that. Are you sure you're a woman?"

I sighed. Sure, I'd love new clothes. But I wasn't just a woman. I was a mother, too. I pushed my barely touched plate away; maybe if I got out of my mother's house I could start eating again.

"Come with me, I'll cheer you up." Jenna stood up and dropped some bills on the table. "Sheryl won't let us pay, but she's getting a big tip."

I added a couple of bills to the pile Jenna left. "You're sure they'll be okay?"

"With the mortgage?"

"Not just that loan."

She sighed. "Siggy'll work with them. And if he won't, I'll refinance them if the rate goes down and get 'em enough extra to pay him off."

"You refinance a lot of people and get them extra cash out." And deeper in debt despite the lower payments. "Are a lot of people in debt to Siggy?"

Jenna didn't answer until we'd waved goodbye to the bustling Sheryl and crossed the street to the car. The black Cadillac gleamed in the midday sun. "Well..."

"You, too?"

She clicked the locks then slid behind the wheel. "Not now."

"But you were?" I asked as I settled against the leather bucket seat. Much higher than the seats in the Bonneville, although that car had probably been nice in its day. Wasn't its fault its day had been long ago.

She started the car and pulled out into traffic with nary a glance. "Sure, I think everybody on the West Side has been in debt to Siggy at some point in their lives."

"To a loan shark?" I couldn't believe it.

She laughed. "Think about the neighborhood, Mary Ellen. More people around here would trust Siggy over a bank. You know Siggy's always gonna be around." True. The old man was probably a hundred years old and still going strong. "Especially after what happened to you with the foreclosure."

"Yeah."

"Rumor has it your dad borrowed money from Siggy when he first married your mom."

"Really?" I couldn't imagine for what. They'd always lived with Grandma. Daddy had always worked in the shop. They hadn't even started their family, with me, until they'd been married for ten years.

Tires squealed as Jenna rounded a corner, heading away from the office. "Yeah, rumor says your dad worked off the money by working for Siggy."

"Dad's always run the shop for Grandma. What could he have done for Siggy?"

"Convince some debtors to pay up."

I shivered. "You're saying my dad beat people up for a loan shark?"

She nodded. "Heard he was good at it, too. Roughed up my old man once."

"God, Jenna, I'm sorry. What your mother must have thought…"

Jenna laughed. "She was pissed, all right, mostly because your dad hadn't hurt him worse. At least that's how she tells it now."

Eddie's black eye flashed through my mind. Was Daddy still good at it? Or had Eddie ticked off someone else? Knowing Eddie better now than I had for the eleven years we were married, anything was possible. "So where are we going?" I asked as she crossed over the Grand River, heading deeper into the heart of Grand Rapids. "Taking me on another appointment?"

"No, we're going to stop by my place a minute." I knew Jenna hadn't moved back home after her divorce. Her mother still lived in the house where Jenna and her brothers had grown up and where Jenna's father had died, but Jenna hadn't moved back home because she was ambitious and driven. She hadn't ever relied on her husband for security, just fidelity.

On the east side of the river, she pulled into a parking garage adjacent to an old warehouse that had been converted to condominiums. Very Jenna-like. She wouldn't want to deal with maintenance or yard work. Toiling with the soil, planting flowers, she'd rather pay someone to do that for her. She wanted convenience.

I wanted comfort. She let me inside the heavy, riveted steel door. "Nice place," I said, my gaze flitting around the cavernous living room. Light hardwood floors met redbrick walls with long windows. Overhead, rafters stretched across the high ceiling, revealing copper pipes and aluminum heat ducts. Very modern, very no-nonsense. Nothing soft or relaxing here.

"Really?" she asked as she dropped her briefcase by the door. "No throw pillows. No wallpaper. No flowers. Aren't you going to have a cow?"

A couple of weeks ago, I'd made the mistake of taking Jenna along while I'd toured the Heritage Hill homes that opened once a year to the public. I'd mentioned some ideas that they could have done to really showcase those gorgeous, historic homes. Instead of that new house we'd bought in Cascade, I would have preferred to move to Heritage Hill from the West Side.

"No, it suits your personality very well, Jenna." And still no pictures, nothing truly personal.

"Well, thanks, I think," she said. "I'll be right back." She headed down the hall beside the door. I stepped out into the room, admiring the spectacular view of the river through the long windows. Then I noticed the rattan stools pulled to the bar at one end of the galley kitchen.

Curiosity driving me, I opened the stainless-steel refrigerator. The contents consisted mostly of cans of beer and a few moldy oranges. Beside the fridge, a wire wine rack sat atop the black marble counter. After glancing around to make sure Jenna hadn't returned, I opened a cherry-wood cabinet. A bottle of whiskey and a box of saltines. My stomach growled, and I reached for the crackers.

"You should have eaten your lunch," she tsked as she draped some clothes over the breakfast bar. "It was good."

"What are those?" I asked around a mouthful of cracker.

"Your new clothes."

I'd lost some weight from my divorce diet, but not enough to fit into Jenna's tiny wardrobe. "I can't wear anything of yours."

"Your clothes are hanging on you. You need a smaller size."

"And I'd say you're still a size smaller, and shorter." While I wasn't tall at five feet five inches, I wasn't Jenna's petite barely five. Nor was I as delicately boned. Grandma said Czerwinski women were big-boned. I liked that theory. Big-boned women could carry more weight. I ate another cracker.

"You're not the only one who lost weight through a divorce."

"So these are your fat clothes?" That would increase my self-confidence, wearing Jenna's fat clothes.

"Some of this stuff I never even wore. I order everything through catalogs. I don't have time for shopping. Malls give me hives."

"Now who's not a woman? Bite your tongue." I'd rather go to the shopping mall than church…and risk God striking me dead in the shoe department.

"Shut up and try this stuff on."

I gestured toward the tall, bare windows. "Not in here."

"Not going to give the noonday fishermen a peep show? Use my bedroom. But make it quick, we gotta get back to work before Vicki blows."

I gathered up an armload of clothes. "I thought you hired me so she could get some rest."

"And she gets more rest at work than home with the other kids underfoot."

"True."

"And you've been doing a good job, really taking the workload and stress off her. Take whatever fits of those clothes and consider it part of your bonus."

She might call it a bonus for working. I still thought of it as charity…until I really looked at some of the clothes as I dropped them on her unmade bed. Tags still hung from the sleeves of suits and dresses in every texture and color. This was nearly as exciting as mall shopping.

Then I glanced around the room, awash with light streaming from the windows. Throw pillows covered the bed, tangled in the rumpled red silk comforter and sheets. Mirrored closet doors were slid half open, reflecting the light and bouncing it back off the redbrick walls.

Here were the pictures, a profusion of them on the walls and scattered about her dresser. I stepped closer, studying faces, recognizing her older brothers. Ronald's beefy arm was wrapped around the shoulders of a bleached blonde, and on her lap sat two towheaded kids. Arthur sat on the hood of a red Corvette, squinting against the sun despite the shadow of the palm tree under which he'd parked. Then Rye…his high-school graduation photo revealed that he'd grown up tall, but still skinny. His big dark eyes shone with youth and innocence. Could he really have changed so much in the six or so years since he'd graduated that he'd wind up in prison? But then, a lot of kids from the neighborhood had.

My gaze skimmed along, but before I could scrutinize any other photos in the row, Jenna called out from the hall. "The pants shouldn't be too short. I always have to have Mom shorten them for me, and she didn't touch any of those. Why don't you try on that red dress. That'd be a great date dress."

I moved back to the pile of clothes on the bed. A red silk dress flashed at me from beneath the sleeve of a purple ray-on suit. "Red? With my hair?" I shuddered.

"Be daring, be adventurous," Jenna taunted, her voice growing louder as she came down the hall.

I didn't know much about myself, not yet, not with the ink hardly dry on the divorce decree. But I did know what I was not. "I'm not daring. I'm not adventurous. And I'm not ready to start dating. Not yet." Maybe not ever. After the girls grew up and left me, I would start taking in stray cats. I'd be the cat lady of…whatever street where I finally found a house of my own.

Jenna stared at me for a minute, then she narrowed her eyes. "Mary Ellen, you're scared!"

"Yes, I am," I admitted with no shame. "Dating is how I wound up pregnant and married to Eddie."

"That won't happen again. You're older, smarter."

I wasn't so sure about that. I shivered at the idea of dating, the risk. "I have two daughters to think about. Perverts prey on divorced women like me, women with beautiful daughters." The beer and two bites of beef noodles rolled around in a sickening wave in my clenching stomach.

"You're spending too much time with your mother."

"Tell me about it." Because Mom told me every horror story she heard on the news or read in the paper, warned me against every danger.

"You need to get out of that house."

"That's what I've been saying. And not to date. I don't want to date. I can't trust a man again. I can't believe anything he says, not after Eddie. So yeah, I'm scared. I'm scared to death of making the same mistake. It's better not to risk it."

"Going in, or going out in this case, you know that. You're in control now, Mary Ellen."

"I'm in control." Repeating it to myself didn't make me believe it any more than I had when Jenna had first told me so over a week ago. "I'm in control."

Vicki whistled to catch my attention, her hand over the mouthpiece of her phone. "I'm still here, you know. You're not in control yet."

I laughed. "Yet? I'll never be in control."

"Just so we understand each other." She smiled at me, probably the first time since I had started working with her.

"I've told you, Vicki, I don't want your job." I would, however, like to be in control. That had a very nice sound to it.

"You're welcome," she said to her caller and flashed me another smile after hanging up the phone. Then she eased back in her chair, resting her feet atop her dented metal wastebasket, and settled her palms on her stomach.

"I understood something else, too. Jenna hired me so you could kick back."

She winced and rubbed her side. "I'm not the one kicking."

"Rib or bladder?"

"Both. This kid's coordinated. More than his father, that's for sure."

"You really should be home getting your rest." The mother in me was always in control; it was the woman who had problems.

She flipped me off, as professionally as Jenna did. This office was full of professionalism and office machinery with as much attitude as the workers. Take the fax machine, for instance, and on a few occasions I'd nearly thrown it out the window so someone could take it. Behind me, a dial tone rang out in sick-sounding tones before the machine choked itself trying to print out the fax on about ten pages at the same time.

"Chewy's hungry, too," Vicki chortled, enjoying my resentment of the malfunctioning machine.

"Chewy…I can't believe you guys named this…"

"Piece of shit?"

"Yeah, and I can't believe that you keep it."

"Can't throw something out once you've named it."

I wrestled the extra pages from Chewy, cursing him under my breath the entire time. "I really can't understand why Jenna keeps this thing!"

"Shit!"

"Yeah, I know…piece of…shit." I always watch my language around the girls to the point that I wasn't comfortable swearing even when they weren't around. But I have a feeling that working with Vicki and Jenna would change that attitude of mine, too.

"Oh, oh, oh!" The cries tore from Vicki's throat in a tortured groan. "My water broke!"

I whirled away from the fax machine, dropping papers all over the counter and the commercial carpet. "Oh my God! Okay, okay, 911. We've gotta call 911."

"Call Bruce first. Call Bruce," Vicki panted as sweat broke out on her forehead. "He's on speed—" She broke off for another tortured groan.

Oh, God. It was going too fast. As a woman who'd suffered through nearly a full twenty-four hours of labor for each child, I knew this wasn't right. Speed dial. That's what she meant, I realized as I rushed over to her and saw the name on her phone. Okay, first I'd call Bruce and then the paramedics. When I reached for the phone, Vicki grabbed my hand, squeezing it tight.

"It's too fast, Mary Ellen—too fast!" She clenched her teeth on another groan.

Tears of sympathy and sheer terror pooled in my eyes, but I blinked them back. She was the one being ripped in two by the birth of, from the size of her stomach, a two-year-old. "I'll call 911!"

"Bruce—Bruce is my breathing partner. He wants to be—" She groaned again.

I punched in Bruce's name, got cell-phone voice mail. "Vicki's in labor…at the office. I'm calling 911," was my harried message before hanging up.

"He'll get it—he keeps checking even when he's on the line," Vicki said. Bruce worked at a local factory, long hours of backbreaking work to support his family. I wished he were here right now instead of me.

"I'll be your partner until he does." Then I dialed 911.

"Calling from First Choice Mortgage at 1300 Walker Avenue. A woman is in labor here…"

"How far apart are her contractions?" asked a nasally, female voice.

"I don't know. There doesn't seem to be any time between them. I don't think we'd make it in the car…"

First off, I didn't think I could get her to the car. Even without being pregnant, Vicki would be no dainty flower. And being, as she ascertained, a year pregnant, she was the size of a big-time wrestler. She screamed as another contraction tore her apart. "He's coming, Mary Ellen. I gotta push!"

"No!" I shouted in unison with the nasal voice on the phone.

"Is this her first pregnancy?"

"No, her fourth…" Her kids' cute faces flashed across her computer terminal as a screen saver. Counting them took my mind off the fact that she was breaking my hand and giving birth in her desk chair.

"Then this baby could come fast—"

"No kidding!" I shouted back. "Send a fucking ambulance!"

"Mary Ellen?" Vicki lifted her sweat-streaked face, her eyes wide with shock. Oh, she was going into shock.

"You just swore," she said, her voice soft with wonder.

"Yeah…"

"The big one," she said, her head rolled back on the chair as she ripped out another agonized scream.

"Where's the ambulance?" I yelled into the phone.

"No need to swear, miss. The ambulance has been dispatched. It should be there soon."

"I gotta push!" Vicki pressed her chin against her chest, bearing down.

The ambulance wouldn't be soon enough…

Jenna pressed a paper cup into my shaking hands, and I sloshed coffee over the brim.

"Damn," she said, taking it back. "Did you get burnt?"

I couldn't stop shaking. The vinyl waiting-room chair vibrated beneath my trembling body.

"Damn!" Jenna cursed again as coffee trailed under the lid and over her fingers. She tossed the cup into a trash bin; she was shaking, too. And pacing. And earlier, when she'd walked into the office as Vicki's baby was crowning, she'd been vomiting. Right there on the office floor, on the commercial carpet, atop the mutilated faxes I'd dropped.

"Who would put themselves through that kind of pain on purpose?" she asked for the hundredth time since she'd emptied her stomach.

"What?"

"You don't count. Amber was an accident."

I hated to hear my oldest referred to that way, but there was some truth in it. "But I wanted her."

"Yeah, yeah, I know you did. But that…" She swallowed hard. "That is cruel and unusual punishment. After you had Amber…"

"I waited a while." Although Mom had asked me in the hospital when I would try for Eddie's boy. Like Eddie had wanted a boy; I wasn't sure Eddie had wanted any kids at all, although in the beginning he had taken pride in our girls.

Poor Bruce. He wanted his babies, and he'd wanted to be a partner for his wife. But despite all the speed limits I'm sure he broke to get to the office, he'd been too late. His wife and baby had already been loaded into the ambulance, on their way to the hospital. Pounding on the doors had stopped the van, and they'd let him climb inside. He'd been shaking, too. And if Vicki hadn't gone so fast, he would have been her partner.

Eddie had never been mine. He'd never made it for either labor, and since each had lasted twenty-four hours, he'd had plenty of time to make it to the hospital. Now I suspected he hadn't wanted to leave the restaurant; then he'd told me he'd loved me too much to see me in that much pain and be helpless to take it away for me. Yeah, right. But back then, I'd been moved by the depth of his feelings.

Daddy had taken me and paced the waiting room while Mom and Grandma had held my hands, Grandma in sympathy and Mom tsking that it wasn't that bad. I'm surprised I didn't kill her then. If I'd gotten a female judge who'd had children, she would have ruled the homicide justified.

"But then you had Shelby," Jenna sighed, "And went through that all over again."

"And wanted to." Eddie and I had tried for two years. "I tried and tried to get pregnant with Shelby."

Jenna shuddered and leaned against the cement block wall, painted a soothing off-white. "On purpose?"

I nodded, and a small smile lifted my lips. "I liked being pregnant."

"You liked doing that?" Her shoulders shook as she fought

a dry heave. I'd had to drive her Cadillac to the hospital, as she'd spent the time with her head between her knees trying to breathe.

"Not *that*. Labor was not fun." Especially not with Mom as coach. "But holding that tiny baby in your arms, holding *your* baby, the one you've carried for nine months—"

"Or in Vicki's case, a whole damn year!" An older lady glared at Jenna and gestured toward the children playing at small tables.

"There's nothing like holding your child for the first time, having her open her eyes and look up at you. She's so small and so new and totally dependent on you to make her life right..." Those tears I'd pushed back earlier slid down my face unchecked.

"Don't cry, Mary Ellen," Jenna said, her voice catching as she fought tears herself. "You're a hero. You brought that baby into the world before the freakin'—" she glared at the older lady "—paramedics put down their doughnuts, and decided to answer their call." She pressed a Kleenex into my hand. "I can't believe you handled that—you were so calm, so controlled..."

I shuddered. Calm and controlled? Hardly. "Vicki brought that baby into the world. She did all the work. I was just there."

"Bullshit!" She shot a hard glance at the offended woman before the old lady could manage another glare. "You're amazing, Mary Ellen."

I didn't feel amazing. I felt sick, and still I couldn't stop shaking. "Jenna," I said it soft so that she leaned closer as I made my horrible confession. "I used the F word."

She erupted, her petite body shaking with laughter. "Oh, God, Mary Ellen!"

Bruce strode into the waiting room, his face split with a wide grin. "They're both okay. Vicki wants to see you!"

Jenna started forward, but I remained sitting, my legs trembling yet.

"You, Mary Ellen."

"Come on," Jenna said, half lifting me from the chair. "You're the hero of the day."

"Sure are," Bruce agreed, grabbing me in a half hug despite the fact the only time we'd met had been outside an ambulance carrying his wife and baby.

With Bruce holding one arm and Jenna the other, I managed to stay on my feet. But when I walked into Vicki's room where she held the tiny baby girl in her arms, I needed no support. I rushed to the bed. "You're okay?"

"Fine. The doctor says we're both fine. Healthy. But I couldn't have—" Vicki's voice broke and tears flowed. "But we wouldn't have been fine without you, Mary Ellen."

"Bull. It was all you. You're one strong lady." Vicki had it all. A job she fought to protect; a husband she loved and who loved her back; a baby and three other beautiful children at home. She was the richest woman I knew.

"You talked me through it. You helped with the cord when it got—" Her breath choked off as she looked down at her sleeping baby, her face soft with awe.

"The ambulance dispatcher talked me through that…" I'd be hearing that nasally voice in my nightmares.

"I know you two have already met, but I want to officially

introduce you," Vicki said, her voice shaking with emotion. "Mary Ellen Black, meet your namesake, Mary Ellen Reynolds."

Tears fell again and not in neat trails down my cheeks. I flooded out and could hardly see the little, dark-haired baby who shared my name. "Vicki, are you sure? You had other names picked out."

Vicki nodded at Bruce. "We decided. You brought her into the world; she should have something of you, too."

Jenna shifted behind me, then fled into the hall before I could turn around. I hoped she wasn't jealous.

"I want to hold the baby," I said, "but I have to get cleaned up first. I'll go home and come back tonight."

Bruce smiled and brushed a kiss against his wife's forehead. Then he winked at me. "And someone will be here that would very much like to meet you."

Oh, God, his brother. I wasn't ready for that. I smiled. "See you both later, then. I'm so glad everybody's fine."

Everybody but Jenna. I found her toward the end of the hall, shoulders shaking as she stared through the glass at the babies in the nursery. In the reflection, I saw tears streaming down her face. "I shouldn't want one, not after seeing what torture it was for Vicki to bring her into the world. I really shouldn't…"

"But you do," I said with sudden understanding. "Ah, Jenna, you'll meet someone. You'll start a family of your own. And there are drugs, you know, that make it so it's not so painful."

I hadn't had any of those drugs, just the ones to speed

things up and make the experience nastier. My HMO hadn't okayed an epidural for me until I was pushing the kid out. But I'd try to make sure Jenna didn't have her baby in the office, although with the hours she worked, she just might.

Her breath shuddered out with another sob. "I can't…"

"Yes, you can. You're the one who told me not all men are jackasses."

"No, Mary Ellen, I can't! Todd stole this from me."

"You can trust again—" I probably couldn't, but Jenna was stronger than I was. She'd be brave enough to trust again. She'd trusted me again.

"No! I can't have kids, Mary Ellen. Todd gave me chlamydia. The infection destroyed my tubes. I can't get pregnant."

The confession was wrenched from her with pain and heartbreak. My arms closed around her, and we stood like that a long time before the nursery window. Hugging and crying…

I stumbled through the back-porch door, my legs leaden now that they'd stopped shaking. Mom glanced up from the stove, her gaze traveling down my suit, the purple one from Jenna. "Oh, look what you've done. You ruined that suit!"

I didn't glance down, knowing that the sight of blood and mucus might unsettle my stomach again after the nerves had finally left it. If one of my children had walked in the door covered in blood, I would have been all over her checking for injuries, consumed with worry. Mom was only consumed with disgust. I pulled out a chair from the metal kitchen table, unsure if I could climb the stairs to the bathroom yet. "Why, Mom?"

"What? Why what? You got all messed up from getting in the paramedics' way. We heard all about Vicki having her baby at the office."

Dad stumbled in the door behind me, his face white with worry. "I heard about it at the store. The paramedics weren't there. Mary Ellen brought that baby into the world."

Like Jenna, uncaring of the blood, he pulled me from the chair and into his arms. "You okay, baby? You must have been so scared."

I'd thought I was all cried out, but with Dad's concern, more emotion leaked out. "I'm fine, Daddy. Really. And Vicki did everything. I'm going to change and go back. Maybe I'll bring the girls."

Dad squeezed me once more before releasing me. "Their mother's a hero. They're gonna be so proud."

As I turned for the stairs, I glanced back at Mom, but she had whirled toward the stove again as she stirred something in a big stockpot. I'd managed only a few steps before I heard her say, "You're going to give her a big head, talking like that."

How many times had I heard that growing up? Every time Daddy had given me a compliment. But what was worse was when she said it to me when I gave compliments to my own children. Mom hadn't answered my question when I'd asked why. Why did she sometimes act as if she hated me? That's what I needed to know.

Grandma gasped as I passed her bedroom on the way to the bathroom. "Mary Ellen, are you all right?"

"Yes, Gram."

She stood in the bathroom doorway. "I heard what you did for Vicki Reynolds. You're an amazing woman, Mary Ellen. Maybe you should become a midwife."

In the vanity mirror, I saw my reflection. Blood had dried on my face in red streaks that matched my hair. My hazel eyes were still glazed, with fatigue or shock. There were spatters of blood from the neck of my suit to the hem. My stomach roiled. "No way."

"You could go back to school…"

I shook my head. "No."

"No, Mary Ellen, I've been thinking about it. This job with Jenna O'Brien isn't permanent, you'll need something else, but when you were interviewing, you said everyone else was more qualified. You need a degree, honey."

"Gram, there's no time…"

"There's plenty of time. You're young. Just thirty…"

"Thirty-one in January."

"Just a baby. Hell, women my age are going back to school every day. You should do this, Mary Ellen, for you."

And Jenna thought I should get sex for me. All I wanted was a place of my own. "I can't, Gram. I don't want to spend my money—"

"You could get financial aid. I was talking to Lorraine at the beauty shop… I'm thinking about going red, too." She patted her blue coif. "And she said she mentioned food stamps to you, and you refused to check into it. Pride—"

"Is all I got left, Gram."

"No, you have two girls you have to take care of. If you

want to get out of here, and I think you do, you're going to have to accept some help."

A sigh of relief shuddered out. "That's why I can't go back to school, Gram. I don't want out in four years. I want out now!"

She nodded. "Your mother's jealous of you, honey. Haven't you figured that out yet?"

"What?" How could a woman be jealous of her own child? Gram must have been into the laced tea again. But I didn't think it was bridge day.

"When your grandfather was alive, we raised German shepherds…" Yeah, she'd been into the tea all right…or she was slipping. "And we had this one bitch, she always ate her female puppies. Didn't want the competition."

Grandma had just called my mother a bitch. I loved it. "Gram!"

"When you're ready to accept some help, I've added to my pin money…"

Grandma had plans for that money. "But your Vegas trip…"

She shook her head. "And miss all the excitement around here? You birthing babies and all? No, Mary Ellen, it's too much fun watching you take yourself back. I don't want to leave now."

Taking myself back. "How did you know?" I asked, tears pooling again.

"Your mother and Morty Schwartz the lawyer, they were the only ones who thought you should keep the name No-wicki. Your father and I actually agreed for once. We knew you had to take back Mary Ellen Black."

"They named the baby after me, Gram…"

She smiled. "That's quite a compliment and quite a responsibility. You're named after me. And the Virgin Mary, of course." She crossed herself.

I nodded. "It's a compliment to *me* that I share your name. And I want it to be a compliment to Mary Ellen Reynolds, Gram. But that little baby is only a few hours old, and she already knows who she is more than I know who I am. Taking myself back isn't easy…"

"Nothing in life ever is, honey, but it sure is an adventure."

As she ambled back down the hall to her bedroom, I glanced down again at my bloodstained suit. It was an adventure all right…

Amber and Shelby hovered close by the chair where I sat, cuddling the sleeping infant.

"She's so beautiful…" Amber sighed.

Shelby wrinkled her nose as she stared down at the baby. "She is?"

"All babies are," Amber insisted in rare defense of her opinion.

"Especially this one," I said, gazing down at the perfect little girl.

"'Cause she's named after you," Amber said with a quiet chuckle and not just in deference to the sleeping mother. Amber always spoke softly.

"Was I a beautiful baby?" Shelby asked, her high, squeaky voice not so quiet.

"A wrinkled little baldy," Amber answered.

"A beautiful baby. Both you girls were and still are." I'd give my daughters the biggest heads on the West Side.

"We're not babies," Shelby argued, but her eyes twinkled. "I want to have a baby sister. Maybe even a brother. Can you have another one, Mom?"

"Yeah, Dad got fixed, but you can have another one, Mom."

I yearned for another tiny bundle, to carry beneath my heart and then deliver, to hold it close to me, as I had held my other two. "I'm so happy with you both. I would be selfish to wish for any more."

"Are you really a hero, Mom, like Vicki's husband said?" Amber asked, her green eyes wide behind her glasses.

I shook my head. "No, I didn't do much of anything. This little girl's mother did all the hard work."

"And she's modest," Bruce said from the doorway as he ushered another man into the room. Oh, boy, he was selling me. And I didn't want to be on the market. I wasn't ready. I wasn't yet in control.

"Mary Ellen, nice to meet you. I've heard so much about you, especially today." He smiled, noticing my arms were full of baby. A gold tooth flashed on the left side of his mouth, and I blinked as the overhead fluorescent light reflected off it. I don't know if the tooth was a vanity or an age thing. He was obviously Bruce's older brother, probably close to fifty. A good ten years older than Eddie, and some people had said Eddie was too old for me. But despite being nine years older, Eddie hadn't been more mature. Maybe this man was.

"I'm sorry I don't remember your name," I confessed, having blocked it from my mind if I'd ever heard it.

"Ted. And no one will forget this little lady's name." He ran a stubby fingertip over the baby's cheek, which was nestled close to my breast. Then he flashed a smile at my girls. "And who are these lovely ladies?"

I fought a shudder and hoped my skin didn't crawl away. "This is Amber and Shelby," I said, not eager to have my children speak to this stranger.

"I have kids, too, actually even a grandbaby now. Can you believe I'm a grandfather?"

Yes, actually, I could. The paunch at his waist and the majority of salt in his pepper hair gave it away. "Really?"

"You're Grandpa's age?" Shelby, ever diplomatic, asked.

His tooth disappeared. "I'm sure I'm not."

I wasn't so sure. "Well, it's a school night. I really have to get the girls home to bed." I stood up, shifting the baby to Bruce's waiting arms. As old Ted glanced down my figure, I suspected he had thoughts of bed, too. He could forget getting me in it with him.

Vicki murmured, her groggy eyes half-open. "Mary Ellen…did you meet Ted?"

"Yes, we met. I really have to get home, though." With a hand on each girl's shoulder, I edged them toward the door.

"Mary Ellen, I'd like to call you sometime," Ted persisted, following me out the door.

"Um…" I hadn't had a man ask me out in eleven years, and even Eddie had had more finesse than this and a helluva lot more charm. "I'm really…not ready yet."

"I've been divorced twice now," he freely admitted. "Trust me—" Sure, with that kind of track record, what woman wouldn't? "It really does get easier to get back out there," he continued. "How about a movie? We can even bring the girls along, see something they might like. My grandson is about this one's age." Despite her gregarious nature, Shelby shot behind me as he reached for one of her pigtails.

"They'd get along great…" Now who was selling? And way too hard? Was he that desperate for number three?

I wasn't comfortable being an ex-wife; I knew I sure wouldn't like being someone's third wife. Or a stepgrandma. No wonder Jenna had never considered dating him.

Jenna… When she'd dropped me home earlier, she'd pulled herself together. She'd been the brash and sassy career woman that the whole West Side knew and feared. But they'd not held her as she wept her broken heart out in front of a hospital nursery. I'd called her before I'd left for the hospital to bring the girls to visit. I'd only gotten her voice mail. But earlier she'd assured me that she'd be okay. That she was fine, really. And Jenna was strong, far stronger than I'd ever realized.

"So I'll call you then," Ted finished his pitch, the one I'd tuned out. He had to be a salesman. Car dealer, I think I remembered Vicki bragging.

Despite the warmth of my sweater, goose bumps rose on my flesh. "No, you'd just be wasting your time." Life might be an adventure, but I wasn't about to find any fun and games with him. The *ding* of the elevator sent me rushing toward it, dragging the girls along until the doors closed between us and his halfhearted, gold-tooth smile.

Silence carried us to the parking garage, but then Amber

spoke, her expression shielded by the dim lighting. "Will you go out with him?"

I shuddered at the thought. "You heard me tell him no."

"He was icky. And he smelled funny," Shelby pointed out the overusage of cologne that still burned in my nostrils.

"So when he calls…"

"He won't call," I tried to reassure Amber as we approached the Bonneville.

"But, Mom, he wasn't listening. He just kept looking at you. You're really pretty now."

Warmth flooded my heart. "Not as pretty as you girls."

Amber paused at the door I'd just unlocked for her. Glancing up, she asked, "We're prettier than you?"

At ten and a half, she didn't have to look up very far. Pretty soon she'd be taller than me. And a teenager. And I'd have to worry about her dating instead of her worrying about my dating. I pulled her close for a hug. "You're very pretty."

"I'm not. I have these stupid glasses and stupid hair and…" A little sob caught in her throat, and I realized my tomboy was gone. Amber had turned the corner. She was no longer a kid; she was edging toward young woman.

CHAPTER L
Leave it alone

"I don't want to talk about it. Leave it alone."

"That's like sticking a sign on the grass to keep off. People inevitably have to walk on it," Jenna pointed out.

"People don't. *You* have to. Other people respect other people's wishes." And I had respected hers. Knowing the raw pain her infertility caused her, I would never bring it up. But I'd always be there if she needed me. And I wished I had been there for her while she'd gone through the whole horrible ordeal. Maybe that's why her brother Rye had been locked away in prison.

He'd killed Todd. And I couldn't blame him. Despite the evidence, the jury must not have really blamed him to sentence him for such a short time. Jenna had only been divorced a year or two.

"You date him then," I offered as Chewy mutilated a sheaf of papers while printing a cruise ad.

"Ted keeps calling, Mary Ellen. Did you really think a man who's been married three times would—"

"Three?" I interrupted, choking on the sip of coffee I'd taken. "He told me he's only gone through two divorces. Did he kill one?"

"No! God, you have a wild imagination…"

If only.

"I guess the third divorce isn't technically final yet."

"And he's hounding me for a date?" Ted wasn't that much different from Eddie. Despite the extra ten or so years, he wasn't any more mature or responsible.

"Should have known that'd turn you off. So Ted is history?"

"Ted never was." But what his unrelenting phone calls had inspired was a matchmaking free-for-all. Sheryl or Jimmy's cousin, George, kept calling; actually, his mother called for him. And now, even my father had gotten involved. "Dad's trying to set me up with some guy he knows through the butcher shop."

"Really? Who?"

I shrugged. "Some deer hunter who will call me once he gets this season's buck. I don't think he bathes until then…"

"Sounds yummy," Jenna taunted. "And Ted probably doesn't sound too bad compared to him."

"All of them make celibacy sound wonderful." And I was used to it, with Eddie's infrequent interest in me toward the end of our marriage. What I couldn't get used to was living with my mother. The men calling had confirmed in her mind that I didn't just have the hair of a tramp, but the morals, as well. Didn't matter that I had yet to go on a date with any of these men…

But I had had Lorraine touch up my roots. "Even Lorraine got in on it. Knows some good husband material. Her accountant."

"Oooh, an accountant. I can't stand the excitement. At least Ted will give you a good deal on a new ride." Jenna wrestled the papers from Chewy and spanked his duct-taped side in punishment.

"I like Grandma's car." Most of all, I liked that it was free. My money was going toward other accommodations. Any other accommodations. If winter wasn't coming, and the beginning of November in western Michigan was pretty much winter, I would have considered the box.

"Vintage is in," she admitted.

"I want to get out," I began.

"So take one of these studs up on a date."

"No, I want to get out of my mother's house. I need to get out. Now. I can't stand it much longer." A week had passed since my mother had chastised me for ruining the suit I'd gotten from Jenna. But that hadn't been the worst of it. The worst of it had been her sewing Shelby's Halloween costume. I'd intended to do it, really, when I found time. But there was never enough time. Maybe she'd only done it to help me, but she'd left me feeling as if I'd failed, not only with my marriage but with motherhood, too.

Jenna squeezed my shoulder. "That bad? Your mother is a piece of work. She loves everybody..."

"But me." And if I'd been a puppy instead of a baby, I didn't doubt that she might have eaten me at birth. "And it's affecting the girls."

"I should have offered before. You and the girls can move in with me." I didn't miss the lack of enthusiasm in her voice.

"I can't do that, Jenna. Your friendship means too much. I don't want to test it."

She suppressed a sigh of relief, but I heard a whisper of it. "Well, let me loan you some money for a security deposit for a house."

"I've got an idea about where to get the money. I just need to find something."

"I'll find a Realtor. Or…" She tapped the calendar barely visible under the pile of paperwork on my desk. "Jeez, Rye's out in a couple of days. He's got a house he's been trying to unload. Hell, he's got a few houses…"

"Rye's got houses?"

"Yeah, he learned the carpentry business from Todd, loves working with his hands. I would have mentioned his business earlier, but I thought it might touch a sore spot with you. He buys repossessed houses from banks and the city for a song, fixes them up and sells them. He's been gone a few months, so he's behind on working on them. In fact, I don't even know what he owns and what he doesn't, but I'm sure he'd rent something to you. He'd probably even do a land contract for you."

And kill me and bury me in the basement of one if I didn't pay up? I'd probably be safer taking my chances with Siggy. Or maybe Lorraine's accountant. He'd have good advice on how to manage my finances into a home purchase.

The first advice the accountant offered when I'd finally taken his call was to eat out on a weeknight because we'd find the cheapest specials. Now, that might have turned off another woman, but after Eddie's financial ineptitude, I happened to find frugality very sexy. But as I stood in front of the medicine cabinet in the bathroom, I stared at my reflection and wondered if the accountant would find anything about me sexy. Maybe the hair. Should I have worn the red dress? But I wasn't dating for a love connection. I was dating for financial advice. I should look sensible. And the black pantsuit was certainly that.

"Who died?" Grandma asked, poking her head of blue hair around the corner.

"Mom's going on a date," Amber said from where she sat on the closed toilet lid, watching me over the top of the book open on her lap. I listened for any hint of resentment or fear in her voice, but her soft tones were bland. She was more interested in the various containers of makeup teetering on the edge of the small vanity, although I don't think she wanted me to notice that. She was growing up too fast.

And I wasn't. My palms sweated, my face flushed, nerves danced around my empty stomach.

"You're not going out with the dickhead that keeps calling?" Grandma asked.

I'd given up on asking her to watch her language. Amber knew not to repeat Grandma's colorful new words. Now, Shelby… But Shelby was downstairs helping Mom bake cookies.

"No, not Ted. And get rid of him if he calls again, please."

"Last time he called Grandma told him you were a lesbian," Amber revealed. Why didn't she ask me what a lesbian was? How did my ten-year-old know?

Grandma shrugged. "Don't think it turned him off any. I think one of his ex-wives was one. So if not him, who's tonight's stiff?"

"Lorraine's accountant, Bernard," I said.

Grandma grimaced. "Your first date in eleven years, and you pick an accountant? How much adventure you going to get with him?"

"I'm not looking for adventure. I want advice."

"I gave you advice. Enjoy yourself. Loosen up. Have fun. Have s—"

I quickly pressed my hand over her mouth. "Gram, Amber's right here and listening. This isn't that kind of date." I stared her down hard, then moved my hand away.

She snorted. "In that outfit, it's definitely not that kind of date."

"I don't want that kind of date. I'm not ready, Gram."

Face wrinkled with disdain, she turned away.

Amber stood up and peered over my shoulder as I leaned forward to apply eyeliner.

I don't think I wanted her to be learning the art of cosmetic application yet. "You don't need makeup, sweetie. You're so pretty just the way you are."

She shoved at a strand of hair that had escaped from her ponytail. "You have to say that because you're my mom."

Why? My mom had never said it. "I'm saying it because it's true, honey."

"Mom, your date's here!" Shelby yelled from the bottom of the kitchen stairs.

My stomach flipped. Suddenly I didn't want to date. I

didn't want adventure. I wanted to stay home with the girls, make sure they ate some real dinner and not just the cookies, the cinnamony scent of which drifted up the stairs with another shout-out from Shelby.

"Mommy! Hurry up! He's waiting!"

"Are you ready, Mom?" Amber asked.

No, not after eleven years of marriage, I wasn't ready to start dating again, not even an accountant for financial advice. "This was a mistake."

"Ignore Grandma Mary. You look really good in black with your new hair, Mom. And when you finish lining your other eye, you'll look really pretty, beautiful."

I grabbed her close for a quick hug. "Okay, I can do this…" I finished up the other eye under her scrutiny. "I can do this, can't I, Amber? You don't care?"

She shrugged. "It's not like you're going to marry him or anything. It's just a date, Mom. No big deal. It's not like you're still married like Dad was."

Bitterness twisted her rosebud lips. So cynical for ten, and way too knowledgeable. "You've overheard your grandmas talking."

"They shout at each other. How can you not hear?" And Amber liked quiet. She was no happier living here than I was.

"Okay, I can do this," I said to us both.

Bernard never made it into the house. Dad had trapped him between his bloody apron-covered stomach and the driver's side of a gray Taurus. Sensible car. I found sensible sexy.

I didn't find anything else sexy about the short man cowering under Daddy's inquisition. From the way the cuffs hung over his thin wrists and bony fingers, it looked as if he was wearing his father's suit. The greenish-brown color was a couple decades old. But hey, maybe he was superstitious, and it was his lucky suit. And it wasn't as though I wasn't wearing hand-me-downs myself. I was just lucky enough to have gotten hand-me-downs from someone with a sense of style.

"Daddy, have you met Bernard?"

Daddy eased a little away and turned toward me. "Yeah, Junior does my taxes since his old man spends his winters in Florida. How's the old man doing, Junior?"

Junior? How old was he? As I stepped closer, hoping to pry Daddy away from him, I noticed a few gray strands in his reddish-brown hair. But no real lines fanned away from his eyes behind his black-framed glasses. And there was no paunch.

Still…I felt nothing but a burning desire to…to have him teach me how to save money for a house. Eddie hadn't turned me on the last couple years of our marriage. Why would I expect another man to?

"You two are going out?" Daddy asked. "I thought you weren't ready to date yet, Mary Ellen?" Oh, God, I'd probably have the deer hunter waiting in the driveway, swilling beer with Dad, when I got back.

"Daddy," I cautioned, narrowing my eyes at him. "You better quick check your oil before Mom calls you in the house for dinner, right?"

His face flushed, maybe he'd already been drinking, or maybe he recognized my threat. Either way, he backed off.

And Bernard held open the passenger's door for me. "Thank you…" I couldn't call a grown man Junior. "Bernard."

"Junior's fine."

"You don't mind?" I must have used up all my tact at work that day.

He laughed, and on the whole, it was a pretty normal-sounding laugh. I relaxed against the seat as he steered out of the alley and down the street. "I'm really glad you decided to have dinner with me, Mary Ellen."

"I'm sorry I didn't call you back the first…" Few times. "…time you called. Then when I was at Lorraine's—"

"Really you could save more money by doing your hair yourself." Now he sounded like my mother.

Because it was still afternoon, the interior was light enough that I could check out his cut. Not even. Short, but a bit shaggy. But this was why I'd agreed to go out with him. This was how Lorraine had sold Bernard to me. He was full of cost-effective advice. I needed cost-effective more than I needed compliments or excitement. Hell, the most excitement I'd had lately was when Shelby had done her back handspring at gymnastics the other night. When she got her round-off back handspring like Amber had a few years ago, she would dip her hand in paint and put it on the wall of fame. That was exciting. Dating was not.

"So…" I said after a long unbroken silence. He didn't even play the radio, probably too big a drain on the battery or the gas tank. "I don't really know much about you. Have you been married? Do you have children?"

"Children?" More terror shook his voice than it had Jenna's when she'd admitted the full extent of what Todd had done to her. "Children are too expensive."

What?

"The price of formula and diapers. Even if a woman breast-feeds and uses cloth diapers, the additional cost of laundry soap and the increase in the water bill…" He shuddered. "And then, when they get older, they outgrow everything. Need clothes, shoes, tuition…"

He stopped at a streetlight, and I thought about jumping out. The only advice I'd get from him on how to afford a house would be to sell my children.

"I'm sorry," he said when he finally drew to the end of his list of expenses. "You have children. And everybody says you're a great mother. I'm sure your child support covers their expenses, and living with your parents is very smart."

Now I shuddered. "Nope, no child support. The ex is broke." The Taurus pulled up to a familiar-looking brick wall. Eddie's restaurant.

"Really? I thought he owned a restaurant."

"He does. This one actually. But I suppose the bank now owns more than he does."

He didn't even blink behind those thick lenses. "Really? He has a great weekday special." And still Eddie was going under. Or maybe that was why. Despite the special, the parking lot was nearly empty. Then, of course, it was early yet for dinner. Good thing I'd skipped lunch.

"So you don't want to go inside?" he asked, his voice heavy with disappointment.

Oh, what the hell. I was over Eddie. And maybe it was

smart to remind myself of why I needed to pay attention to Bernard's advice. Eddie was the poster child for what could happen if one didn't budget wisely.

When we entered the restaurant I saw that the poster child had another black eye. I think it was a different eye. The one that wasn't swollen narrowed as I entered the foyer with Bernard.

"What do you want now, Mary Ellen?" he murmured, and I noticed that his lip was swollen, too. He'd really been worked over this time. Was Daddy still capable of that kind of muscle?

"Just a table for my…" I couldn't call Bernard a date, not to anyone. "…friend and I."

"Friend?"

"If it's going to be a problem…" Bernard offered him the right to refuse to seat us. But the empty tables in the dining room spoke of the slow business that was driving Eddie to bankruptcy.

He couldn't afford to turn us away. "No, no problem. Pick any table." As we turned toward the dining room, Eddie caught my arm, fingering the material of the jacket sleeve. "Nice suit, Mary Ellen. I heard you were working for Jenna O'Brien."

She'd been right about the alimony. Good thing the court had decreed all the debts Eddie's responsibility, or I could imagine he'd be slipping me a few overdue bills right now.

"Just helping out while her processor's on maternity leave."

"Maybe if you'd gotten a job while we were married, we

wouldn't have lost everything." He said that now, but when we'd been married, he hadn't wanted me to work. He'd wanted to take care of me and our children. He'd done some job. In some ways, I was angrier about his keeping our dire financial situation from me than his mistress. If he'd told me how the debt was mounting, I would have gone to work then. I would have fought to save the life I'd thought we'd built. I jerked my arm free and stalked to a table with Junior.

"I heard about you delivering that baby," Junior said, his voice awed. "I can't imagine how you held it together…"

But hadn't your marriage. I heard what he left unsaid. Or what he should have said. But little Mary Ellen, the infant, had brains. She'd known which way to get out.

And so did I. I would find a way to take back my life. "So, Junior, tell me how to buy a house."

"If you filed bankruptcy with your husband, you're not going to qualify for a conventional mortgage, not for—"

"I know, Junior. I work for Jenna, remember."

"Do you draw a salary? Without child support, you're going to have to have some means of proving income even to rent an apartment. But a house… Mary Ellen, the best advice I can give you is to continue living with your parents."

I should have stood up and walked out then. I wanted to; I knew Junior wasn't going to tell me anything I wanted to hear. And later, when he held out his hand for my part of the bill, I wished I had walked out.

At least I wouldn't have to worry about his calling again. As he'd said when he'd dropped me off in the alley behind the house, he didn't really want to start dating before the holidays. If we were dating, I might expect presents, and not only for myself but for my children. And he didn't want to fill in for the financial responsibilities that my ex-husband was neglecting. I hadn't expected anything but some advice on how to handle my own financial responsibilities. So my first date in eleven years didn't end in a good-night kiss but a kiss-off.

Because Chewy had decided to repeatedly check his power source and dial tone instead of work, I wound up having to run some closing papers downtown. The loan in question was for Sheryl and Jimmy, and I didn't trust a courier to not get mixed up. But downtown wasn't familiar to me. I wound up parking around the corner from the Grand Rapids Press building, the only open meter I could find, on a side street near a deserted-looking warehouse. Crime in Grand Rapids…well, is like crime in any moderately sized city. After dark I wouldn't have risked it, but it was broad daylight.

I shouldn't have worn the heels. By the time I'd dropped off the papers and headed back toward the car, my feet were screaming. I had just turned toward the side street when a long, black Lincoln limousine pulled up beside me. I couldn't understand why a wedding party would drive through a warehouse district. I waited for it to pass me before I crossed to Grandma's car, but the limo stopped. A door flew open.

I stumbled back, twisted my ankle and thought about screaming and swinging my purse. Then Dougie, the guy I'd seen at Eddie's restaurant, stepped out. His unibrow lowered over eyes full of concern. "Mary Ellen, are you all right? We didn't mean to scare you."

Then I had sure missed the point. "I'm fine. My car's across the street, though."

He cupped my elbow, but instead of leading me to my car as I expected, he steered me to the open door he'd jumped out of. "Mr. Ignatius would like a minute with you," he said.

Mr. Sigmund Ignatius? Siggy?

"Mary Ellen Black," a voice emanated from a wrinkled man who barely sat upright on the rear seat.

"Sir…" My voice cracked with fear.

"I'd just like a word with you. Help her in, Dougie, and we'll take a little ride."

They were taking me for a ride. Oh, God… I looked around for the cement blocks they'd tie to my feet before they dropped me in the Grand River. Before I could think of a protest, I was sitting on a seat so soft it made Grandma's bench seat feel like a steel bleacher. The door closed behind Dougie's muscle-bound body and the car slid into smooth motion.

"Um…" I cast around for something to say, but all I could think of asking was if they were going to beat me up. And I didn't know what the proper etiquette was in such situations.

"How's your family, Mary Ellen?"

"Good." My voice cracked as I formed the word. That's all I could manage.

"Good. Your grandmother's well, then?"

"Yes, good."

"You favor her. She was a stunner at your age, too."

Well, hell, if he was going to compliment me… I relaxed a bit into the leather. "She's always on the go." Meaning Mom was, too, driving her to bingo and meetings.

"No surprise. She was always full of energy. I'm slowing down a bit now, hate to admit it. I'd like her secret." I didn't think her secret to vitality was why he'd picked me up.

"You look great…" For a hundred-year-old man. "And I know you're really involved in the community, too."

He nodded, accepting my compliment with grace. I had to learn that. "I heard what you did for Vicki Reynolds's baby, delivering it. That took a great deal of courage."

And wherever I'd found it for that day, I hadn't been able to tap in again.

"Your girls must be proud of you. You have two?"

I stiffened in my seat. "Yes, I do." My voice cracked again.

"Beautiful girls," Dougie added. "I saw them at the restaurant a couple of months ago."

What the hell was happening? What had Eddie done? "Please…tell me what this is about," I pleaded, and if he threatened my children, he wouldn't live to see a hundred and one.

He groaned, or maybe his bones just creaked as he shifted on his seat. "I have to ask, Mary Ellen, just to clear this up…"

I swallowed hard. "What's this about, Mr. Ignatius?"

"It's regrettable that your ex-husband seems unable to repay a rather sizable investment I made in his restaurant. He claims you're the reason he can't, that you took him for everything in the divorce."

An hysterical laugh escaped before I could swallow it.

"I'm sorry, but that's really…and excuse my language, a load of crap. Check with Mortimer Schwartz. He'll tell you what I got for a divorce settlement—nothing, except an exemption from all Eddie's debts. The bank took the house and my vehicle. Why else would I be living with my parents?"

Siggy leaned forward and squeezed my knee. For an old man, he had a fierce grip. "I'm sorry, dear. I suspected he was lying. But he told the boys that you couldn't live alone, that your daddy had to take care of you."

And the sad part was that until I got a place of my own, he was probably right.

"You look very nice lately, too, dear…"

I touched my hair and the jacket of my navy, wool suit. "Lorraine cuts me a break, and these are Jenna's clothes. I have nothing but my girls, Mr. Ignatius. Eddie has no interest in them—"

"They're safe. You're safe, dear."

And I had no interest in what happened to Eddie. Though I did almost ask why they'd stopped breaking legs. Wasn't that what loan sharks did in the movies?

"And this little meeting, Mary Ellen…"

I nodded as the car slowed. It wasn't a total loss. "I had wanted to ask about your interest rates, anyway." And I never would have figured out where to find him. I could have waited on street corners all day.

"You want a loan, dear?"

"No!" God, no! "But I did wonder about your rates."

"For you, fifteen percent. Less than some credit cards…"

If you were a lousy credit risk. Oh, yeah, I was. "Thank

you, Mr. Ignatius. I enjoyed riding in your car." And not going for a ride.

The car stopped on the street where they'd picked me up. "And dear," he said, a slight quaver in his voice. "Your father…Frank Black's a fine man, a loyal man. He doesn't need to know about this, does he? We just had to check the facts."

"Please, feel free to check with Morty the lawyer. But my father won't know about any of this…" Because he would break Eddie's legs for putting me in this situation. Or maybe he'd make good on that old threat to grind him up into hamburger. And while I didn't worry about what happened to Eddie, I didn't want Daddy winding up in jail.

As I stood beside Grandma's Bonneville, my knees shaking from another adventure, I realized just what the last exchange meant. A loan shark was afraid of my father.

Damn. I didn't know nearly enough about my family. But in this case, I suspected ignorance just might be bliss.

I had one call waiting on hold while Jenna checked in with me. "Mary Ellen, come down to Charlie's tonight. Rye might stop by, and he'd like to see you again. It's been years."

He was out. Had been for a week or so now. Out. What the hell did that mean? Out of where and for what had he been 'in'? I wanted to ask, but the phone, while someone waited on hold, hardly seemed like the appropriate place.

"I have plans with the girls, Jenna." Movie night where we'd nibble popcorn while watching one of their favorite videos that we'd only watched a hundred times before. "After I lock up here, I have to head home."

Jenna had knocked off early in order to schmooze Realtors for referrals. She even worked on her "off" time.

"You have to get with Rye. I asked him about his houses, and he has quite a few, some right in the neighborhood, that you could look at. And he'd work a deal for you, Mary Ellen, you're like family."

I was so glad that she felt that way again even after eleven years of silence. After my date with the accountant, I knew my options had dwindled. I did need to talk to Rye. "I'll wait until he gets used to being…out. Then we can talk. And you don't even know if he's going down there. You said he didn't make it last week." Maybe he wasn't ready for hanging out socially. Not after being "in."

"There're some cute Realtors here," she said, trying to tempt me.

I wasn't tempted. My dismal date with Junior had brought about the realization that dating wasn't worth it. "Not ready. Not interested."

"Your one date in eleven years, and you picked a dud. Pick another one."

"Take your own advice, Jenna. Pick one. Have some pleasure instead of business."

"Hmm…" The considering tone of her voice almost tempted me to stop by and check out whatever she was checking out. "Maybe," she said.

"Have fun!" The phone light flickered off as the person on hold gave up. He would call back and rant and rave for my rudeness in leaving him on hold. What would a Friday afternoon be without someone throwing a major hissy fit? And usually at five minutes to five. I had just shut down all the computers and gathered up my purse when the door opened. Had the caller come in person to harass me? Oh, joy.

I glanced up…and then up some more. A wall of muscle filled the doorway, and atop the broadest shoulders I'd ever seen was a well-shaped head shaved bald. Oh, God, first an abduction by a loan shark; now a mugging by a skinhead. This adventure could end any time now. And if he had a knife or gun maybe it would.

"I'm sorry. Are you the gentleman I left on hold? I was tied up with another caller..." My voice trembled a bit in my haste to apologize and explain, but I didn't think he'd thank me for my efforts.

"No, you didn't leave me on hold. I didn't call first, I just stopped by." To mug or rape or murder me?

What was the proper protocol for that? Should I just hand him the petty cash? I glanced again to those broad shoulders; a white thermal shirt was molded to them and the sculpted muscles of his chest. Faded, ripped jeans clung tight to those long legs. I probably should just hand over my purse, so then he could get to the raping. What the hell was I thinking?

"Mary Ellen? Mary Ellen Black, right?"

How did a skinhead know my name? Oh, God, was that group after Eddie, too? Just what had he done to *them*?

"I'm sorry...do I know you?"

A smile lifted his mouth, and a dimple winked at me from his left cheek. His big, heavily lashed brown eyes warmed with laughter. My stomach flipped. He was still scary. Just a really sexy scary.

"Um..." I stammered.

"I guess I have grown up some since you saw me last, huh?"

"Grown?" Then I remembered the graduation photo on Jenna's dresser. A tall, thin Rye in his cap and gown. He had grown up since I'd seen him in person and had grown out, musclewise, since his high-school graduation. "Rye?"

He ran a broad hand over his bald head and nodded. "Yeah, it's me."

"Ryan O'Brien?"

He winced, the dimple winking with that facial expression, too. "Yeah, I think they were still letting women use major drugs during labor when I was born."

I laughed. "I always thought it was cute."

And he'd been a cute kid. He wasn't a kid anymore. Damn, he was big. And bald. And scary. Had to be why I was trembling.

"Um…Jenna's not here," I said after a long silence during which we just continued to stare.

"I know. She's down at Charlie's…schmoozing." He grimaced, and again the dimple winked at me.

I resisted the urge to wink back. "That's Jenna. But she thought you were going to meet her there."

He shook his head. "Not my thing. I don't really fit in with her crowd." Where did he fit in? A prison yard?

I shivered. "She wanted me to stop by, meet some of the Realtors. But…"

"You weren't interested?"

I shrugged. "Vicki will be back in a couple of weeks. I'm just filling in while she's on maternity leave."

He stepped closer, and with proximity, he was even bigger. "I heard what you did, delivering her baby. Everybody's talking about it."

I tried not to think about it, the terror and helplessness I'd felt. "You know how that goes, every time the story gets told, it gets bigger."

And so did he, as he took another step toward me. Even with heels, my eye level was at his chest, where the shirt was stretched taut across muscles. He cupped my shoulder with one of those huge hands, then squeezed. Gently. If he'd applied any real pressure, he probably could have broken the bone. "You stayed in control. That's impressive."

And so was he. And so was the fact that I was controlling my urge to run screaming out the back door. This was Jenna's brother; I'd helped her babysit him when he was younger. He wouldn't hurt me. No matter who else he'd hurt…

"I heard Jenna lost it," he continued with a little brother's enjoyment of his sister's embarrassment. "Threw up all over the place." Only a brother could find pleasure in that.

But I found myself chuckling a little. "Just when you think she's so tough that nothing'll bother her…" Then you find out how much hurt she's really hiding…

He squeezed my shoulder again, the heat of his palm penetrating my wool jacket and silk blouse. "She's not so tough." He knew.

"No, she's not." I sighed.

"So how are you doing?" His brown eyes softened with real interest; those weren't the eyes of a criminal. And he had really gotten an earful from the gossips. Had he caught wind of Grandma's lesbian excuse for my not dating Ted the car dealer? I hoped not.

"I'm fine." And I really was starting to believe it. "Or at least I will be when I get out of my mother's house."

"She still hard on you?"

How had he known that? Then I remembered the times Jenna and I had pulled him from his hiding spot under her bed where he listened to our conversations. He'd been such a little pest back then. He wasn't little now. I doubt he'd fit under any bed, but he'd probably seen quite a bit of action on top of some. Heat rushed into my face. This was Jenna's little brother. I couldn't think of him that way.

"Mary Ellen?"

I roused myself. "Sorry. It's my fault. I shouldn't let her get to me. I'm an adult now. I'm a mother myself."

He leaned forward, his chest brushing against mine as he reached around me and picked up the two-fold picture frame from my desk. My breath caught, but then he moved away, lifting the pictures into the fluorescent light. "Beautiful girls. The little one has your smile, so full of sunshine."

Me? Full of sunshine? That sun had set long ago... "They're great girls. Very smart. Very sweet."

"They have a great mom."

"A totally biased one, too," I said, taking the frame from his hands before he could reach around me to set it back on the desk. My fingers trembled against the glass and wood.

He'd asked me about my life. I could ask about his, could ask where he'd been. But I didn't think I could handle knowing. If not prison, had he joined the Michigan militia or something?

"You should be proud," he said.

And I was...of my girls. Just not myself. Yet. But I would be. I didn't hold my breath that Mom would ever be, though. "Thanks."

He nodded.

Another silence fell. I felt the need to fill it. "So, if you knew Jenna was at Charlie's...why'd you stop by?"

"You."

"Me?" My voice squeaked.

He nodded again, the fluorescent lights reflecting off his bald head. "I meant to stop by sooner and talk to you, but I've been busy the last couple weeks. I left a lot of stuff unfinished when I had to go back in."

Oh, God. It got worse. He'd been in before and he'd had to go back? For what? Violating parole? I edged away until the backs of my thighs met the desk. "Why did you want to talk to me?"

"Jenna mentioned that you need a house. I'd be happy to show you some."

"You'd rent to me?"

"Do you want to rent?"

"I really want to buy."

"Then I'll sell you one."

"But Rye, I have no hope of getting a mortgage. I don't even have a steady job."

His hand touched my face, nudging up my chin until our eyes met. "Would you promise to make the payments?"

I didn't know how, but I knew that I would…even if it meant a quarter a beer at the VFW. "Yes."

"That's good enough for me."

"Why?" I asked, very conscious of the brush of rough fingertips against my skin. Then he dropped his hand and stepped back. "You haven't known me for years," I persisted. "How can you trust me?"

"Even as a teenager, you always kept your word. I can't imagine you've changed that much, Mary Ellen."

But I had…I think.

"Don't get your hopes up, though," he said. "These houses aren't much. Except for a few bank foreclosures, most of them I buy back from the city are either condemned or close to. I make them structurally sound, but I don't have time for much else. If I was smart, I'd take you through some tonight so you *can't* tell just how much work they really need." The dimple winked at me as he grinned.

I hated to wait; I was so close to getting out myself. Out of the prison of my mother's house. That feeling of suffocation from living there did recall my youth; as a teenager, I'd felt the same urgency to get away from her. I guess that was why I'd fallen for Eddie so fast. But I wasn't a teenager anymore. I was a single mom of two dependent children. "If I didn't have to get home to my girls, I wouldn't care how dark it is already. You've gotta love autumn in Michigan, short, cold days…"

"Compared to where I've been, I don't mind it here. But you're right. It did get dark. I'll walk you to your car. You were just locking up, right?" He stayed close while I shut off the lights and locked the door, too close as I fumbled with the lock. His big body blocked the force of a brisk wind as we stood on the sidewalk outside the office. Then his hand closed over mine, sliding the key home. "You're too cold."

"What about you? You're not even wearing a coat." I had the protection of a wool jacket over a wool suit. He just had that skintight thermal shirt. And no hat.

He turned toward the car parked in front of the office. "I'm fine. Is that your grandma's car?"

"You recognize it?" My heels kicked through dead leaves and a dusting of snow flurries as I walked to the driver's side.

"She nearly took me out a few times while I was riding my bike. She can barely see over the wheel."

"Well, that might be more the seat than the fact that she's shrinking. But you're safe. She stopped driving. Cataracts. Never loses at bingo, though."

"Or cards."

I laughed a bit triumphantly. "Until she played against me."

"You beat Czerwinski the cardsharp?" He wasn't the first to call Grandma that. And then there was Siggy asking about the woman he referred to as a stunner. The cardsharp and the loan shark. Maybe a little romance in her own life would get her off my back about dating and sex.

"So how about tomorrow?"

"What?" I asked. For sex? What was I thinking?

"To look at some of the houses."

"The girls want to go to open gym, but after that, we're free."

"You want to bring them?"

Despite the wool over wool, I shivered. I really didn't want to go alone…with him. "Yeah, they're in this with me."

"Some of these places aren't very nice…"

Then I couldn't risk them. And they wouldn't have the vision I would. I had always had the ability to look at a house and see it the way it should be. That was another reason I had to leave home; there was too much that needed changing there. But change wasn't something my mother had ever known and wasn't likely to accept especially not from me.

"You're right. I'll leave them with Gram. She's teaching them to play cards."

"Like she taught you?"

I smiled. "Yes."

"I've been wanting to play her. I've gotten better over the years, but if you're the new queen of hearts, maybe you're the one I need to play."

I swallowed hard. Then something irreverent bubbled out. "I'll play you for a house."

He laughed. "I never mix business with pleasure."

Which was I? I shivered again.

"You're getting cold. Get in your car. I'll stay here to make sure it starts." Just the way Daddy had always done whenever we drove separately anywhere, even if just to church on Easter Sunday and midnight mass on Christmas Eve.

I blinked back moisture. The cold had to be making my eyes water. Then I opened the door and settled onto the bench seat. The key turned in the ignition, but nothing happened. Not a clank, click or clunk. Not a damn thing.

Knuckles rapped on the glass near my head. I rolled down the window. "It won't do anything."

"Probably a dead battery. I've got cables in my truck. Pop the hood, and I'll check your connections first."

I tugged at the open hood lever, but it didn't budge. "I can't get it—"

His hand reached through the window and fumbled blind for the lever. Fingers brushed over my knee before locating the hard plastic. A sharp pull, and the hood popped.

"Do you have a flashlight?" he asked. The dim streetlight overhead offered little in the way of illumination.

I reached into the glove box, sure my dad had equipped

the car, at least when he knew I'd be driving it. Besides a flashlight, he usually stashed a crowbar under the seat for my protection; something he'd never told me, but I'd discovered when, as a teenager, someone had rear-ended my car and the crowbar had shot forward and broken my ankle.

Daddy's always looking out for his little girl.

Sure enough, I pulled a metal flashlight from the glove box and passed it to Rye. He palmed it. "Heavy. You could use this as a weapon."

Rye shone the light under the hood, then muttered something under his breath. "These cables are so corroded. The battery's probably as old as the car..."

"So you won't be able to jump it?"

He leaned around the hood. "How about I drop you home and bring your dad back? We can clean up the cables and get the car going again."

"I hate to put you out..." I hated getting in a car with him alone after dark. But since he'd stopped by, Rye had done nothing but offer to help me. Still, I couldn't trust him, and it had nothing to do with the bald head and his past and everything to do with my past. I couldn't trust anyone. Not after Eddie.

"It's no problem, Mary Ellen. My truck's just behind yours."

I glanced behind me at the enormous four-wheel drive with the snow tire mounted to the grill. Better than antlers, I guess. Dad hadn't given up on hooking me up with the deer hunter, despite my many protests. I didn't want to date anyone who enjoyed killing animals. But what had Rye done?

Maybe I should just ask. Or better yet, maybe I should start listening to the beauty parlor gossip, and if that failed, Grandma. She knew everything.

I could walk. It wouldn't be the first time I had since borrowing Grandma's vehicle. The gas gauge stuck on full, and if I didn't carefully make note of mileage, I wound up on empty. But that wasn't the problem tonight. I'd filled the tank that morning. And because of that, I'd thought it safe to wear heels. I wasn't walking in these, not in dead leaves and snow flurries. "Okay…"

He opened the door of the car and then the truck for me, and when my heel slipped on the running board, he half lifted me onto the seat of the big pickup. Eddie hadn't even been able to carry me over the threshold on our wedding night. But at five months pregnant, I'd been carrying a little extra weight then. And now the divorce diet and avoiding Mom's cooking had me lighter than I'd been since my early teens.

Rye noticed. "You're too skinny, Mary Ellen."

Despite the bald head and the possible criminal past, I fell a little in love with him. "Don't get used to it. If we strike a deal over a house and I get to do my own cooking, I'll be packing it back on."

He chuckled. "You're not like Jenna, then. She doesn't even know how to cook."

"And doesn't want to learn."

"All work and no play…" He sighed. "I've been wanting to talk to you about her, too. I'm worried." He hadn't had to say it. I had heard it in his deep voice and seen it in the clenching of his hard jaw. The dimple wasn't winking now.

"Me, too," I confessed. Then I reached out, laying my hand on his hard forearm. The muscles tensed beneath my hand. I snatched my hand back. We pulled through the alley and up to Daddy's garage.

"Maybe we can talk tomorrow...while we look at houses," he said as he killed the rumbling engine.

I'd be alone with him tomorrow. Totally alone. But then, I'd been alone with him just now, and I'd survived.

"Rye!" Daddy tossed a cigarette on the ground as he came out of the garage. "I'd heard you were home! Glad you got out!"

Out of what? I wanted to shout the question but held my tongue. I could wait until Rye left and then pump Daddy for information. It was about damn time I started getting interested in other people instead of just my own troubles. Of course, I was worried about Jenna, too. I'd pried into her life; I'd searched her house. I intended to do more; I intended to help her. And Rye could help me do that...while he was helping me out of this house.

Because Daddy had him in a bear hug, I hopped down from the truck myself, just as Mom pulled up in the minivan with the girls and Grandma. "Another date, Mary Ellen?" she asked, probably thinking I was a tramp.

I knew it was a mistake asking her to watch the girls after school. They jumped out of the sliding door with Happy Meals clutched in their hands. But then maybe I was being too hard on her. While she was a pain in the neck, she was a terrific grandmother. The girls adored her.

"The Bonneville broke down at work, so Rye gave me a ride home."

"Rye? Ryan O'Brien?" she asked, her voice lifting with approval. Sure, she could approve of a guy who just got *out* of something, but she couldn't approve of her own daughter.

"Yeah, Daddy's got him on the other side of the truck."

She and Grandma both rounded the hood of the four-wheel drive and joined Daddy in hugging and petting Rye. "I'm so glad you're home," Mom said, giving him more of a welcome than she had her own daughter when I'd moved home.

Grandma reached up to pat his bald head. "You must be so cold." Only Grandma. On the off chance that Rye would have a house I could afford, I had to talk to her, had to ask a favor.

Daddy slapped Rye on the back. "Thanks for getting Mary Ellen home. Did you run out of gas again?"

"Just filled it this morning," I said. I wasn't an idiot. Anymore.

"I think it's the battery," Rye said.

Daddy nodded, accepting Rye's wisdom. "I'll go back down to the office with you and get it home. Louie…why don't you get some dinner going for Rye. Kid must be half starved. They give you anything to eat while you were…"

I missed it as Daddy rounded the hood and Mom started yammering about what fast food she'd picked up.

Where? While he was *where?*

Daddy came back alone in the Bonneville. No high beams of a four-wheel drive followed him down the alley. Even the girls, who had been too timid to approach the bald giant, breathed a disappointed sigh that he hadn't returned. Mom rattled the pans of leftovers she'd heated to fill up that O'Brien boy.

"From the size of him, that wouldn't have been easy anyhow," Gram commiserated.

"Daddy'll eat it, Mom," I reminded her, knowing she'd be disappointed she hadn't been able to feed Rye. She loved feeding people.

"But I brought him back a couple of Big Macs."

"He'll eat those, too." As clogged as his arteries probably already were, it wasn't as if any more fat could get into them. Since I'd moved back I'd harped on them all about fat and exercise, but I'd wasted my breath. They hadn't changed. Nothing ever changed in this house. Not the faded yellow countertops. Not the teapot wallpaper. And not me if I stayed here. "Gram, can I talk to you a minute?"

I steered her into the living room, out of my mother's earshot. Funny how sometimes she seemed as deaf as Grandma, unless you were talking about something you didn't want her to hear. Grandma settled onto the rarely used couch. "What is it?"

"I need to get out of this house, Gram. I love you all, I really do, but the girls and I need a place of our own. I want to take you up on your earlier offer."

"My pin money?"

I nodded. "I'll pay you back. Siggy would charge me fifteen percent interest—"

"That crook!"

"I'd rather give you the interest than Siggy. You can use it for Vegas."

Grandma leaned forward and squeezed my hands. "You don't need to do that, honey. The money is yours whenever you want it. Just tell me. All I want is for you to be happy. And you're not going to be happy living here—"

"Thank you!"

"And you're not going to be happy with boring accountants. If I was looking for a good time in the sack, I'd look at that Ryan O'Brien—"

"He's my best friend's little brother."

"So? He's not *your* little brother."

No, he wasn't. But I didn't know what else he was. And if I asked Grandma about him now, she'd think I had more than normal curiosity about a friend's brother. She'd think I was interested in him as a man.

And I wasn't. How could I be? Rye was six years younger than me, my best friend's little brother, and out of something. I had no idea what. So no, I wasn't interested in him as a man.

Even when he showed up at the warehouse where the girls took gymnastics. Today was open gym, a mad scene of a bunch of squealing girls and a few boys. Unlike a lot of the parents who dropped off their kids and left, I stayed to watch. I'd missed some of their lessons because of work, and the guilt had been eating at me. I leaned over the railing that separated the spectator area from the equipment, watching as Shelby called out to me, "Mom, watch!" before she performed each new stunt she'd learned.

"I took gymnastics here," a deep voice rumbled near my ear as a broad shoulder bumped mine. Rye leaned over the railing next to me.

"You did?"

His bald head nodded. "Mom did extra sewing on the side to pay for them. She thought I might make it to the Olympics someday."

If he had, I would have heard about it. "I just want my girls to have fun, build confidence. I'm not hoping for gold."

He chuckled as Shelby called out again before doing a cartwheel on the balance beam. "That one doesn't need much more confidence." His head swiveled toward where Amber waited her turn for the trampoline, but she kept letting younger kids cut in front of her. "But that one…needs to stick up for herself."

But he was looking at me now. I sighed. "I know. Like mother, like daughter. I need to, too."

"Jenna tells me you got nothing in the divorce—"

"None of the mountain of debt. The restaurant's losing money—"

"Don't defend him! He still has the place, doesn't he? You should have made him sell it to pay you back." Anger vibrated in Rye's deep voice.

A lot of people had felt sorry for me; few had gotten this angry on my behalf. I smiled. "Besides the bank, who owns more of it than he does, seems he had someone else invest, a lot. And I'm not the only one he hasn't been making payments to."

"Siggy?"

I nodded, shivering as I relived my car ride with the hundred-year-old loan shark.

"How bad's Eddie hurting?"

Not bad enough in my opinion. "He's probably been seeing double for quite a while."

"That's not where you're going to get money for a house, are you?"

"Siggy? No, I'd rather give Grandma the interest."

"I said we could work something out, Mary Ellen," he reminded me, his deep voice soft with understanding.

"I don't want charity." Especially not from him.

"I'm not *giving* you a house. He—heck, you might not even like any of the ones I have."

"How many do you own?"

His broad shoulder shrugged, brushing up against mine again. "Some. Here and there." So his ex-brother-in-law's body could be buried anywhere and maybe in more than one place. He sighed. "I was away for a few months, or I'd have less…"

"Your Realtor—"

"I sell them myself. Or in this case, I don't."

I wasn't the only one with trust and control issues. Had Rye been burned, too, and in love or just business?

"So if you buy one of these, you'll be doing me a favor, taking it off my hands. Okay?"

"Sure."

He moved away from me toward the trampoline. Amber's eyes widened behind her lenses as he approached. "Hey, kids, give Amber a turn," he told them. "I want to see if she can do a back handspring."

The smaller kids scrambled away, leaving Amber alone. She rose to the challenge, faultlessly performing the handspring and then a flip. "You're very good," Rye praised her.

I had to blink moisture from my eyes when Amber smiled. She was so beautiful. Rye stayed through the whole open gym, praising both girls as Shelby sought his attention, too. That wasn't unusual; Shelby always sought to be the center of attention. What was different was that Amber didn't back into the shadows and let Shelby shine alone. She continued pushing herself, and I finally realized her potential. With some more self-confidence, she *could* be a gold medal contender.

The manager of the gym approached me with that very thought before we left. "She should be on the team," the middle-aged woman said. "She's that good."

But the team was so expensive. Then Amber flashed another triumphant smile as she did a handstand dismount off the beam, and I knew I'd find the money.

Later, after we'd dropped the girls at the house with Grandma shuffling her deck of cards in anticipation of more lessons, Rye agreed. "The little one's good, too. It's gonna cost you. Eddie should be helping."

"I'll find a way." Saying the words aloud reinforced my belief that I would. Heck, if I had to, I'd apply at the strip club yet. Anything for my girls.

"Why does that scare me?" Rye said with a fake shudder.

I laughed and realized that I wasn't scared of him anymore. I was scared of a few of the houses he showed me, though. Some were in obviously depressed neighborhoods that made the West Side look affluent; the adjoining properties, multifamily rentals. But families didn't appear to be renting them. Drug gangs, maybe, but no families. Without getting out of the car, I shook my head. "No. I don't want to become a statistic."

"Drive-by shooting? Fire bomb?"

"No preference. I wouldn't want to risk my kids or myself, either way."

He nodded. "I know. I was just gauging how desperate you are."

"Not that desperate."

"You'll learn to love your mother's cooking," he teased.

"I didn't in nineteen years. I don't think I can now."

"Okay, I'll take you to the possibles now."

I slugged his shoulder, the muscles not even bunching beneath my fist. "You were just teasing me!"

"Why would I stop doing that? It was always so much fun." He chuckled. "I don't even own those houses."

"Smart-ass!" I hit him again, and this time he pretended to cower behind the steering wheel. "What if I'd wanted to see inside one of them?"

He shook his head. "I know how smart you are. And what a good mother. You wouldn't have considered it."

He knew me better than I thought, better than I knew him. Maybe it was time I started asking some questions. But then he pulled onto a street just a few blocks down from my folks' and close to John Ball Park. The girls would love it; they'd be in the same school. And we'd be close to their grandparents, too. Not to mention the park and zoo.

But would I love it? I'd moved into one house because it was what Eddie wanted; I couldn't shortchange myself again, not even for the girls. For nineteen years I'd wanted out of the West Side, but since being back, I'd come to accept it, accept that I'd learned a lot growing up here. About friendship and hard work and support. Because, despite their sometimes hurtful comments, my family and the neighborhood supported me. I wasn't strong enough to leave it. Yet. Maybe not ever.

"Which one?" I asked, leaning toward the dash.

Rye's big hand closed over my shoulder, holding me back in my seat as he braked the truck on the street. "I thought my little prank would get you thinking more realistically."

He thought I was a dreamer? Okay, so he didn't know me. "What do you mean?" I asked.

"I told you not to expect much. It's the worst house on the street."

But the brick and white clapboard–sided bungalow he pointed to wasn't the worst house. It had character and potential. "It's cute."

"Cute? It's a house."

"A house can be cute." The enclosed front porch covered the front of it. I could imagine hanging plants from it, could imagine Daddy smoking on it when I did our family Christmas party. The new black shingles shone under a sprinkling of flurries. "New roof. Some new windows. You said you've made it structurally sound."

He nodded. "Yes. And done some outside stuff. But it's definitely not cute inside."

He jumped down from the truck and came around to the passenger's side to help me out. But in my excitement, I'd already opened the door and jumped down. Today I wore tennis shoes and old jeans. Rye wore old jeans, too, so old they were worn white at the seams and ragged at the knees. Another white thermal shirt was topped by a quilted flannel jacket, the red plaid making his shoulders and chest even more massive. No wonder all the kids had cleared the trampoline when he'd asked. I swung my gaze back to the porch as I rounded the hood of the truck. "I can see it with those overgrown bushes pulled out of there, flowers blooming."

"If you take this one, be careful where you dig in the yard," he cautioned.

I shivered despite the sweatshirt and down jacket that topped my jeans. "Why?"

"I don't know where she buried..." His face flushed. "Never mind. Sounds crazy. Let's go inside. You'll probably change your mind about the flowers then."

If there was a body buried in the yard, I sure as hell would.

A shared driveway opened up to a single-stall detached garage, which needed painting, and a nice-size backyard. One big enough to accommodate the girls' trampoline that was currently stowed away in the rafters of Daddy's garage, along with the antique chest and end tables I'd smuggled out of my old house.

"A shared driveway is a drawback, usually. But Mrs. Jacques doesn't have a car. She never knew how to drive, and her husband, Elmer, passed away ten years ago."

I smiled at Rye's knowledge of the neighbors. But he was the kind of guy to get involved, who knew about other people's lives. Not a gossip. Just a caring individual. More so than me. I needed to ask him those kinds of questions, but it was easier to ask about my potential neighbor than about him. "How old is she?"

"Somewhere between your mom and grandma. Maybe seventy or so. Nice lady. You'd like her."

Rye worked the locks on the back-porch door as I visually measured the yard. It was fenced in, and besides the trampoline, there'd be room enough for both a vegetable and flower garden. If I dared to disturb the soil...

The locks clicked, and Rye held the door open for me. The back porch was small, but roomy enough for muddy shoes, and would be a good place to start plant shoots that I might never work up the nerve to plant. Rye unlocked the kitchen door; I barely waited for the click before I turned the knob and stepped inside. The linoleum was worn, the cupboards painted a faded pink, the wallpaper reminiscent of Grandma's teapots.

"Now do you think it's cute?" Rye teased.

I touched a cupboard. Metal. Real vintage. The countertop was ceramic and needed new grout, but it was workable. The whole place had potential. An archway led me into a dining room, which would have been small but for the large bay window, with new glazed glass, that opened it up into the fenced side yard. Through another archway was the living room, the rust-colored, sculptured carpet threadbare in some spots. But the room was huge. French doors led to the foyer where an oak staircase rose to the second story. My rubber soles hammered the stairs with the worn rose-colored shag runner as I climbed up to the second story. Three bedrooms and a large bathroom with the tub built into another archway. Two of the bedrooms were small but overlooked the backyard with built-in window seats. The new windows shone, and patched areas of drywall showed why the new roof had been necessary.

"What do you think?" Rye asked, following me back down the hall as I again poked my head into the bathroom with the lime-green ceramic tiles, and then I stopped in the front bedroom, the largest one. One bathroom, but that was the norm with old houses.

"It needs work." I expelled a shuddery sigh of anticipation. "A lot of work."

Rye sighed, too. "I have some others you can look at. Not as close to your folks', but they might not need as much work as this one."

I couldn't jump at the first one. After marrying Eddie, the man who'd taken my virginity, I knew that now. "Okay, let's take a look at them."

So he trailed me through house after house as I ran from room to room, mentally, and then as I grew more comfortable with Rye, verbally, listing all the necessary improvements.

When he pulled into the Heritage Hill area, I knew he was having fun at my expense again. "Okay, joke over. You can take me—" Back to the first house because I knew that little brick and clapboard bungalow was mine.

"No, I own one of these monsters now." He pulled onto a street where I'd toured some of the houses, dragging an uninterested Jenna along with me. All of the houses, but one eyesore, had been redone on the block. Of course, he pulled up to the eyesore.

"Oh, Rye, this needs a lot of work..." An outside stairwell leaned like a three-day drunk against the side of the old Queen Anne. The turret had some fraternity insignia painted around it, windows and all. But those were about the only ones not boarded up.

"Don't I know it..." And his heavy sigh was no joke. "I got an extension...since I'd been called away. But I don't have long to get some major repairs done."

Flurries drifted down and melted against the windshield. Any heavier snow and the sagging roof might give up. "This was one of those condemned ones, huh?"

"All of those I showed you were. Remember the basement of the one by the park?"

Despite loving the rest of the house, the basement had made me uneasy. If Todd had been buried anywhere, I suspected that was it. The fresh cement would effectively conceal whatever crime had been committed there.

"That foundation had caved in. I had to jack up the house and repour the walls and floor. As a result, most of the drywall cracked. Not a fun job. And this one looks like more work." But it wasn't discouragement that quivered in his voice. Excitement. He loved houses as much as I did.

He squeezed my hand. "Come inside. Check it out."

Oh, yeah... The house. I was interested in the house. That was all. The gracious old home had been chopped into five apartments. The structure was sagging like the roof. Holes gaped in the foundation. The yard was a mess of empty beer cans and liquor bottles.

"Careful," he cautioned, grabbing my arm as we walked around the house.

"I bet you can't dig around here either," I said.

"Dig around? Oh, you mean like the others..." His face flushed again. "Yeah, well...Mom's not been here yet."

"Your mother?" She was the one who had buried Todd?

Considering most of the neighborhood thought she'd pushed her husband down the basement steps, I guess that made sense.

When he opened the front door, the scurry of rodent feet scratched across the abused hardwood floors. "Yeah, I haven't had a chance to bomb this place yet."

Now I realized what the metallic odor had been in the other houses. "You bomb them?"

He shuddered. "Have you seen the cockroaches on the West Side? They could drag off a dog. Not to mention some of the other bugs I've found in those places."

"I won't ask." I'm sure I'd sleep better at night if I didn't know. But I had to ask about Rye. It was now or never. "It was nice that they gave you an extension, Rye. Why were you called away?"

"You didn't hear?" He laughed. "That's probably good. From the way your dad acted last night, I guess the story's gotten all stretched out."

"So what is the story?" I persisted as I followed him from room to room. I would bet that the stained drop ceilings covered high ceilings and crown moldings. I would also bet that the layers of paint covered burled oak or walnut trim. And somewhere in the walls that separated apartments, I suspected pocket doors hid.

"About this house?"

"About you, Rye."

"I was in the Marine Corps for four years, went in right after high-school graduation at seventeen. And I've been called back a few times for special operations. Nothing big."

Nothing big. He was Special Ops with the Marine Corps.

He was a hero, and I had thought him a criminal. Now Jenna's excitement over his coming home made sense. There had been a very real possibility that he might not have. That he might not have made it out alive. "Rye..."

"Don't do it," he threatened, backing me up against drywall that already bore a body-shaped dent.

"Don't do what?"

"Don't treat me like a hero." His jaw, darkened with stumble, tightened. "I hate it."

He hadn't appeared to hate it last night when Mom and Dad had been hugging him. Was it just me he didn't want hugging him? I lifted my hands, and as he stepped closer yet, settled them onto his broad shoulders. "I'm not treating you any different than I ever have. Promise."

"Damn!" His hand stroked over my cheek and down my neck to where my pulse pounded madly against his caressing fingers. "I don't want you treating me like Jenna's pesky little brother, either."

I had already asked about his past; I didn't want to ask about his present, about what it meant that he had me backed against a wall, stroking my skin. My knees shook, and my breath caught in my throat. I couldn't have formed a question if I'd tried. And I didn't want to try. *Chicken*.

He dropped his hand and stepped away from me. "Sorry. I'm still getting used to being back..."

Me, too. Marriage had seemed like a foreign country to me. Being back in the neighborhood, back with my family despite how crazy they drove me, and back with friends was all that mattered. But it had been so, so long since a man, a real man, had touched me. Maybe a real one never had. I sighed.

"I'm sorry, Mary Ellen. I didn't mean to scare you."

I don't know if he'd scared me or if I had, with the unfamiliar desires that still quaked inside my body. "It's okay, really." My lips tipped up into a smile. "You think you can get away with it, being a hero and all!"

I squealed and ran toward the stairs as he turned on me with a banshee cry. I'd cleared the first few steps when the next gave way under my feet. Strong hands closed over my leg, stopping me from dropping through the staircase.

"Put your hand on my shoulder." It was already there, clutching at the flannel-clad muscle. "Now you gone and done it, Mary Ellen." He had me in his arms, tight against his hard, warm body. Oh, yeah, I'd gone and done it. "You broke it, you're gonna have to fix it."

"What?"

He settled me on my shaky legs. "I'll get the hammer and nails."

"I can't fix that staircase."

He laughed. "Okay, I'll handle that, but I need your help here."

"What?"

"Probably not just here. I think I figured out why the houses aren't selling."

"Terrible unemployment rate, salary cuts, slow economy," I said.

He nodded. "Those, too, so I have to make my houses more presentable. And you're going to help me."

"I am? What do I get out of this?" I knew what I wanted. Bald head and all. God, I knew what I wanted.

"The house by the park," he said.

"What?"

"For starters. If this works out well, I'll give you a share of each sale. What do you think?"

"I think you're crazy!" But I loved it. "You'll give me a house for decorating tips?"

He shook his head. "Not just tips. You're going to do the work, princess."

Remember the pesky little brother, remember the pesky little brother, I chanted to myself, hoping to slow my racing heart. Maybe it only raced over his outrageous offer. "You want me to do the work? I'm not kidding about the stairwell. I'm not very good with a hammer, unless I'm using it for hanging pictures or shelves."

"That's a start. How are you with paint and papering?"

"Awesome," I said with pride and honesty. "I can decorate a mean house."

"I believe you can. When you were telling me what you'd do to each house, I could see it…" He shook his head, and a smile spread across his face, the dimple winking at me.

I really, really wanted to wink back.

"I want them to look like that, Mary Ellen. It's going to be a lot of hard work. Are you up for it?"

"For a free house? Hell, yes!" I reined in my excitement, though. "This isn't charity?"

He grabbed my hands, holding them palm up between us.

"When these are full of calluses, you're not going to call it charity. Are we okay?"

With his big hands wrapped around my wrist where my pulse jumped wildly, I think he knew. "Sure, we're okay. I can't wait to get started." I meant the houses. Really.

"I bet you can't wait to move out."

I nodded, my head bobbing back and forth with my vehemence. "Telling Mom won't be fun." But working with Rye would be.

Working two jobs and moving was not fun. The days with Jenna wore on me. The irate callers, the overload of work without Vicki, all was proving to me that I'd found my true calling with Rye, working on the houses.

As part of our new partnership, we'd started with the house by the park. He'd known that I would have to do that first, before I could concentrate on the others. He hadn't figured on pulling up carpet and sanding floors. And I hadn't figured how irresistible he'd look in a ribbed undershirt and sawdust.

"Problem?" Jenna asked.

"When isn't there?" I countered with a weary sigh.

"Working with Rye is wearing you out. I hear you're even working the girls."

"Amber's good with a paintbrush." And she loved listening to Rye talk about the places he'd been, the locations he could tell us about. There were places he'd been that he could tell no one about, and I could see the pain in his big, brown eyes.

Despite his protests, the neighborhood was right. He was a hero. But he couldn't be my hero. I still needed to find Mary Ellen Black. I couldn't get sidetracked now, not when I was so close.

When Vicki came back and Jenna didn't need me as much, I intended to do more than work with Rye. I intended to go back to school as Gram had suggested. I wanted to become a professional interior decorator. Finally, after nearly thirty-one years, I knew what I wanted to be when I grew up.

"Look who's here!" Jenna exclaimed, rushing to open the door.

Vicki staggered through the doorway, the weight of the blanket-covered car seat knocking her off balance. "Remember me? Or am I old news?"

I jumped to my feet, taking off the blanket to see my little namesake. "Oh, Mary Ellen…"

"We call her M.E., sounds like Emmy," Vicki explained. "She's such a good baby, has your sweet disposition, Mary Ellen."

Yeah, right. "Still worried I'm trying to steal your job?" I teased.

"Well," Vicki said, "I'll be ready to come back soon, at least part-time. Maybe we can job share, Mary Ellen."

Jenna nodded. "She needs to cut back, either here or with Rye."

"I heard you're helping him with houses," Vicki said, with a wink for me that Jenna, thankfully, missed.

"I've always loved decorating."

"Playing house like Todd did," Jenna grumbled, and her eyes grew moist as she stared at the squirming infant. "She's really pretty, Vicki. Doesn't look like she did here in the office." She shuddered at the bloody memory.

So did I.

"Where's my chair?" Vicki asked with a laugh.

"We burned it," Jenna admitted. "But I ordered a new one. Come back soon."

"After the baptism. Which is Sunday after next. You ready, Mary Ellen?"

I assumed she was talking to the baby but then caught her questioning stare on me. "What?"

"You, Mary Ellen, I want you to be M.E.'s godmother."

Godmother. The honor and responsibility awed me. "Vicki, are you sure? I know you and Bruce have a lot of family."

"And of all of them, you're the best role model for little M.E. Speaking of role models, I just figured out who her godfather should be."

"Not Ted?" I grimaced. A man with three exes?

She laughed. "Hell, no. I was thinking of the neighborhood hero, Rye."

Jenna snorted. "Hero? Don't give him a big head."

I winced, recalling Mom's oft-repeated comment after anyone's compliment. But Jenna's dark eyes shone with pride.

"You think he'd be interested?" Vicki asked.

I assumed she'd asked Jenna, but once again, she was staring at me. "He seems to like kids." He was great with the girls. Better than Eddie had ever been.

Jenna laughed. "Rye is still a kid, a big, dumb one."

A kid? A big sister might still see him that way, but the big sister's friend was having a little bit of trouble maintaining that image…especially when it was replaced with other ones. Images of bare arms, muscles rippling, as he sanded the floor; images of a dimple winking as he smiled at my daughters; images of paint streaked across his bald head as I whirled with a paintbrush and splattered him…

"Mary Ellen?"

"Hmm…"

"She's not getting enough sleep," Jenna explained.

With the dreams I was having, those images playing through my head at night too, no, I wasn't.

"Don't forget next Sunday, okay?" Vicki reminded me, "The baptism?"

"Of course I won't forget. I'm very honored, and I bet Rye will be, too." And we would be parents together, godparents. Jeez, what was I thinking? I had to get it together. And I would, then I'd pack it up and move it out. And maybe I'd get up the nerve to tell Mom. About moving…not about Rye.

"Can you really afford this?" Mom asked as we sat down to dinner at the Coppertop.

Thanksgiving was still a week away, but the restaurant already had their Christmas lights up, thousands upon thousands of them twinkling around us. And Santas, snowmen and reindeer smiled down at us from the walls and the bar. "I can afford this, really. It's on me."

Since it was a weeknight and early, the bar was pretty quiet. I was hoping a public spot would bring about some restraint when I told her and Daddy the news. Grandma and the girls had done well at keeping the secret, and I'd left them home with a pizza as their reward.

Daddy slid into the booth. "What's the occasion?" he asked. "And why not bring the girls and the old woman?"

"I brought the girls for lunch on Saturday." With Rye. He'd treated us for our hard work on one of his houses.

"I bet they liked the lights," Mom said with a genuine smile. She never faulted me for treating the girls.

"They did." I swallowed hard, then started my speech, "I brought you two here...first, to thank you."

"Sweetheart, you don't have to do that," Daddy said, reaching across to squeeze my hand. "That's what parents do. You'll do for your own kids someday."

I would do for my own kids *now*. "No, I do have to thank you. It's been a tough year."

"And you're doing good. Working for Jenna, working for Rye. I'm proud of you." Daddy said that; Mom hid behind a menu.

"I'm proud of me, too," I admitted with a smile. "And because I'm doing so well, I think...no, I know, it's time the girls and I move out."

"Move out?" The menu dropped as Mom fixed me with a disbelieving stare. "How can you move out? Where will you go?"

"The first house I worked on with Rye, it's mine."

"You borrowed your grandmother's pin money?" she asked.

I shook my head. "I'm working a deal with Rye. Decorating his other houses—"

"And he's going to give you a house for that?" She snorted her disbelief. "Is that all you're using to pay him?"

"Louie," Dad cautioned. "You know Mary Ellen better than that."

She sighed. "I do know. Ryan O'Brien is not like that. But he's really paying you for doing a little painting?"

I'd stripped floors right along with him, covering my skin and hair in sawdust and grime. I'd painted, yes, backbreaking, neck-aching work, spattering paint in my eyes, inhaling it into my nose and pores. I'd regrouted tiles. I'd repaired sheet after sheet of drywall. I'd laid floors. But I didn't ache over the work. My problem was that I hadn't yet laid what I wanted to—Rye. My face flushed, and I pushed the candle farther away.

"Mary Ellen?" Daddy asked.

"Hmm?"

"So, when are you moving?"

"I've taken some of my stuff over already. The girls are packing up the rest of their stuff. We'll be out by the weekend."

"Before Thanksgiving? Before Christmas?" Mom asked, her eyes wide with horror. I hadn't realized how much she'd wanted us with her, at least the girls.

"Where's the house?" Dad asked. "Good neighborhood?"

I gave him the address. "Right next to Mrs. Jacques. She says she's one of your customers."

He nodded. "Lean hamburger. Jesus delivers to her since she doesn't drive. I think she gives it to her cats, though. Nice lady."

"It's a great house, Daddy. You'll love it." I reached across, sliding my hand over Mom's. I hadn't wanted to hurt her, but I could see that I had. "And I'll have Christmas, Mom. The living room is perfect for an enormous tree. The girls have already decided where it'll go."

"They like it?" she asked, voice breaking.

I nodded. "They love it. They have a yard, and Mrs. Jacques's cats." Since Grandma was allergic to animal hair, we'd never been allowed any pets.

"You're happy, Mary Ellen," Dad said, his eyes shining with satisfaction. "I'm glad. Be happy for her, Louie."

"Sure. You did it. You got out again, just like you said you would," Mom said, but she rose from the table. "I can't eat right now. I'm going home."

I sighed. Since I'd driven them, we were all going home. Except it wasn't my home anymore. It truly hadn't been since I was nineteen. And Eddie's house hadn't been mine, either, despite my decorating it. I'd finally made my own home. On the West Side. How about that?

Later that night I brought over another box. Because it was a school night, the girls had gone to bed early. Probably their last night sleeping together. Tomorrow they'd each have their own room, even if they only had mattresses on the floor. I hadn't managed to move much from Eddie's house before the foreclosure. I had grabbed their mattresses, their clothes, toys and the small furniture that I'd stored in the attic of Dad's garage. While I'd had Daddy and Mom at the Coppertop, Rye had moved the first load. I hadn't asked him; he had just done it. That was Rye.

He couldn't keep doing for me. He'd brought by some other things, too. Things left in other houses, or so he claimed. The couch had been in surprisingly good shape for something left in a condemned house. I suspected it was his. And I suspected charity was involved. I should have made him take it back, but I'd decided to bury my pride...and work it off instead.

We'd nearly finished another house in the neighborhood. And I knew it'd get a good price with the new tile we'd laid and the hardwood floors that we'd buffed until they gleamed. No one who saw it now would be able to resist. And maybe when it did sell, I wouldn't feel so indebted to Rye.

I fumbled with the lock as I juggled the box in my arms. Before I could grasp the knob, the door opened and Rye filled the entrance. "Speak of the devil..." I murmured.

"You calling me names?"

"You shouldn't have moved my stuff. I was going to have Daddy help—"

He reached for the box in my arms, but I wouldn't release it. "Your dad's not as young as he used to be. Now, strong... that I can vouch for. He lifted me off my feet that night your car broke down."

And lifting Rye off his feet was not an easy task. "No, Daddy is too old to be moving furniture. I could have found someone else, though." Maybe my younger brother, Bart, when he came home for Thanksgiving next week. But then it hardly seemed fair to put him to work during a holiday, especially when I saw him, his wife and young baby so rarely.

"Who?" He pulled harder on the box.

I shrugged but held tight. Then I remembered Ted, M.E.'s

uncle. With three exes, he had to have some moving experience.

"Eddie?" he asked, his voice unusually hard.

I snorted. "Eddie didn't even pack his own bag when he left me. I can't see him helping us move, not when he has yet to pay me any child support."

"I can't believe he doesn't give you anything." His voice got harder, his dimple nowhere in evidence.

"There's nothing to give." If he had anything, he'd probably give it to Siggy before me, and I really didn't blame him. "But even if he could…"

I managed to wrest the box from Rye's arms, push past him and set it on the kitchen counter. I'd regrouted the antique white tiles, using terra-cotta, which matched the walls in the living room. From the kitchen walls, I'd stripped the old grotesque paper, patched the places where the drywall had come off with the paper, and painted it a soft yellow. Through the archway, the dining room bore the same sunny walls. The house looked happy…even if I wasn't.

"What do you mean?" Rye asked, his dark eyes narrowed.

I wasn't exactly sure what he'd done in those Special Operations, and I knew he could never tell me. But sometimes I suspected it had something to do with interrogation. He was damn good at it. "Nothing."

"That's not true."

"Just a bitter ex-wife comment, okay?" I pulled some kitchen utensils from the box, automatically stowing them in the locations I'd used in my old kitchen. Spatulas by the stove. Silverware in the drawer closest to the dining room.

"You're not a bitter ex-wife, Mary Ellen."

I laughed. "Where have you been?"

He sighed. "Gone too long and then sometimes not long enough."

I abandoned my unpacking and stared at him. His handsome face was taut with some unidentifiable emotion. "I don't understand."

"I guess that makes two of us then. Why can't I help you?"

I blew out a ragged breath. "I appreciate everything you're doing. I love working on all the houses. I love this house, but it's too much, Rye. And the moving...you're doing too much for me."

"What are you saying? I'm smothering you?"

God, I wish, the weight of his big body driving me into a mattress. "No!"

"Then what's the problem?"

"I feel like a charity case, Rye. You gave me a house, for crying out loud!"

"I didn't give it to you. I sold the place on Garfield today. I got twenty thousand more than I was originally asking. That's because of you. I stopped by your house to share the news, but your grandma told me you were out telling your folks that you were leaving. So she asked me to move some of your stuff. I'm sorry."

Guilt clenched my stomach. "I'm sorry, Rye. Ever since Eddie left and I found out about...everything, I keep jumping to conclusions. I guess I'm overcompensating for being so stupid."

"Stop doing that!" he shouted.

"What?" His anger shocked me, and I edged back against the cupboards.

"Stop blaming yourself. You weren't stupid, Mary Ellen. Eddie was the stupid one!"

My madly beating heart warmed. "Rye…"

But he stepped away from my outstretched hand, his anger still gripping him. "And I'm not Eddie!"

The door slammed behind him, the windows rattling with the force of it. And I trembled from the strength of his anger. Why was he so mad? Because I was so ungrateful? I owed Rye more than an apology…

I was still thinking about it at the office, late Friday afternoon. How could I apologize? Especially since he was avoiding me. I hadn't seen him since our argument Tuesday night.

Rather than angry, I'd been scared. I didn't want Rye doing too much for me. I didn't want to become dependent on him. After Eddie had let me down, I didn't want to depend on anyone but myself.

Moving out felt good. Sleeping on the floor didn't even seem bad, not compared to the lumpy foldout bed in Daddy's den. The girls were happy. The house looked happy. I should have been happy. But guilt stole my happiness. I'd hurt Rye. I'd been ungrateful, oversensitive.

Instead of unpacking all our stuff, I'd had Mrs. Jacques sit with the girls after they'd gone to bed, and I'd used the extra keys Rye had given me for the other houses. I hadn't found him at any of them, at least the ones I'd checked. I hadn't checked the one in Heritage Hill. That was still all structural work. He didn't need me there. But I made use of my talents in the other houses. I sanded and revarnished trim. I finished up painting. Like Mrs. Jacques, who stayed up all night reading romance novels, I couldn't sleep. And I owed Rye the work on those houses.

Had it been just a few weeks ago that he'd come into Jenna's office and turned my world right side up?

When someone rattled the knob of the office door, I turned toward the entrance, hoping Rye had stopped avoiding me. But there was no bald head, no broad shoulders…just Eddie, sporting some new, more colorful bruises. He limped inside.

I leaned back in my chair. "Coming to see if I'm alive after you sicced your loan shark on me?"

That seemed like a lifetime ago. But then Eddie wouldn't have had the nerve to approach me soon after. And he would never apologize. He never had. He lifted an eyebrow at my sharp tone. Why hadn't I yelled at him more? Mom nagged constantly at Dad, and he still loved her. Maybe it wasn't Eddie's fault he'd treated me like a doormat; I'd acted like one. Then I remembered Rye's anger over my willingness to take the blame for the failure of my marriage. But he'd never been married. He didn't understand that it took two, one to dish the dirt, and one to take it. I was sick of taking it.

"You're mad?" he asked.

Why was he surprised? "Of course I'm mad. I've been mad at you a long time—"

"Over the house. I understand that, and over the…"

Twenty-year-old tramp? "No, why would I be mad about

any of that? But you know, I'm really not as mad at you as I am at myself."

"You're finally taking some responsibility here?"

From the man who'd lost us everything, that was really ironic. "Yeah, it is my fault, Eddie." Despite Rye's righteous anger, I couldn't shrug off all the blame.

Eddie raised that eyebrow again; he probably thought it was sexy. And maybe in the beginning of our relationship, I'd thought it was. But that had been a lifetime ago. I'd started a new life now.

"I never should have trusted you. I believed you loved me. I believed you were paying the bills. I should have known you were a liar and a cheat."

"You can't judge our whole marriage by how it ended. That's not fair, Mary Ellen."

"Life's not fair, Eddie. Isn't that what you told me when you left?" I dragged in a deep breath. That was old news, and there were parts of my life with Eddie that I could never regret, such as Amber and Shelby. "But despite how everything turned out, there are things I wouldn't have changed."

His swollen mouth slid up into a smile.

"But don't sic your loan shark on me again."

The smile fell off his bruised face. "I am sorry about that. I didn't think he'd care if you owed him…"

Because of Daddy. Just what had my father done in his youth? "The court ruled that the debts, all the debts, are yours, Eddie."

He nodded. "I'm sorry about other things, Mary Ellen." An apology? Maybe they'd given him a concussion this time. "I should have given you some money. I should be paying child support. The girls are my daughters, too. A man should take responsibility."

Was I dreaming? Was this Eddie or had Siggy killed him and hired someone to impersonate him? Someone with a more developed sense of responsibility. "A man should, Eddie, but you never did."

He shoved his hand in his pocket and pulled out some crinkled bills. "It's not much…but it's long overdue."

This was definitely an impostor. I closed my hands around the money he pressed against my palm. The bills felt real. But nothing else about this encounter did.

"But…" And I know I should have just taken the money and demanded more, but that wasn't me. "You owe other people, Eddie. Siggy wants his money."

He grimaced, pain tightening his face. "I know that. We've worked a deal. He's taking over the restaurant—"

"But…" That was all Eddie had ever wanted, ever loved, more than me, more than his daughters.

He shrugged. "I'm still managing…sort of. What he lets me do. It's probably for the best, Mary Ellen. We both know I was never good with money."

And we shared a laugh. I couldn't believe it. He left with nothing more, no request to see his daughters, not even on Thanksgiving, despite my offer. I might have believed that I'd imagined the encounter if not for the bills clutched in my hand. The court had not been my friend. My friend was a hundred-year-old loan shark named Siggy.

Thanksgiving was hardly a happy occasion despite the extra money in my pocket from Eddie and the visit from my brother and his family. Because she and Elmer had never had any kids of their own, I'd brought Mrs. Jacques along with me. She had nowhere else to go. If not for Bart's visit, I might have made dinner at my own house for the girls and her.

The rest of the Black family had gotten too large for all of us to get together. Dad's brothers and sisters had each had such large families of their own that they could barely fit in a house. But seeing Bart's new baby boy toddling around the living room, playing a hand of cards with Grandma and hanging out with the rest of my family was worth it. Even Mom's attitude didn't detract from that. The only thing detracting from my happiness was Rye and my guilt over the way I'd treated him. And the way I'd since avoided him.

"Is it hard?" my sister-in-law asked, her voice lowered to a conspiratorial tone as she sat next to me on the couch in the front room.

Mom had shooed us both out of her kitchen, which was fine with me. I'd had enough of her silent treatment in response to my moving out—and enough of her fawning over Barb. My sister-in-law was an exceptional woman, though: a great mother, a smart business professional, and my brother's dream woman. I couldn't be happier for them. "Hmm?" I asked, not understanding.

"Your first holiday without your husband?"

I laughed. "My ex? He was never around for the holidays. He always kept the restaurant open, made some of the biggest receipts on those days."

"So he really is as bad as Bart says, huh?"

I nodded, then thought of the money he'd given me. "I don't know. We'd go see him at the restaurant then. We used to spend a lot of time up there until the last couple of years when he changed so much. But maybe he's changing again now."

At the threat from a hundred-year-old loan shark's henchmen. But hey, change was change. I knew intimately how hard it was.

"You wouldn't—"

"Go back to him? God, no."

Barb laughed and looped an arm around my shoulders. "It's nice to see you like this, Mary Ellen. You're stronger than I remember."

Mrs. Jacques glanced up from the book she'd brought along to read while waiting for my mother's turkey to finish cooking. "That's what I keep telling her—she's strong."

I shook my head. "No, you tell me that I work too hard."

"Hey, Mrs. J.," Amber called out. "Want to play cards with Grandma and me and Shelby?"

"How much will it cost me?" she asked, putting her book

back into her purse and rising from her chair. She moved a little slower than I remembered when I'd first met her. But I'd driven her to the doctor last week. And next week, she had a follow-up. I was pretty sure everything was fine. I think she'd tell me if it wasn't. We'd grown really close in a short time.

"Did you bring your checkbook?" Grandma asked with enough seriousness in her teasing tone that I would have to watch her. I wasn't entirely sure that she didn't cheat.

Barb squeezed my shoulder. "You're always watching over them. That's hard to understand…" But her gaze was trained on her toddler. "…until you have kids of your own."

"Kids?" Was she? And why did I feel a flash of envy at the thought of my sister-in-law being pregnant? I didn't want to be married and pregnant again. I didn't want her life.

"Well, you know Bart's a big kid." Then she laughed. "And so am I. Why don't you come down some weekend soon. The city's all decked out for Christmas. It's gorgeous."

I shrugged, but I was tempted. Shopping trips to Chicago were tradition. I'd often gone with my mother and Grandma on the church bus tours. But even with two jobs and a free house, I had other bills: utilities, gymnastics lessons. Unlike Eddie, I believed in paying my bills. "I doubt Grandma's car would make the trip."

"The train—"

"Next year for sure, but we're still a little shorthanded around the office."

She smiled. "Can't get away from work. Did you think last

year that you'd be saying that this year?" Then she blushed.
"I'm sorry. My big mouth—"

I squeezed her hand, feeling closer to her than ever before,
and certainly less inadequate, too. "I know what you meant."
And no, I could have told her, there was a lot I hadn't fore-
seen last Thanksgiving: the divorce, the repossession, the
foreclosure. But there were good things, too: my job and my
independence, for starters. I had a lot to be thankful for. And
a lot of it I owed to Rye.

Dinner was one of the more relaxing meals I'd enjoyed in
my mother's house. She only made a few cracks about my
bland cooking, which Mrs. Jacques took exception to because
she liked the food she'd shared with us. I invited her often,
hating the thought of her being all alone. Which was silly,
really, she'd been alone since her Elmer had died ten years
ago. She probably liked being alone. I didn't. If I didn't have
the girls, would I be so desperate for companionship that I
would have taken up with Ted of the three exes? Or would I
act on these strange feelings I have for Rye?

We were clearing the table when I heard the rumble of an
engine. I glanced out the kitchen window and saw Rye alight
from the truck and head toward the garage where Daddy and
Bart were checking the oil. Well, not Bart. He didn't smoke,
but I think he'd missed Daddy, because he'd gone out with
him despite how much he hated smoke. And Rye must have
stopped by because he'd heard Bart was in town. They'd been
friends despite Rye's being a year or two younger than Bart.
God, Rye was even younger than my younger brother. I

wouldn't go outside. Rye probably wasn't ready to see me yet, or accept the apology I knew I had to make.

"Rye's here!" Shelby squealed, heading out the door before I could yell at her to grab her coat. Amber picked both coats off the hooks by the back door and headed after her. They'd missed him, too.

"You're not going out?" Mrs. Jacques asked, picking up the gravy boat from the dining-room table.

"No, I have to help Mom clean up. You can go, though, if you'd like. Or if you're tired, I can drive you home now."

She shook her head. "No, I want a piece of that pumpkin pie. And to try to win back my money from your grandmother."

"You do make good pie," my mother admitted, the compliment not even sticking in her throat. "Maybe Rye would like a slice. Why don't you ask him, Mary Ellen?"

I shook my head. "I'm sure the girls will ask him. You've done all the work cooking. I can't let you clean up by yourself." And I shoved my hands into the soapy dishwater in the kitchen sink. From there, I had a good vantage point to watch the girls…and Rye. He never did come in…for pie or to say happy Thanksgiving to me.

Later that afternoon, after dropping off Mrs. Jacques next door, I showed Bart through my house. "Nice place," he complimented with appropriate enthusiasm. "Really nice."

I held in a giggle. "Thanks."

"You worked hard on it, as you do on the other houses. Rye says you have a real passion for it." From the curious way he studied me, his blue eyes narrowed, I figured he had guessed what else I had a passion for. "Is that all you and Rye do together? Work?" he asked, his words confirming my suspicions.

I snorted. "Get your mind out of the gutter, little brother. You were the playboy in this family. I'm just working with Rye."

"Is that all you want?"

"We're friends, too."

"Friends let friends do stuff for them."

Rye had evidently told him about our argument. "It can't be all one-sided," I maintained. "It can't be charity."

"Do the other houses look like this when you're done?"

I nodded.

"Then his help's not charity. It's a reward for hard work. Accept it gracefully," he advised, repeating something Mrs. Jacques told me often. I knew I shouldn't have had her sit beside him at dinner.

I snorted, showing him just how graceful I can be.

He smiled with no real amusement. "I know you've been hurt, Mary Ellen." And he would have been there, would have beaten up Eddie for me, if I would have accepted his help. But he had a life of his own; I couldn't interfere with that.

"I'm doing fine," I swore, and realized the words were pretty much true this time.

He studied me a long moment before nodding in agreement. "I believe that. I see that you are. You're getting back to your old self."

"Slowly, I'm finding my way back."

"I know you, Mary Ellen. Even though you've been hurt,

you'd never purposely hurt someone else." He sighed. "Not even Eddie."

"No, I wouldn't," I admitted.

"So be careful. You'd feel really bad if you hurt someone without meaning to."

His advice came too late. I'd already hurt Rye, and Bart knew it. "What if it's already done?"

"Do what I've heard you tell the girls. Fix it."

The three of us stood shoulder to shoulder in the bathroom. Well, Amber and I did. Shelby came about to my elbow. She might stay petite, but her size was about the only thing little about her.

"I look even prettier," she said as she ran some of the glitter over her eyelid. I'd gotten the glitter for Amber who had become quite fascinated with my makeup over the last couple of months. But Amber, as always, was unfailingly generous with her sister.

"You look very pretty, too, Amber," I said, pleased that she'd left her sun-streaked blond hair down around her shoulders. In its perpetual ponytail, I tended to forget how long and thick it was. "You should wear your hair down for school. It's so beautiful."

"Amber has a boyfriend," Shelby singsonged. "His name is Jordan."

Shelby's other big feature, besides her ego, was her mouth. Amber's deep blush caused a sensation like a rubber band snapping against my heart. How would I survive their dating? Their marriages? Their giving birth?

I could remember Daddy running up and down the hospital corridors, screaming for someone to give me something for the pain while I suffered through hour after hour of natural childbirth. And it had hurt Daddy as much to see me in pain as it had hurt me to feel it. My girls would get a damn epidural and not suffer through all that. But to have children, they'd have to have boyfriends, lovers, husbands... Oh, God. My knees weakened, and I sank onto the toilet-seat lid. "Oh, boy..."

"Mom, we're just friends. Big mouth's got it all wrong. And she was eavesdropping on my phone call with..."

"Jordan," Shelby supplied with a triumphant smirk.

Jordan. She talks to him on the phone? Amber talks to no one on the phone. Heck, she rarely speaks in person. If not for Shelby's expert spying, I'd know nothing of Amber's life. But I'd been closemouthed, just like her, growing up. And I'd wound up with Eddie, love struck because he'd lavished attention on me. God, I worried about Amber.

"Mom," Amber said, her voice tentative as usual. "We're just like you and Rye. Just friends."

And did I get that soft look in my eyes when I talked about Rye? Did I care more about makeup and hair? Oh, God, I did. And today would be the first day I'd seen him since our fight, or whatever it had been. And since we'd be in a church, standing beside a baptismal font, he would have to forgive me. Right? We'd be able to be friends again. Just friends. Why wasn't I happier about that?

"Amber, I think that's great that you have a friend like Rye."

"Why hasn't Rye been around, Mom?"

I shrugged. "He's busy. We're busy."

"Have you seen him when you go to the houses at night, after we're in bed?" Amber asked.

I shook my head. "Not yet. He must be working on some other ones. That's okay, though. We're still friends." I hoped.

Shelby stepped closer to me, running her small hand over my cheek. "Close your eyes, Mommy."

Reflex had me doing just that. Something swiped across my lid. "You're going to look so pretty, Mommy."

Amber giggled. "You sparkle, Mom. You look like an angel."

Maybe. If I grew wings. I wore a cream-colored suit, which brought out the fiery highlights in my hair. I loved Lorraine. The woman was a genius. But as I glanced in the mirror at the gold glitter Shelby had swiped over my respectable taupe shadow, I liked what I saw. And I hoped Rye would, too. At least enough to forgive me.

An hour later, as we stood behind Bruce and Vicki who held M.E., I kept chancing glances at Rye. He wore a suit. Dark navy, which led me to all kinds of fantasies about what he might look like in his uniform—and out of it. The roof creaked, and my gaze flew up, checking for lightning strikes and cave-ins.

Rye's broad hand settled against the small of my back, causing my hips to twitch. "Okay?" he asked.

I don't know if he meant my inspection for lightning or us. "Okay," I whispered back.

He smiled, the dimple winking at me...right there, in church. My heart flipped. His hand slipped lower, riding the rise of my butt, but he nudged me forward. We stood shoulder to shoulder, hip to hip, watching while Father Michael poured holy water over M.E. She endured this sacrament with quiet acceptance. I didn't want to be quiet. I wanted to express my apology to Rye…and my feelings, as soon as I figured out what they were.

Friendship? Was that all I wanted? The way his touch burned through my suit, causing trembling inside me; I didn't think I could quietly accept only friendship. I wanted more. I wanted Rye.

But could I trust myself?

Father Michael asked us to repeat after him our pledge to help raise this child in the Holy Spirit. As we vowed that we would, I remembered another pledge I'd made in this church to Eddie.

I hadn't held on to him or our marriage. How did I think I could hang on to a guy over six years younger than me? And the neighborhood hero. I was delusional. Hair dye and glitter wouldn't attract a man like Rye, let alone hold his interest. I'd mistaken the friendship he'd offered me for something more; no wonder he'd spent the last several days avoiding me.

Later, in Vicki and Bruce's rec room, Rye leaned over me as I refilled a paper cup of coffee from the urn on the Ping-Pong table. "I thought we were okay," he said.

I dragged in a deep breath of air and Rye, that particular scent of man and musk that wasn't from a bottle, that was just him. "Not until I apologize," I said, tipping my head back to look up at him. Our faces were very close, lips only inches apart.

"For what?" he asked, drawing back. "You don't owe me an apology. But I owe you for your work, finishing the house on Pine. I couldn't believe it when I saw that you'd laid the bathroom tile, too."

"Was it...okay?" I asked.

He nodded. "Excellent. I like the color you dyed the grout, too."

"Not too much?"

"Dark brown with tan? I had my doubts, but you pulled it together. I've already got an offer on the place."

I nodded as satisfaction poured through me. "Good. Maybe I'll pay off the house yet."

"That reminds me. I have something for you. The deed for your house."

My house? Free and clear? No mortgage? All mine? But...had I done enough to earn it? I didn't think so. "No, not yet. Keep it."

"Mary Ellen, I know how much you want that house..." He did, probably more than anyone. He knew what I'd invested in it, and what it had invested in me.

"When you sell the house on Pine and maybe the Heritage Hill one."

He shook his head. "There's a lot of work to be done there. That's going to take a long while."

"And most people have thirty-year mortgages. I know, I work with your sister."

"You want to owe me for thirty years?"

"Enough shoptalk," Jenna said as she stepped up to us. Then she laughed at her own joke. "Sorry, couldn't help it.

I should thank you for bringing me business. The Garfield buyers went through me, and the Pine ones called this morning. Sell the house on the hill, and we'll all be in the money."

Rye shrugged those broad shoulders. "I don't know if I'll sell that one or not."

"You'll live there?" Jenna asked. "In that big old house all by yourself? That's ridiculous…or are you seeing someone, little brother? I heard you've been scarce the last couple of weeks."

I fought the blush that rose to my face. I hadn't asked about him…much. Then another emotion rushed forward, turning the coffee to acid in my stomach. *Was* he seeing someone?

It made sense that he had stopped coming around then. Not only had I jumped on him for helping me, but a new girlfriend would probably not be thrilled with the amount of time he spent with a divorcée and her two daughters.

"The house on the hill has become my mistress, Jenna," he said with a chuckle. Like the restaurant had been Eddie's. And Rye claimed before slamming out of my house that he wasn't like Eddie.

"Still a bit burned from that girl with the big eyes?"

I pictured some little china doll with huge, cornflower-blue eyes.

Rye laughed again. "Big eyes?"

"Yeah, the way she looked at what everyone else had and wanted that. Isn't she why you quit college and got so big into the houses? You wanted to make all the money she wanted?"

"You should talk about making money. I guess that's an-other O'Brien-family addiction, sis. I like what I do."

I could vouch for that. Rye took great pride in breathing life back into those condemned properties. It was about more than money to him. And why hadn't the girl with big eyes used them to see the treasure she'd possessed if she'd had Rye's love?

And why did something eat away at my stomach lining, leaving me queasy. Jealousy? I had no right to it. Rye and I were just friends…if we were even that.

"Me, too," Jenna said. "So back off, both of you. I'll relax when I'm dead."

"That's what we worry about," I said, comfortable with my concern for Jenna. "You should take a vacation, and not a working one. Start with a weekend and then work your way up. Maybe a cruise."

She waved a hand in dismissal. "I don't have time for va-cations. I'd go crazy sitting by a pool doing nothing."

Nothing but thinking. That's what scared Jenna. Ironic that I'd been scared that I couldn't think on my own, with-out Daddy's guidance or Eddie's. And Jenna was scared to let herself think about all she'd lost in the past and the future.

"You need to do nothing, absolutely nothing, for a while," I maintained.

She snorted. "Hypocrite. Look at you. You're hardly sleep-ing, hardly eating, you're working yourself too hard. We O'Bri-ens are way too hard on you, Mary Ellen. Aren't we, Rye?"

He caught my hand, running the rough pad of his thumb over the row of calluses on my palm. "I warned her what working with me would do to her hands."

"Ryan O'Brien, you're a slave driver," Father Michael teased as he walked up to us, slapping a hand on the ex-marine's back. "I heard you and Mary Ellen have joined forces. She's helping you sell those houses. Does that mean your mother will stop bringing statues of St. Joseph for me to bless so that she can bury them in the yards?"

Rye laughed as his skin flushed over his mother's religious superstition, and Jenna shook her head. "Mom's still trying to buy her way in, huh, Father?"

"Jenna, you watch yourself. Your mother is a wonderful woman, loves her children loyally."

"Especially her baby," Jenna taunted her brother, totally unaffected by the priest's holy presence.

"She's probably trying to buy your way in, Jenna," Rye teased. "You're not going to get there on your own."

Her face scrunched into a sneer. "More likely yours, hero."

"You two play nice," I said. "Father Michael will think your mother did a poor job of raising you if you don't show the proper respect in front of the father."

Behind Father Michael's head, Jenna scowled at me and mouthed, "Suck-up."

"You're doing a fine job with your girls, Mary Ellen," the priest praised, warming my heart with the words every mother wants to hear. "They are such sweet young women. A real credit to your patience and love."

Rye reached for my hand, squeezing with a gentle pressure.

"Thank you, Father," I said, gratified.

"She's a super mom," Jenna said.

The priest nodded his agreement, then answered someone's call, and crossed the basement.

"But being a mom isn't enough, Mary Ellen," Jenna said. "You've gotta be a woman, too."

I jerked my hand from Rye's. I didn't want her to think what I was thinking about her brother. Our renewed friendship was still too fragile to withstand such a test.

Ted, loading up a dish from the banquet table behind Jenna, snorted his derision. "He thinks I'm a lesbian," I quietly told Rye, who narrowed his eyes at the older man's reaction.

Rye laughed. "How the hell would he get a crazy idea like that?"

"Grandma told him."

"Oh."

Funny how illogical things made sense once someone knew Grandma was involved. But Grandma wasn't involved with Rye and me. And so any match between us remained illogical. Friendship was all I could hope for—his and Jenna's.

While Rye worked on the house on the hill, I worked close to the neighborhood. The house on Garfield had closed; the one on Pine sold. I'd processed the paperwork for the loans. I knew the appraisals were high because of Rye's and my hard work. Seeing tangible proof of my success energized me, that and the fact that dreams of Rye kept me awake all night. I kept replaying in my mind Grandma's suggestion to use Rye for sex. Maybe instead of pushing a man off on me, she needed one of her own. And I knew one who thought she was a stunner, full of energy. The office door opened with a creak and a groan, or maybe that was the joints of the hundred-year-old man who walked through it. I didn't dare say speak of the devil to him, because he might just be.

"Hi, Mr. Ignatius," I said in the loud tone I reserved for Grandma.

His hearing aid screeched, and he reached up to adjust the volume. Outside the door, Dougie stood beside the idling limo. He waved at me, and I waved back.

"Good afternoon, Mary Ellen," Siggy greeted me with a wrinkled smile. "Nice to see you again, dear."

"What can I help you with, sir?" I asked, hoping he didn't want me to go for another ride. I didn't think my heart could handle it.

"I have a check for you."

Had he broken Eddie's leg this time, so that my ex couldn't bring it in himself? "For me?"

"Well, for the buyers of the house on Pine, Ryan O'Brien's house."

"Oh, they borrowed money from you?" Another gift we'd have to explain to the mortgage company.

He shook his head. "Not a loan. It's my great-niece and nephew-in-law. Nice kids. I'm helping them out. My Edna and I never had any kids of our own."

Like Mrs. Jacques and Elmer. And from the soft tone of her voice when she spoke of her husband and Siggy's when he spoke of his Edna, neither's love had been lessened by the inability to have children. I made a mental note to bring these examples up to Jenna. Not that she would listen. I talked myself blue in the face, and she hadn't listened yet.

"That's very nice of you to help them," I said.

He shrugged a thin shoulder. "I try to help where I can. You never came to me for a loan."

"I'm fine. Grandma had some pin money, but I didn't even have to borrow hers."

"Your grandmother is quite a woman. She likes to play cards."

"She's good at it."

"An independent woman. Had to be. Her husband was a fool. If not for your father…"

What had my father done to Grandfather? I didn't want to know. "You should call my grandma. I'm sure she'd love to catch up with you."

He shrugged again. "I don't know about that."

"What can it hurt to find out?"

He smiled. "You're right, Mary Ellen. Life is short."

He thought a hundred years short? I liked his math. "Yes, it is. Call her."

"I just might do that."

"Good."

"I also wanted to ask you about something else, Mary Ellen."

"Anything. I owe you a favor, I understand."

His faded eyes narrowed. "For what?"

"For…talking to Eddie…about child support. He brought me some money last week."

"He did?" He chuckled. "Well, I'll be damned. Maybe there's hope for that boy yet."

"Well, I don't think he would have made the gesture on his own. He had help. Thank you."

He shook his gray head. "Don't thank me, dear. I had nothing to do with it. I wouldn't get involved in something like that. That could be taken as an insult toward your father, that I think he can't take care of his own. I wouldn't do that."

I almost believed Siggy, but I really didn't believe Eddie had found his conscience on his own. He had to have had help, a lot of it.

"Okay," I said.

"The question I had for you was about your decorating. I saw what you did to the house on Pine. It's quite lovely. You have a real talent for interior design. Ryan O'Brien is lucky to have you working for him."

"Thank you." And I was lucky to have Rye as a friend. That should be enough, but I still didn't have him in the way I wanted him, the way I dreamed of having him.

"My house is getting old, dated. It needs updating. I'd like to hire you," Siggy stated.

"Me?"

He nodded. "We can work out the details after the holidays. I know it's a busy time, so we can put it off for now." How long could a man his age put off anything? But then, that was up to him. Maybe making plans for the future kept him going.

"I'd love to work on your house."

"I'll pay you very well, dear. I'll be in touch with you after the holidays. And maybe with your grandmother... soon."

He left with a smile and a twinkle in his eye.

CHAPTER P
Paint Stains & Pestilence

Because of those odd thoughts I'd been having, I didn't even try sleeping that night. Instead, I had Mrs. Jacques watching the girls while I finished up the house on Atlantic. It needed distinct colors. The gorgeous maple floors that we'd stripped and revarnished needed a sharply contrasting hue that would bring the living room alive. So I used sage, rolling on a flat shade of it with a rag over the semigloss I'd already applied.

I had the radio blasting, singing along with Shania Twain about the kind of man I'd need, when someone chuckled from behind me. I whirled on the ladder and nearly fell off the step.

Rye steadied it by closing his arms around the ladder and me. "Careful, careful."

I swung at his shoulder, swiping it with the paint-sopped rag and getting some on the side of his neck and bald head. "Don't sneak up on me like that!"

"I knocked twice. But your singing must have drowned it out."

Heat rose to my face, but instead of giving in to the embarrassment, I swiped at him again. "How dare you mock my singing."

He caught my wrist, his fingers overlapping it and then some. "I wasn't. You're really good."

"Yeah right. I couldn't even sing my babies to sleep. My lullabies made them cry."

He chuckled, and his dimple winked at me. I'd missed that dimple.

"You think I'm exaggerating? Ask them now if they let me sing in the car? They yell at me not to." I stuck out my lip in an imitation of Shelby's pout.

"There's just no accounting for taste."

I laughed. "No, there's not. And you obviously have none."

He shook his head. "No, I love your singing. You sound happy, very happy, slapping paint on walls…" He touched his neck and head with his free hand. "And me."

I wrestled with him over the rag, trying to dab more on him. "You deserve it…for scaring me." And for avoiding me. I'd missed him more than I should have. But friends missed friends. That's all it was.

"Are you scared, Mary Ellen? Is that what's wrong?"

I didn't think we were talking about the paint anymore. "What do you mean?"

"We were getting close before, and you accused me of smothering you—"

"No, I didn't. I—" Wanted that, wanted it too much even though I wanted my independence, too.

"You were mad, so I backed off," he said.

"You were mad!"

"Still am!"

"Why?" I asked, aroused by the heat of our illogical argument and his closeness. He hadn't released me yet.

"I'm not Eddie."

"I never said you were. I know you're not."

"Then why won't you trust me?"

"I do."

"No, you don't. You're holding me back, Mary Ellen."

"No, I'm holding myself back. From doing this." I threw my free arm around his neck and pressed my mouth to his.

His lips were cool, then grew warm. He groaned. And still our lips stayed fused, heat on heat, as we consumed each other. His arms lifted me from the ladder, pressing me tight against the hard, long length of his body. To get closer, I wrapped my legs around his waist, felt the nudge of his erection pressing against the front of his worn jeans.

Oh, God... Even through two layers of denim, his heat branded me. I rocked my hips against his and moaned. I wanted less—less clothes between us. And more—all of Rye, driving into me.

"Mary Ellen," he groaned, his lips slipping from mine to graze my cheek and nuzzle my neck. His tongue lapped at the pulse jumping wildly in my throat.

I clutched at his back, dragging up his flannel jacket and thermal shirt, so that my fingers could graze the rippling muscles. He was so much muscle and man. I needed to know how much; I needed every detail. Through my cotton shirt, his hand closed over my breast, kneading the flesh that ached for his touch. "More, Rye..."

He pulled the shirt up and over my head, tossing it behind

me. I didn't care if it fell in the paint. I didn't care if I fell in the paint, as long as Rye fell with me. A quick snap of the clasp between my breasts, and my bra fell away, the light washing over my throbbing breasts. Rye's breath caught, then shuddered out.

"You're so beautiful…"

Nobody had ever said it that way, as if he meant it. And in Rye's eyes I was. I was.

I arched my back, and then cupped a breast and lifted it for his touch. He dipped his head toward me, his tongue darting out to trace around the hardened nipple before lapping at it, then suckling me into his mouth. Heat shot through me. I panted, desperate for more. It had been so, so long. And it had never been Rye. While he suckled at my other breast, he teased my damp nipple with his rough thumb. Stroking back and forth. "Rye…" I sobbed his name. "Rye…"

"What do you want, Mary Ellen?" He rasped the question out, his voice choked with desire for me.

"You, Rye. I want you." Maybe it was all the years we'd known each other or how close we'd grown working on the houses together, but I was totally comfortable with him. Maybe being older, a woman who'd been married and divorced, I felt more experienced, which was probably a laugh. But it didn't stop me from being able to tell him exactly what I wanted and how.

The hand, braced on my back, slid over my hip and buttocks until he stroked my heat through my jeans. "Here?"

I whimpered and moved against his hand. Still, it wasn't enough. "More."

We were lying on the drop cloths on the floor, side by side. I was bare to the waist, he, fully clothed. I tugged at his jacket until he shrugged it off his shoulders. Then I pulled up his thermal shirt, baring skin and rippling muscle. Aside from models in magazines and actors in movies, I'd never seen a man so well built, with a washboard stomach. My fingers caressed it, and he shuddered.

"More," he said, obviously comfortable with me, too.

I fumbled with the snap of his jeans as he reached for mine. His hand was already inside my unzipped jeans before I'd eased his zipper down. My hand trembled as I reached out. His fingers stroked the cotton crotch of my panties until he eased the fabric aside, and eased inside. "Tight. You're so tight, Mary Ellen."

My body shuddered and squeezed Rye's fingers. For a minute the room spun. Heat flooded me. Mindless cries spilled from my lips as I had my first orgasm in years.

"Touch me," he ordered as he kicked off his jeans and pulled down his boxers. His penis sprang free, long, thick and so very hard.

I wriggled free of my jeans and panties. I wanted skin on skin. A part of me marveled at my greed. I closed one hand over him, stroking back toward his bulging scrotum.

He threw his head back and groaned. Then he lifted me away and rolled me onto my back, kissing me again and again, soft kisses, drinking from my lips, my mouth. Desire lifted me up, so that I arched against him, rubbing my breasts against the hard wall of his chest. He groaned, the muscles in his arms straining while he held his weight above me. "Mary Ellen…"

"What?" I asked, as I lifted my hips to his pulsing penis.

"You're making it hard to go…slow…"

I wrapped my arms around his neck, pulling him down for a hot, wet kiss. When I could breathe, I asked, "Why slow?"

"You deserve slow," he murmured, his lips gliding across my face to nuzzle my ear. "You deserve everything…"

His hot breath caressed my lobe, making me shiver in anticipation. "I don't want slow…and I only want you, Rye. Fast and hard!" But before I could wrap my legs around him, Rye gently pushed me back on the drop cloth, his lips continuing a slow, wet journey along my sensitive skin. He kissed every inch of my shoulders, my arms… Who knew the inside of my elbow was so sensitive?

Until Rye, I hadn't known how greedy I was…that I could lie back and take everything he had to give. And Rye, being Rye, had a lot to give. With every kiss of his firm, silky lips, with every touch of his hot, wet tongue…he gave. To my arms, my legs, my breasts, and then to the part of me that throbbed for more.

I convulsed, shuddering as another orgasm slammed into me.

Looking up at me, his eyes dilated with passion. His hands slid over my hips and waist to cup my breasts, his thumbs teasing at the hardened nipples. I came again. "Rye…" I moaned. "Now, please…"

I couldn't stand it; I had to be closer to him.

"Mary Ellen, so polite, so sweet," he said.

Polite. I was too polite. I took what I was given. I asked if I wanted more. Why didn't I just take? I wriggled around and took his long, throbbing penis into my mouth.

"Mary—" His voice caught in his throat. He groaned, his face contorted, and his hands shook as he gripped my shoulders, trying to pull me up. I held tight to his strong thighs, my hands gripping as my mouth slid up and down, my tongue lapping.

His fingers tangled in my hair, tugging me up. "No…" he groaned. "Slow…"

A broad hand cupped my cheek, and he lifted my gaze to his. Then he grabbed at his jeans, rifling through his pocket for a foil packet. Rye, ever responsible, a real Boy Scout— no, better than that, a marine, a hero, and tonight, all mine.

"Mary Ellen…" He reached for me. His lips slid over mine, stealing away my doubts and fears with silken kisses and the seductive slide of his tongue in and out of my mouth.

My hands slid over his shoulders, wide, broad, strong, capable of holding anyone's burdens, even the world's. I moaned, my tongue tangling with his.

His hands, skin rough, glided over me in gentle strokes. My back, my hips, my breasts…my thighs, which I opened for him. We'd risen to our knees on the drop cloth, and he pulled me up and over, onto his lap and his erection. His sheathed head slipped into the heat and wetness he'd created with the touch of his hands and mouth. I locked my legs around his waist and rode up and down as I opened more and more with each of his thrusts, driving me into a frenzy as I convulsed around him, squeezing all of him that I could hold. Squeezing as I came, squeezing as I held him. He cried out, his head dropping against my forehead. When I thought I could come no more, I came again on his last hard thrust. And I screamed his name.

He kissed me, kissed me hard and long. Still joined, he pulsed between my legs, hot and alive. It was more than I'd ever hoped for, more than I'd ever dreamed.

"Mary Ellen..." Rye said on a ragged sigh as he pulled me tight, cradling my head into the crook of his neck and broad shoulder. "It's been so long..." His hand stroked my hair.

So long that he'd take a sex-starved divorcée up on her wanton offer? Had I seduced him? A smile teased my lips despite a wave of embarrassment. I could seduce a man? Who knew? But then I'd never wanted anyone the way I'd wanted Rye, the way I still wanted him. And with Rye, I felt safe, confident for once. But what had I been for him? Convenient?

"I'm sorry, Rye."

He held me away from him, staring intently into my face. "For what? For fulfilling a dream I've had since I first hit puberty?"

"What?"

With a chuckle, he said, "You've been my fantasy since I was ten years old."

"Ten?" Boys hit puberty at ten? Amber was ten, almost eleven, and so was her friend Jordan. Then it dawned on me what he'd said. I had been someone's fantasy?

"O'Briens start young. Mom was sixteen, Pop seventeen when they had Arthur," he explained without really explaining anything.

"But me?"

"Hell yes! You were so hot when you were sixteen, or so I thought..." Then he'd gotten around and seen something of the world and realized I hadn't been hot. So much for the fantasy...

"Then I came home and found you in Jenna's office, and you're hotter now than you ever were as a teenager." His dark eyes burned with intensity.

I fingered a strand of my new red hair. "I am?"

"I'm sorry, Mary Ellen, that I was so fast. I rushed it, and that's the last thing I wanted to do. I wanted to take my time. I wanted you every which way I've fantasized about since I was ten…" He pressed a soft kiss against my mouth, which hung open in amazement.

"That's a long time," I mumbled against his lips.

"A long time…" He kissed me again and traced a pattern over my bare shoulder with the tip of his finger. "And that's what I intend to take now…a long time…loving you."

Loving me? My breath caught in my throat. I wasn't ready for love. I couldn't risk that again, loving someone or having someone love me. But his finger traced on, over the slope of my breast, over the nipple until it hardened and pressed against him. Making love was fine. For me making love was long overdue. But I wasn't ready for more.

Rye showed me positions Eddie had never known, and since my experience was limited to Eddie, it was very limited. While we'd been more adventurous in the beginning, in the end it had always been missionary in the dark, if at all.

Rye never turned off the lights. And I was grateful because I loved the way the light danced off his rippling muscles. All of them. One condom was disposed of in the drop cloth, another rolled on by my hand. "Do you have to special order these?" I asked with a nervous tremor in my voice and hand. "Extra thick, extra long."

Rye laughed, and his very busy hands stilled for a moment. "We fit, Mary Ellen."

"I can't take all of you…" Not now, not yet, maybe not ever. But I'd take as much as I could… And I did. I took it in ways I'd never known existed. And with props; the ladder playing the most significant role. By my stepping up a couple of treads, we were level. And level brought about all kinds of possibilities.

Then Rye wanted me higher, wanted to torture me again with his mouth and tongue, so that I nearly slipped through the rungs and onto the floor in a liquid puddle. And when I believed I couldn't feel anymore, he made me. He turned me and slipped his hard penis between my wet folds, and despite his promise of slow and easy, he thrust fast and hard, pounding against me until I came again.

And then again, my legs wrapped around his waist, he leaned against the wall, then braced me there as he hammered into me. Wet paint seeped into the skin of my bare back and tangled my hair, but I didn't care. Because still there was more. He sank to the drop cloth and showed me how to take the ride of my life. Up and down, back and forth, as I learned what felt best, what brought us both the most pleasure.

For me…it was Rye. No matter where, no matter how. And I took as much of him as I could. And I lost count, orgasm after orgasm, until I sank to his chest in a boneless, exhausted heap.

Then his hands, shaking, swept over my paint-streaked hair and back. "You're a mess." He sighed, contented and not at all regretful.

"Thanks, you're pretty wonderful, too." And he was, paint-stained bald head and all.

"This green—"

"Sage," I corrected him.

"Well, sage is now my favorite color. You'll have to use this in the master bedroom for the hill house."

"Bedroom? What's that?" I teased.

"Maybe next time we can find a bed."

He wasn't making any promises, and I didn't want any. "Next time?"

He tipped up my chin, his hot, dark gaze meeting mine. "There will be a next time, Mary Ellen."

I sighed and shifted against his sweat-slick chest. "I don't have a lot of time for this, Rye…"

He started, rousing himself. "My God, the kids. Are they alone?"

"Of course not."

"No, of course not. Is your grandma watching them?"

"No, Mrs. Jacques is my new sitter. She comes over to the house and reads while they sleep."

"She leaves her house?"

I nodded. "Yeah. And in exchange for her babysitting, I take her for her errands. Before that, she always had everyone deliver everything. Dad used to send Jesus to her. I'm even teaching her how to drive. We practice in the park while the girls play on the equipment, but we have to be careful."

He chuckled and kissed my nose. "You're amazing."

"Why? Because I'm using an old lady for free babysitting?"

"Free? Do you know what you're doing for her?"

I shrugged. "So? I'm teaching her to drive. Giving her a little independence." Like I wanted.

"A little? She hasn't left her house since her husband died. She'd hardly even come out in the yard. Everybody said, and she even admitted it while I was fixing some plumbing for her." Of course he had fixed it for free, too, I'm sure. And Rye had undoubtedly helped her around the house, as he helped everyone, the world included. He was a hero.

"But someone takes care of her yard. I thought she…"

"I took care of it." The way he was trying to take care of me.

I nodded. "That's sweet of you. But I don't really think leaving the house is such a big issue for her. She enjoys spending time with the girls, and she's having fun—"

He kissed me again. "With you, of course. Is it any wonder I—" He broke off the last of his sentence with another kiss.

I pulled back. "Rye, that's what we're having, right?"

"What?" His dark eyes narrowed on the question.

"Fun. We're just having fun." With the serious tone I used to state this, it didn't sound very fun.

He studied me silently for a minute. "Is that all you want?"

"Rye, I'm not ready for more. I don't know how I'd tell the girls or…Jenna."

"You're her best friend."

Guilt churned in my stomach; Jenna and I had just regained our friendship and now I'd betrayed it again. "Yeah, I am. Trust me on this. I have a younger brother. She won't be happy about this."

"So you want to sneak around?"

He made it sound so nasty. "Yeah," I said with a smile.

He chuckled, even though the humor didn't reach his eyes. "Okay, it's just fun and games right now. And in the spirit of such, you really need to go to karaoke with me."

"Karaoke?"

"Yeah, I know an out-of-the-way little bar where they have it. Nobody would recognize us there."

"So you don't think strangers would hate my singing as much as the girls do?"

He shook his head. "You'll have fun. Isn't that what we're all about?"

Fun and games. "And work. We have houses to finish. I need to finish paying you off."

A naughty gleam twinkled in his eyes, and I swung at his shoulder, not even jarring the muscles. "You're a feisty little thing lately."

Hardly. "I want to pay you off, Rye, financially."

He reached for his jeans again. How many condoms did he carry? We'd used three or four. At least. Instead of a foil packet, he handed over a folded document. "The deed. I told you—it's yours. You just need to sign it and have Jenna notarize it. File it with the registrar of deeds, and the house is yours. Free and clear."

My fingers itched to take the document; to accept that the house was mine and I was indebted to no one. But I was indebted still, and for more than the house. I owed Rye more money. And I owed myself more respect. "A few more houses, and I'll take that."

Maybe.

"Take it now." He shoved the deed into the pocket of my discarded jeans, crumpling the paper that meant so much to me. "When you're ready," he continued, "have Jenna notarize it. But I want you to know that I'm a man of my word. I promised you the house."

I already knew he was a man of his word, a man of honor. I'd never known anyone with as much integrity. But I couldn't take advantage of that. "No, you keep it...for now."

He shook his head. "You are so stubborn."

Not enough, not yet. But I would be, stubborn enough to take care of myself. "I'm not ready to accept it yet, Rye. After I've decorated more houses for you..."

"Decorated for me? It's for us, Mary Ellen. I consider you my partner."

"But Rye, it's your money. Your hard work—"

"Not anymore. It's yours, too." He caught my hand. "I told you it was going to be work."

I nodded. "You warned me about that." He hadn't warned me about this, though.

"You should have warned me," he said, "that you were going to work yourself half to death. I never expected that, and I never expected to make so much more money because of your hard work."

Warmth washed over me as I accepted his compliment. I had brought something to this partnership, if I dared accept that's what we had. I didn't dare; I wasn't that brave yet. "Did you expect this?" the devil made me ask as I bumped my naked breasts against his chest.

A grin slid across his mouth, and the dimple winked at me. "I didn't expect but I sure as hell hoped."

I laughed at the expression he wore, one of a ten-year-old boy who, on Christmas morning, had found the BB gun under the tree that he'd wanted but hadn't dreamed his mother would ever let Santa bring. Strangely enough, it was fun to be the BB gun. And that's all I could let this be...fun. Nothing more. And no one needed to know, except us.

He stuffed the deed back in his pocket. "We're not going to be about all work, you know. You will go to karaoke with me."

I considered the idea. "Fun and games..."

I slipped through the back-porch door, hoping Mrs. Jacques had nodded off in the easy chair she'd had brought over from her extra room. It was her reading chair, now in my house. Was it true that she hadn't left home after her husband's death? Was it true that I'd done something good for her, something I hadn't known I'd done?

"He followed you home," drifted a voice from the living room.

Barefoot, I padded through the kitchen and dining room to lean against the living-room archway. I was still too weak to stand. "Who?"

"I saw the lights, he made sure you got home. So he's some sort of gentleman."

"I wasn't on a date, Mrs. Jacques. I was working on the house on Atlantic."

"You're covered in paint sure enough," she said with a devilish smile. "But you weren't working. I may be old, but I remember that expression you're wearing, and I remember what causes it: a good man."

"No, really…I was working." A lie well told and stuck to is just as good as the truth. Wasn't that one of Grandma's sayings? Or maybe it was Eddie's—it sure was what he lived by.

"With Ryan O'Brien?"

"He was there," I admitted.

She laughed. "Oh, yes, I bet he was."

"Mrs. Jacques…"

"Don't bother, dear. I won't tell anyone. I'm not a gossip. You know that."

I sighed. "I know you're not. But I'm not ready to tell, so…"

She rose from her chair. "If you need someone to talk to, you can come to me, Mary Ellen. I know I can come to you, that I can count on you."

Tears stung my eyes. The assurance in her voice, the faith in our friendship, moved me. But not enough to share my new sex life with her…or anyone.

Getting paint out wasn't easy. I still had a green tinge to my skin and hair the next morning when I woke the girls for school.

"Mom," Amber called out from the bathroom while I stood propped against my bedroom doorjamb, still feeling boneless. "I can't find a ponytail holder."

"Ponytail? You've been wearing your hair down." And

she'd been looking adorable, with the long, thick blond waves framing her face.

But now, knowing what I did about the hormones of ten-year-old boys, maybe a ponytail was a good idea. Maybe baggier jeans and a big sweater was a good idea, too.

"Did you see the note I brought home yesterday?" she asked.

"Note?" I had glanced at a couple of items from the girls' backpacks and had attached some papers and drawings to the fridge to admire later.

"The lice note."

My heart clenched. "The pink note?" Oh, God, no…

"Yeah, one of the twins in my class has 'em. Maybe both. They had to go home early yesterday. Things were jumping."

"No, no, they're not supposed to jump." The school nurse had explained that the last time lice had shown up at school. But that had been at the girls' old school. Maybe inner-city-school lice were different, more talented.

"These were jumping, Mom. Or that's what Mrs. Senecki said."

I joined Amber in the bathroom; Shelby was there, too, swinging her legs as she sat on the closed toilet. "Okay, let me make sure none jumped onto you." Not that I knew what I was looking for. The instructions that were sent home last time said to look for gray or light-colored eggs, small and near the base of the hair shaft.

But as soon as I lifted her hair away from her neck, I noticed—not any eggs, but little bugs scurrying around. Bugs on my child! Bugs laying eggs to produce more bugs.

"Mom?" Amber asked, fear evident in her tone.

"Amber, has your head itched?"

"Yeah, but…"

I caught one of the little insects and smashed it between my fingers, but when I opened them, it moved again. Was it impossible to kill the beasts?

"Mom, do I have 'em?"

"I see a few." And a few more than that. I kept trying to catch them between my fingers, but they scurried deeper into the thick tresses.

Shelby screamed, a high-pitched wail. "Ewwww… You've got bugs, Amber."

"You probably have 'em, too, big mouth," Amber retorted.

Oh, God, they were probably on my baby, too.

"Mom! Check! Check my hair!" Shelby shouted, bouncing up and down on the toilet seat.

I dropped Amber's hair and quickly washed my hands. "Amber, take a shower. A long one."

Scratching her head with one hand, she turned on the shower with the other. "Will that kill 'em?"

God, I hoped so, but I seriously doubted it. "Try it."

"But I took a shower last night…" Despite her protest, she stepped under the water.

I turned toward Shelby, closing my eyes as I picked up the long, silky fall of her hair. I couldn't look. I couldn't handle the thought of parasites on Shelby. Amber was bad enough. Seeing those tiny creatures running through her hair, over her scalp…

"Mom, you can't see with your eyes closed."

"I know, Shelby. I need a minute."

"First you check me, then I'll check you. Okay, Mom?"

I opened my eyes and checked closely. No bugs. But I did see what could be eggs, but with Shelby's fair hair, it was hard to tell. Maybe I needed to bring the girls in somewhere, where a professional could take care of this pestilence. Like an exterminator. Or Lorraine! Lorraine would know.

"Do I have 'em, too, Mommy?" Shelby asked.

"I don't think so, baby."

"Can I go to school then?"

I shook my head. "Neither of you can go right now. We have to make sure we get rid of these things."

Amber poked her wet head around the shower curtain. "But, Mom, I don't want to miss school. I have a project due today."

I wouldn't be going into the office today. I lifted my hand, scratching my head.

"Let me check you, Mommy," Shelby said, clambering on top of the closed toilet seat and reaching for my hair. "Mom, your hair's sticky and kinda green. Is that what the bugs do?"

"That's paint, sweetie."

"How'd you get paint in your hair?"

"How do you think, stupid?" Amber yelled out in an unusually grumpy mood. But then the bugs running over her head gave her a reason for grumpiness.

"She got the paint in her hair painting," Amber finished. Incorrectly.

My knees weakened at the memory of how I'd gotten the

paint in my hair. But I didn't have time for the afterglow now. I had to do some exterminating. "See anything, Shelby?"

"Just paint," she said with a giggle.

But I wasn't trusting Shelby's inspection. My skin crawled thinking about bugs on my scalp. "I'm going to call and find out how to get rid of these things, okay?"

Lorraine's advice was concise. Don't take any chances, she said.

Wash everything in hot water to make sure the bugs were dead and the eggs too fried to hatch, load after load of wash; blankets, clothes, coats, hats, even stuffed animals.

In Lorraine's opinion, the chemical pesticide was dangerous to skin and the effects might not be long lasting enough to withstand a repeat infestation, so I shouldn't take any chances. As had been passed on to her, the best precaution was to use baby oil. Soak the hair in baby oil, let it set for a couple hours and comb out with a special lice comb, to make sure all oil-soaked bugs and eggs were removed. And the only effective thing to remove the oil was Dawn dish soap. So I had to make a run to the store.

Since Mrs. Jacques had already been exposed, she had no problem watching the children while I ran out for supplies. But I'd have to check her for bugs, too. Between loads of laundry and combing, there wouldn't be time for Rye. My children had bugs.

We were on the second oil treatment and fifth load of laundry when a knock came at the door. "Is it safe?" a deep voice called out.

Not from bugs, not from feminine tears of frustration and exhaustion. This was definitely not fun and games. "Enter at your own risk," I called back.

Shelby sniffed back her tears as Rye strode through the back door and into the dining room where we sat around the towel-covered table. "We've got bugs, Rye."

His dark eyes warmed with sympathy. "Oh, baby, I heard. That's terrible."

"We missed school today," Amber sniffed as I pulled the long, metal-toothed comb through her hair and dipped it in a bowl of water.

"That's too bad, Amber. I know you really like school. And your mom missed work, too. Jenna told me why," he said.

Alarm skittered through me. "You asked Jenna about me?" That wasn't exactly sneaking around.

"I called to ask about the closing date for Pine. She answered the phone. No big deal."

But it was. After last night and the lice this morning, I couldn't handle anything more. Tears threatened, and I was nearly too exhausted to fight them. "You didn't need to stop by," I said, fighting the temptation to rely on him.

"Friends help each other." He pulled out a chair by the table and pointed toward the comb in my hand. "Have another one of those? I can do Shelby's hair."

He found it before I could reply, and with the quiet intensity with which he did everything, he went to work on the slicked-up tresses that reached past Shelby's waist.

She sniffled and glared at me. "It doesn't hurt when Rye does it."

I studied his technique. He pulled the comb from the base of her scalp, all the way down the shaft and then dipped it in the bowl of water. He knew what he was doing. Did I feel that no one could do anything right for my children except me? In the early days of their lives, when Eddie had tried to help, I'd gotten frustrated with leaky, loose diapers and hadn't wanted him to do anything else. Had I always wanted to do everything myself?

"You've done this before," I commented as I continued working Amber's thick hair.

He nodded. "Oh, yeah. Mom put me to work on Jenna's once, when we were kids. And—" he ran one hand over his bald head "—I had some experience with these buggers not too long ago. I didn't have time to bomb the house on the hill before I moved in. Slept on the floor one night, and they must have been in the carpet."

And I'd thought the shaved head was a military requirement.

Shelby's blue eyes widened with horror. "You're not going to shave our heads, are you?"

I was tempted. "No, honey, I'm not. We'll get rid of these things." Even if I had to do as Lorraine had recommended and repeat the oil treatment once a week.

"So will you let your hair grow back?" I asked Rye, curious what he would look like with hair when he was already so handsome without.

The dimple winked at me as he grinned. "I thought you liked the Mr. Clean look."

I liked the feel of his bald head rubbing against my inner thighs. Just the memory had me clenching my legs together as I throbbed for him. Last night was too much—and not enough. I wanted more.

When the girls were done and had headed up to shower, Rye touched a strand of my oil-soaked hair. "How were you going to do this yourself?"

"I can comb my own hair, Rye." I wasn't that helpless.

"Why is it such a struggle for you to let people—no, to let *me* help you?"

I shrugged. "Because I'm stubborn? Isn't that what you told me?"

"You are stubborn. And you might have bugs. Want me to check?"

I shivered at the thought of those parasites running around my head. I saw the critters when I closed my eyes. I was going to have some nightmares over this. "Let me help the girls get the oil out, and I'll be right back."

I did need to help them and do another load of laundry. And while I stalled, I almost hoped he'd left. As exhausted, physically and emotionally, as I was, I was too vulnerable to deal with Rye.

But he was still waiting at the dining-room table when I returned. "Ready now?" he asked. "Or do you have to run a marathon?"

I felt as if I already had. "Funny."

"No, I've never met anyone with as much energy as you have, Mary Ellen." The dimple flashed. "Especially last night."

"You don't have to stick around, Rye. This isn't fun."

"Why do you keep trying to get rid of me?"

Why did I? I sank onto the chair next to him and laid my head on the towel the same way the girls had done. As he gently combed through, checking for bugs, making sure no eggs had been left in my hair, I let myself enjoy his attention, his care. And I let myself fall a little in love with Rye.

Debugged, life returned to normal. At least, as normal as it could be when I worked two jobs, raised two daughters alone…and lived two lives: one in which Rye was just my friend, for whom I worked decorating houses; and one in which Rye was my lover, who met me at those houses and made love to me in every conceivable position. That first night, he'd given me more orgasms than Eddie had in eleven years. The rest was extra. And there were a lot of extras with Rye. Hair combing was only one skill he possessed. Another was as a lover. He was also my best friend's little brother, as I was reminded when Jenna interrogated me a few weeks before Christmas.

Jenna dropped to the corner of my desk and let out a lusty sigh. "I just can't understand him."

"Who?" I asked, hopeful she'd found a man. I'd been pestering her to do so, as much as Jenna let anyone pester her.

Rye had also added his concerns about her workaholism to mine, but she'd merely flipped him off. And then pointed out that neither of us was in a position to criticize.

She snorted. "Rye. Who else? You see more of him than I

do since you're working with him, you must know what he's gone and done."

"What?" I asked, dread roiling through my stomach.

"Gotten involved with some woman with kids. Can you imagine?"

Actually I could. "What's wrong with that?"

"Nothing personal, Mary Ellen. But this is Rye we're talking about. He's too young to hook up with a woman with all kinds of baggage."

"What do you mean?"

"Kids," she said again, a wealth of meaning in the word.

"What's wrong with kids?"

"Nothing, but Rye doesn't need to be raising some other man's kids. He's too young to take on that kind of responsibility."

I'd known older men who couldn't handle it. My daughters' father, for example. "Rye's a responsible guy."

"Exactly. And that's why this desperate single mother latched on to him, I'm sure."

Heat flushed my face, and I stammered something.

"I'm not talking about you, Mary Ellen. You're not desperate. You're doing really good on your own. And you would never take up with Rye, he probably seems like your little brother, too."

Nothing about Rye made him seem like my brother. "To me, he's just Rye."

"Exactly," Jenna said triumphantly, missing my point. "But you see a lot of him, have you got a load of this woman yet? I want to have a little talk with her."

Already done. "Um, if you haven't seen her, how do you know about her and that she has kids?" What had Rye said? For a Special Ops marine, he didn't know much about sneaking around.

"I found some Christmas gifts at his house on the hill. As usual, his generosity knows no bounds…"

Didn't I know it? What had he done now? "Really?"

"He was putting together some bikes, and he had some books and DVDs." Exactly what my daughters wanted. How did he know them so well? Because he cared. We were obviously far enough beyond fun and games to make Jenna nervous. And she didn't know the half of it. Sadly enough, neither did I.

Jenna jumped up from the desk and paced the office, full of nervous energy. "I just hate to see him get involved in something like this—sharing kids with an ex, sharing the woman with him, too, probably."

Not if the guy was Eddie, which he was. I opened my mouth, almost ready to confess.

"Don't ever say this to Rye," she continued, "because I'll deny it, but he's a great guy."

The best man I'd ever known, Daddy included. I nodded, fighting emotion, fighting the love I felt for him.

"He deserves to be number one," she said. "You know, some lucky girl's first, last and only. He doesn't deserve someone else's sloppy seconds."

Sloppy seconds. I swallowed hard at the sting of that. But wasn't that the truth? Wouldn't that be all I could be to him?

Jenna was being honest. If my little brother were involved

with a divorced woman, I might have the same emotions, the same conviction that he was being cheated.

"I think he's in deep this time, deeper than he was with old Big Eyes. But I don't want to see him doing something stupid. Rye deserves the best, you know…" She sighed. "I've gotta find out who this woman is."

Now I was too chicken to tell her. Because now I knew when before I'd only suspected, if I admitted to Jenna how involved Rye and I were, I wouldn't just lose Rye, I'd lose her, too.

Breaking off with Rye wasn't something that I wanted to do, or knew how to do. All I knew was being dumped. Why couldn't Rye just dump me?

"Karaoke tonight," he said as he swept in the back door, while I was starting dinner for the girls. "Mrs. Jacques agreed to sit."

I shook my head, wishing we had the privacy for another discussion, the one I'd decided was necessary since my talk with Jenna. "I don't think that's a good idea." For anybody…from Mrs. Jacques to the poor unsuspecting bar patrons whose ears I would assault with my singing.

"Chicken," he clucked.

The girls giggled as they set the table.

I shook my head. "No, that's not it." Not all of it. "Mrs. Jacques just doesn't seem herself lately. She doesn't have much energy. She's been sleeping most of the day. She's not even interested in our driving lessons."

Rye rubbed a hand over his head, where some hair had

grown back. It was short, dark and soft-looking. I wanted to feel that against my thighs, too. I swallowed my longing sigh.

"You don't think she's feeling well?"

"I don't know. I've taken her to a doctor a couple of times. She hasn't said anything was up." But I was worried. My elderly neighbor had come to mean a lot to me.

"She loves spending time with the girls. She said they make her feel young again," Rye said, using the phrase Mrs. Jacques had oft repeated.

I couldn't deny that. "Okay, but about the singing…"

Both of the girls covered their ears. "Don't sing, Mom. Don't sing!"

"Very funny," Rye said, his dimple winking at them. "Your mom has a beautiful voice."

"You must be tone-deaf," I said. When I'd taken the musical-aptitude test in school, to see what instrument I should play, my music teacher had advised me, "Don't." And Rye wanted me to sing.

"I know what I like," he said, his gaze burning as it traveled over my body.

I snorted. "Yeah, right." And because I was tempted to lean across the counter and kiss him, I pulled back, turning to the girls who were watching the two of us with little smiles playing across their mouths. "Girls, please go see if Mrs. Jacques wants to join us for dinner."

They shot past Rye and out the back door.

"You really are worried about her," Rye observed. "Is that why you haven't been coming to the houses alone lately?"

I'd been bringing the girls and leaving before their bedtime, usually missing Rye or spending only a little time with him, supervised by two smart little girls who had started to wonder just how close Rye and I were. "She's been really tired lately, and I hated thinking that might have been because she watched the girls so late some nights." Those delicious nights I'd been with Rye as more than friends.

He blew out a sigh of relief. "And I thought you were avoiding being alone with me."

Guilty. And I *was* a chicken. But who was I more scared of? Rye or Jenna? Should I give up my pleasure being with Rye for my friendship with Jenna? Maybe I was scared that she was right—that Rye deserved better than me.

Rye and Mrs. Jacques joined forces and talked me into trying karaoke. The girls kept groaning, until I reminded them that they weren't coming. Then they offered Rye earplugs, the little smart alecks. Mrs. Jacques followed me upstairs when I went to change.

"You're sure you're up to babysitting?" I asked, concerned about the dark circles around her sunken eyes. With all the sleep she'd been getting, how could she still look so tired?

She nodded. "Of course I am. It's movie night with the girls. I haven't seen *Home Alone* enough times yet."

I laughed. "They do get into a rut."

"You know I love them. I love spending time with them." She blinked hard. "They have come to mean a lot to me. Elmer and I never had any kids of our own. They're like the grandchildren I never had. And you're like my daughter, Mary Ellen."

Now I blinked back tears and pulled her into a tight hug.

"That's so sweet." And if I'd had a loving, supportive mother, she'd be Mrs. Jacques. "You're very important to us, too. Although sometimes, I feel like I take unfair advantage of you."

She patted my cheek. "You have no idea yet what kind of person you are. You're always going to give more than you take. That's just you, Mary Ellen Black."

I shook my head. "No, you do much more for—"

She pressed her fingers over my mouth. "When Elmer died, I did, too. I locked myself away in that house and refused to live. I think I felt guilty that I was still breathing. But I wasn't living. I wouldn't let myself. You made me live again, Mary Ellen. I can never repay you for that."

I hugged her again and let the tears roll.

She patted my back now. "I didn't come up here to mess you up, dear. I came up here to give you some advice."

People had done a lot of that lately. Jenna's still burned in my ears. "Okay."

"Wear something sexy, dear. Have fun. Enjoy life the way you made me enjoy it again."

"I do enjoy life."

"And that boy's had a lot to do with it. But you've been avoiding him lately."

"It's getting too serious, Mrs. Jacques. And that's not fair to him." My heart hurt, admitting it aloud, but I had to face the facts.

"Think of yourself for once, Mary Ellen. Do something because you deserve it! Have fun tonight!"

Be selfish? Wasn't that all I ever was? Wasn't that why I hadn't had that discussion yet with Rye? Because I didn't want to hurt myself, more than him? But fun was all this was supposed to be, this thing between Rye and me. So what would it hurt to have fun one more night?

Then tomorrow I could let him go… Maybe.

Happy hour was over, but the crowd hadn't thinned any at the hole in the wall where Rye had taken me, northwest of Grand Rapids, in a little town called Nunica. Smoke filled the air, hiding our identities. Not that it was needed, since, at Mrs. Jacques's urging, I'd done more than ever before with my hair, makeup and clothes. If anyone I knew saw me, I wouldn't be recognizable anyway.

The way Rye kept staring made me wonder if he liked what he saw. Did he appreciate the extra mascara, shadow and lipstick, and the hot red dress that I'd taken from Jenna's closet and worn tonight just for him?

Maybe tomorrow I'd have that discussion with him that I knew I had to have. But I deserved tonight, I decided, just as Mrs. Jacques had said. She'd brought her toothbrush, pajamas and bathrobe and had advised me to do the same when I went home with Rye. God, I loved that widow woman. And tonight I'd follow her advice, and there were no worries, just a sloe gin fizz, a smoke-filled bar and a drop-dead-gorgeous man at my side…rubbing his knee against mine under the table as he played with my hand.

"So, you ready?"

I'd never be ready for this to end. "To go back to your place?" I asked, dipping my head close to his.

He shuddered. "Oh, yeah…but first you're going to sing."

I shook my head and took another sip of the drink, enjoying the warmth of the alcohol as it spread through me. Or was that the warmth from Rye's lazy caresses? "You really don't want me to sing." I continued the argument we'd started at the house and hadn't finished all the way to this remote corner of the world.

He chuckled. "Looking as you do, I don't know if I want you up on that stage. I'll have to fight off all the guys who'll want to steal you from me."

I shook my head at his outrageous compliment. "I doubt that…at least, once they hear me sing. They'll feel sorry for you then." Up onstage, not far from where we sat, an older guy in bib overalls killed a Frank Sinatra song. But compared to my singing, his voice was as smooth as Pavarotti's.

"The whole point of karaoke is to have fun, Mary Ellen. No one cares how you sound." His fingers tightened on mine. "Isn't that what we're all about?" That last question carried a trace of bitterness. We'd gone beyond that, and we both knew it.

"You first," I challenged him.

He laughed. "First, I'm going to use the little boys' room." Another challenge flickered in his dark eyes; is that how he thought I saw him? As a little boy? I'd never known more man than Ryan O'Brien, and I'd begun to suspect that I never would. "Can I leave you alone, or should I take you with me?" he teased, even more fire rising in his eyes.

I waved him off. "I'll be fine."

No one who'd seen me come in with Rye was likely to accost me. The glare he threw around the room before he stood up and strode to the restroom was just extra. I finished my drink while I waited for him, knowing that I'd need the false courage if I was going to get up on that stage. And given Rye's challenging mood, I knew there was no way he'd let me out of it.

Someone else had gone up. A new voice cut through the smoke, a deep, dark voice, rich with emotion, singing Roy Orbison's "Pretty Woman"—much better than Roy ever had. I turned to find Rye onstage, gesturing toward me. Oh, he was singing "Pretty Woman," and tonight I fit the title. I stood up, swayed a bit on my heels, then strode toward the stage where Rye dropped to his knees and lifted me onto the stage, to an explosion of applause and shrill whistles, mostly for Rye. He was gorgeous and he could sing. But a few of those whistles were for me. Tonight I wasn't a mother or divorcée or a disappointing daughter. Tonight I was just a sexy woman…about to make a fool of herself. More applause followed the end of Rye's song, giving me a little time to tell the woman running the machine what I wanted to sing. Then, voice cracking with nerves, I broke into Shania Twain's "Any Man of Mine." Laughter broke out, women laughing with me, not at me. So my nerves settled a bit, although my palms were still damp on the microphone. I may not have sung the song well, but I belted it out with enthusiasm and got a standing ovation at the end.

Rye spun me around and coerced me into a duet of Tim McGraw and Faith Hill's "Let's Make Love." More than my palms got damp during that number…with Rye staring deep into my eyes as his sexy voice rumbled close to my ear. Above the applause after the song, someone called out, "Get a room!"

We didn't need a room. We had a few houses to choose from, and I was wondering which was closest. But after helping me from the stage, Rye didn't head toward the door, but stopped in the middle of the dance floor and pulled me into his arms. A new performer onstage was singing Dolly's "Always." I melted against Rye's chest and feared the reality of that song as I admitted to myself what I felt for him: love. And despite knowing that I had to let him go to be fair to him, I would love him always.

He drove faster than I'd ever known him to go. When he pulled into his driveway, he didn't come around to open my door, in his usual gentlemanly fashion. He pulled me under the steering wheel and out on his side, then kept me pressed tight against him as he unlocked the door to his house.

I barely had time to admire that he'd opened up the porch so that it now wrapped around the house as it had when the place had been built over a hundred years ago. But Rye didn't want to talk houses, anyway. He was in no mood to talk. He lifted me up and threw me over his broad shoulder, patting my behind as he climbed the stairs to the second floor.

"We might fall through—"

"I fixed it. And I'm going to fix you in a minute."

"Promises. Promises."

"I'd make you promises, but you're not ready to hear them."

He was right. "So just shut up and kiss me."

He gently swatted my butt again before tossing me onto a soft mattress. I bounced once; then his body covered mine.

And I wasn't bouncing for a while. Something silky slipped around my wrists, then tugged at them. Rye trailed kisses down my body, then something silky bound my ankles, anchoring me to his new, antique four-poster bed. "Rye!"

"Scared, Mary Ellen?" he taunted as his fingers trailed up my legs. I wasn't scared of him or what he was doing to me, but of what I felt for him, yes, that terrified me.

"Come on, this isn't a good idea. I can't touch you back." I struggled against the bonds. "Hey, just what did you do for Special Operations? Torture?"

He chuckled. "I'll never tell. But if you're a very good girl, I'll give you a chance to be bad, and I'll let you tie me up."

With that kind of incentive, how could I continue to resist? Especially when his torture began…

"I love this dress," he said as he slipped a hand beneath me to tug at the zipper. He loved the dress so much that he didn't entirely remove it, but worked around it. And boy, did he work! Kiss after kiss, on my lips, my throat, my breasts.

My fingers clenched, aching to touch him, to feel the softness of his new hair, the stubble of his dark jaw, the satiny smoothness of his rippling muscles. He knew about torture…intimately. As he knew me. He kissed the inside of my elbows, the backs of my knees…all the places that had me shifting convulsively against the sheets and murmuring his name.

"Rye, please…"

"What do you want, Mary Ellen?"

"Untie me!"

"No." And his lips brushed over mine, his teeth plucking

at the fullness of the bottom one, then soothing the spot with his tongue. My tongue met his, stroking it, tempting it. He entered my mouth, tasting me, groaning as his fingers stroked my breasts, rolling the nipples, making me arch as close to him as my bonds would allow. As he would allow...

But I didn't feel controlled. I felt free, free to enjoy every sensation and give nothing back, free to take. And I took. First he drove me into a frenzy with the nimble stroke of his fingers, while suckling my breasts. I whimpered as I came. Then his mouth trailed down my body, and his tongue replaced his fingers, playing over my creases and folds before diving into me. His soft hair brushed the quivering muscles of my inner thighs. I screamed as I came.

Then he sheathed himself with a condom and drove into me, again and again until I exploded...physically and verbally, screaming his name. When we had recovered, we reversed positions. I bound him to the four-poster bed and showed him my love. I trailed my hair and lips over every inch of his magnificently muscled body. I took him in my mouth, deep in my throat and milked him until tears leaked from his eyes and he groaned my name. But Rye didn't hold in his passion. When I rode him to ecstasy, he shouted his love.

To be fair, I couldn't reciprocate.

My mom's minivan was parked in my shared driveway when Rye dropped me off early Saturday morning. "Save yourself," I said with a sigh as I hopped down from the truck.

Despite our night of passion, he was subdued. More than

physically tired, he was emotionally exhausted, probably from giving so much and getting so little in return. I couldn't speak the words he wanted to hear even though they dwelled in my aching heart.

He nodded, then said, "Don't let her get to you."

Easier said than done. But it was easier than it had been because I now had friends, like him and Jenna and Mrs. Jacques. "I need to talk to you," I said, gathering up my courage for later.

"I know." He pulled the door shut and drove off before setting a time and place.

I dragged in a deep breath before I stumbled through my back door, probably looking like something the cat dragged in. And Mrs. Jacques's cats could really drag in some nasty-looking things.

"Finally," my mother said from her vigil at the kitchen table. "I can't believe you stayed out all night. What kind of example does that set for your children?"

"Are they up?"

"No, not now."

But they had been. Oh, God. "Is one of them sick? Hurt? Are they all right?"

"Now you worry," she scoffed.

After nearly thirty-one years, my patience with my mother had finally run out. "Cut it out and tell me why you're here!"

My tone brought her to her feet. "Amber called me late last night. Nobody knew how to reach you."

"They have Rye's cell-phone number." Had the battery run out? Had we been out of area? "Is she all right?"

She finally relented. "The girls are fine. Mrs. Jacques is not. When I got here, I called an ambulance."

"Where is she? Which hospital?"

"Butterworth." Mom called it by its old name, like most of the West Siders did, ignoring the merger that had changed its name to Spectrum Downtown.

I jingled my keys. "You can stay, right? I have to be there for her." She had no one else.

Mom nodded, and her face softened. She reached out, squeezing my hand. "I'll keep praying for her. But it doesn't look good, Mary Ellen."

The doctor repeated this diagnosis when I found Mrs. Jacques in the ICU. "The cancer's progressed even faster than we suspected it would."

"Cancer?"

"You didn't know?"

I shook my head. "She never said a word."

His mouth tightened. "If she would have gotten to us sooner…but by the time she did, it was too late. All we could do was wait."

For her to die? I fought back tears. "But…" She'd never said anything, never told me.

"If she didn't tell you, she probably didn't want to be treated differently."

"Can I see her?"

He nodded. "She comes in and out. And she's heavily sedated."

"The pain?"

"It hasn't been bad…until now. But she won't—" Last.

The pain would be over soon. And so would my friendship with one of the sweetest people I'd ever known.

Tears rolled down my face as I settled onto the chair by her bed. I took her hand in mine, squeezing the wrinkled flesh, as my mom had squeezed my hand before I'd left, offering support. Knowing I'd need it. "Mrs. Jacques, I'm here…"

Her lids fluttered, then opened. "Mary Ellen…did you have a good time last night?"

I nodded and answered honestly because I knew it was important to her. "The best." Then I asked, "Why didn't you tell me…about this?"

She smiled faintly. "You know why. You got me living again. I didn't want to stop." She grimaced and shifted in the bed. "But it's quitting time now, Mary Ellen. Time to be with Elmer. You'll take care of the cats, won't you?"

I held tighter to her hand, hoping to hold her in this world. Elmer had had her for over thirty years. I wanted her just a little while longer. "I'll take care of the cats and you. You have to stick around for Christmas."

She shook her head. "It would have been fun with the girls. But it's over now. I think I just waited for you…"

As she said the words, her last breath sighed out. The buzzing machine confirmed what I already knew. She was dead.

It was quitting time.

Stunned, disbelieving, I sat in the chair nearest Mrs. Jacques's casket. Morty Schwartz the lawyer shifted against the back of the chair next to me.

"It's true, Mary Ellen," he insisted. "She left you everything." And everything was more than the cats, more than the modest house next to mine. Everything included a small fortune. "Elmer Jacques was an investment banker who had done very well. They lived modestly, never using a tenth of what they had. I'd suggest getting a good financial adviser. Or if you leave the money where it is, you can live quite nicely off the interest and never work again."

But I liked working. My job with Jenna wasn't all irate calls. Some of it was gratitude, the kind that Sheryl and Jimmy had shown when they'd moved into their new house to await their baby's birth. Happy, healthy, bright futures full of possibilities! Mrs. Jacques had given me that and so much more. "Why me?" I asked for the tenth time.

Morty smiled. "She may not have known you long, but you made quite an impression on her. You taught her to drive."

I wouldn't call parking in the zoo parking lot driving. "That was nothing."

"It was something no one else had taken the time to do. You gave her time."

Not enough. More tears fell, despite the fact that I thought I'd cried them all. "I don't feel right about this."

"I talked to her at length. She wasn't reacting from the cancer or from gratitude. She really wanted you to have this. It meant more to her than anything had in a long time. Accept it gracefully, Mary Ellen."

Accept it gracefully, I'd heard that before. Maybe it was time I took the advice. "Okay, but I'm not sure I want to use the inheritance." I'd probably save it for the girls, for college, for weddings, for their epidurals, if their HMOs wouldn't approve them.

In carrying out the rest of Mrs. Jacques's wishes, there was no visiting time, just a quick service before we laid her in the ground. Rye came, as did my girls and my mom and dad and grandma. Jesus even came, as they'd closed the shop that day. I appreciated how the neighborhood rallied around.

After the small meal following the service, I sent the girls home with Mom and Grandma. Although Rye tried to come back home with me, I waved off his concern and his love. I couldn't deal with it now. I was too weak. I might say what was in my heart. So I went home alone, as alone as Mrs. Jacques had been for the ten years after Elmer had died. The silence was so deafening I almost went next door to get the cats. Anything would be better than this relentless quiet with only the company of my own thoughts And nowadays I had a lot more going on than a cricket orchestra.

The doorbell pealed. I scrambled to answer it, hoping Rye had ignored my request to be alone. But it wasn't Rye.

Eddie stood in the doorway, his eyes taking in the place he hadn't seen yet. Had he heard about my inheritance already and come with his hand out? Maybe hoping I'd give him enough to buy his mistress back from Siggy? I'd heard the restaurant was doing better. If he was smart, he'd be grateful Siggy was running it. But Eddie had never been smart.

"If you came to see the girls—" which would be a first "—they're at my mom's."

"I came to see you, Mary Ellen."

I was too tired to fight, so I simply walked away from the door and reclaimed my chair, Mrs. Jacques's reading chair. Uninvited, Eddie stepped inside, at least having the sense to close the door against the snow that swirled around outside. The girls would love it. It just might be a white Christmas if the stuff stayed on the ground for another week and a half.

"You don't have your tree up yet," Eddie observed. "That's not like you."

I merely shrugged despite the thoughts rolling through my head.

"But then, you're doing a lot of things that aren't like you…like singing in a dive bar."

I laughed. I couldn't help it. "How the hell did you hear about that?" Despite being just a couple of days ago, it seemed a lifetime away. So did Eddie.

"I was there."

"Only place they don't card your girlfriend?" The flush on his face confirmed my wild guess. I laughed again.

"You think it's funny? A mother of two crawling all over some young stud in the bar?"

He should have seen how I'd crawled over Rye later. "I get enough criticism from my mother, Eddie. If that's all you came to do, get out!"

He started again. "You weren't that woman for me, Mary Ellen, the woman you are for him."

"What?"

"Even at nineteen, you were never that wild. You were never that fun." Like Eddie would know fun. But we'd had some good times, had two good kids. For a while I'd forgotten that; Eddie had yet to remember.

"If you could be that woman for me, I'd want you back," he said, his eyes dark and intense.

I snorted. "Really moving, Eddie."

"Come on, Mary Ellen. We have kids together. It would be the right thing to do."

If I could be some wild, sexy thing… But that wasn't me. At least not all the time. "You remembered the kids, Eddie? I'm surprised. You never see them, never have anything to do with them. What did you buy them for Christmas?"

"What?"

"Did you get them presents?"

"You always buy the presents." And put his name on them. He'd never picked out a single gift since he'd married me, not the way Rye had, on his own.

Eddie dragged a hand through his thinning hair. "You don't want to give him up? O'Brien?" He grimaced. "When he roughed me up to pay the child support, I thought Jenna had put him up to it. That's just the kind of thing that bitch would do. But I didn't think you would."

"I wouldn't."

He nodded. "I didn't think so. So he did it on his own. And from the look on your face, you didn't know about it."

Taking care of me or taking over? Why did Rye constantly want to help me, by whatever means...sex, violence, love? He was too much. And Eddie was not enough. "That's none of your business, Eddie. My life is none of your business."

"Mary Ellen—"

"You had me for eleven years and never knew who I was. It's too late for you to find out. I'm not this woman for Rye. I'm this woman for me." And when I had that discussion with Rye, and now I had the strength to do it, it would be true.

After the door slammed behind Eddie, I sank into the silence...and for the first time in my life, I enjoyed being alone.

After a few days of packing up Mrs. Jacques's clothes and books for Goodwill, I stopped by the mortgage brokerage office. Vicki gave me a quick, pained smile, then grabbed up her purse and headed for the door. "Where are you going?" I asked, but she was already gone. I turned around to find Jenna leaning against the doorjamb, her arms crossed over her chest.

"I'm sorry about Mrs. Jacques." She'd told me that already but had been too busy to attend the funeral of a woman she'd never met. I understood that. But from the expression on her face, there was something she didn't understand.

"Thanks," I said.

She nodded, all sympathy gone, as her expression hardened even more. "So you found Mary Ellen Black, and she's a lying slut."

Now I knew what she knew. "Maybe."

"So you're not going to bother denying it?"

"What's to deny?"

"That you've been sneaking around with my brother. That you've been using him."

I winced but met her gaze head-on. "You think I'd do that? You think I'd use him?"

She shrugged. "I don't know what to think. I can't believe you could get involved with him at all."

"You were the one who told me to find a young stud for sex."

"Not Rye!"

No, I hadn't used Rye as a young stud.

"I made you choose between my friendship and a man once before," Jenna went on, "and you chose the man. What will you do this time?"

I sighed. "Don't bother issuing ultimatums, Jenna. I heard you before. I don't want Rye to be anyone's second, either, not even mine. I'm ending it." I didn't need anyone. I wanted Rye, but I didn't need him. And maybe when he saw that, he wouldn't want me. Because maybe it was just the hero in Rye that made him think he loved me because he thought I was weak and helpless. I wasn't.

"It never should have started."

"At least I had the balls to try," I retorted. "Mine. Not someone else's in a jar."

"What are you talking about?"

"Todd."

She dissolved in laughter, sliding down the doorway to sit on the floor. "You think I have Todd's balls in a jar?"

"For cheating on you. You would, Jenna."

The laughter dried up, and she got to her feet. She ducked into her office, then came back, handing me a Christmas card. A nice-looking family stared back at me: handsome, smiling husband, young adoring wife and twin babies clasped in their arms. We'd gotten several of these, thank-yous for loans Jenna had done. But when I flipped over the card and read the message, it wasn't a thank-you. "*It takes two, Jenna. Todd,*" I read aloud. "That little prick. He should be ground up into hamburger in the shop."

She nodded. "I should've asked your dad, but Todd was already gone."

Gone but not forgotten. He made sure of that. I hugged her tight, forgetting the grievances between us. "You'll be okay. You'll meet someone. You'll be happy like Mrs. Jacques and her Elmer. Like Siggy and his Edna. You just have to try."

"What about you, Mary Ellen? If you dump Rye, will you be happy?"

I was touched that she cared. But I knew she was more concerned about Rye than me. I smiled. "Sure, I found out being alone isn't that bad. I can handle it."

I couldn't handle breaking up with Rye, but I couldn't put it off any longer, for Jenna, him or me. It wasn't fair to any of us. When I drove the Bonneville up to the house on the hill, the first thing I noticed was the ladder leaning against the turret. My gaze traveled up the rungs, then over long, denim-clad legs and the tightest, sweetest butt any man had a right to possess.

Rye glanced down as I sat in the car. Then, slowly, he climbed down. He was a smart man. He probably knew what was coming, had probably known since the first night we'd gone from friends to lovers. Now could we go from lovers back to friends? Or was that as impossible as everyone always swore it was?

He pulled open the passenger's door and dropped onto the bench seat next to me. "So this is it?" he asked, his tone heavy with dread.

I nodded. How like Rye to make it this easy. And if it was easy, why did it still hurt so much?

He sighed. "So Eddie told you. I figured he would when I saw him at the bar that night."

"You should have told me, but you were protecting me again."

He shrugged one broad shoulder, nearly brushing it against mine. If he touched me, my resolve would fold. Despite my brave claims, I was that weak because I was that in love. "Why does that make you so mad?"

Was I brave enough to be as honest as I needed to be, as Rye deserved? I summoned my courage. "Because I think protecting me is the only interest you have in me."

He laughed, with bitterness rather than humor. "You think what we do together, you think I'm protecting you?"

Better than Eddie ever had. Rye never forgot condoms, never put me at any risk. "Yes."

He sighed and squeezed the bridge of his nose, as if he had a headache. Maybe I gave him one. "So that's why you're ending this? Because I protect you?"

I shook my head in denial and at how silly that sounded. "It's not about me really." If it were, I'd never let him go. "It's about you, about what you deserve. You deserve to be someone's first."

"You think I need a virgin?"

Now I laughed. "Medically that might not be possible nowadays, not unless you go quite a few years younger. I meant first…"

"Husband? We've never talked marriage, Mary Ellen. All you agreed to was fun and games."

"And we both know it went further than it should have." At least for me it had. And our last time together Rye had used the L word.

"Why?" he asked.

"I've got baggage, Rye." And sometimes it got damn heavy to carry around alone. But then, alone wasn't as scary as it used to be.

"And with my childhood, crazy family and the job I did in the service, I don't?"

"No ex-wife. No kids. Not like my baggage, no, you don't."

"So if I'd been married and divorced, too, then you wouldn't be breaking up with me?"

"I don't know…but as it is, it's not fair to you…"

"So you're protecting me…from you?"

I groaned and pushed my fingertips against my eyelids as a headache threatened. And there was no doubt he was responsible for it. "You're twisting everything I'm saying."

"No, I'm telling it like it is, and I wish you would, too. Where did you get all these half-baked ideas? Jenna? My big sister trying to protect me? You're trying to protect me? I'm a freakin' marine, Mary Ellen. I can take care of myself and—"

"Me? And the girls?" I shook my head. "No, I don't want that. I want to take care of myself and the girls." And the amazing thing was that I was doing it.

"So you're cutting me out? Just like that?"

The most painful thing I'd ever done? Just like that? Hardly. My heart hurt so bad that I finally understood the breaking analogy. That's exactly how it felt. It hadn't felt that way when I'd packed Eddie's bag so he could leave me for another woman. And we'd had eleven years together. But ending my short time with Rye was the hardest thing I'd ever done, harder even than moving back in with my parents. "Rye…"

He jumped out of the car, slamming the door with such force that the old Bonneville shook. Despite his reaction, I knew he wasn't mad. He was hurt. I'd hurt him.

All these weeks of rebuilding my self-esteem was kind of shot to hell in that moment. But in the long run, he'd thank me. He'd see that I wasn't what he wanted. If he needed to make up for the abuse his mother had suffered at the hands of his drunken father, then he needed a wounded woman to help, to protect. I couldn't help him work through his past, through his childhood…but I could help him build a wonderful future, working at his side. Partners. Not hero and waif. I was no waif.

I was Mary Ellen Black.

"So you broke up with him?" Jenna asked as we slid into a booth at the Coppertop. The twinkling Christmas lights didn't lift my mood. These days nothing did, not even with Christmas only days away.

I nodded, even though she couldn't see me around our menus. "Hope he can take back those Christmas presents."

"Why? He'll give 'em to the girls. He didn't break up with them."

He didn't break up with me either. This time I did it. And I didn't feel very good about it. "That's really nice of him. The girls will love the presents."

Jenna sighed. "I guess I should be happier about all this. First time you chose me over a man and followed my advice, but I… Hell, I don't know." She lifted her frosty mug full of red beer. Better than green, I guess.

"I didn't choose you over a man," I maintained.

"But you did. I can't believe you dumped me for Eddie last time, but this time you'd dump Rye…" She shook her head. "Even a sister can see that he's quite a catch."

How much beer had she had? "I didn't dump you for Eddie."

"But you married him."

And Rye hadn't asked. I squeezed my eyes shut and prayed for sanity. "Yes, because I thought I loved him. Now I wonder if it was ever really love." Because I know I'd never felt about Eddie the way I did about Rye. "Or marrying him was just a way to get out of my mother's house. Eddie was the booby prize."

"You can say that again." She snorted. "But that makes sense. I always wondered if you really loved him that much… enough to give up years and years of friendship."

"I'm a good little Catholic girl." Who had tied a marine to a bed just a couple of weeks ago. "I was raised to do the right thing. Marrying the father of my baby was the right thing, at least that's what my parents said."

"If they told you to marry Rye, would you?"

"I'm not nineteen anymore." And after what I'd done to the marine I'd had tied to the bed, I was hardly a good girl.

Jenna sighed heavily. "Thank God. Don't think I could live through all that again."

This was worse. Losing Rye, especially so soon after Mrs. Jacques. One of my grandmother's superstitions popped into my head. You always lose people in threes. First Mrs. Jacques, then Rye…now who? Jenna? Could our friendship overcome my sleeping with her little brother and not telling her? So far we seemed fine. But then, I'd been preoccupied by the gaping hole in my chest and might have missed something.

"Mary Ellen?"

"What?"

"Are you okay?"

I nodded. "Oh, yeah, fine."

"You look like shit. Did you love him? And don't lie to me."

I nodded. "Still do."

"Then why choose me over him?" The wail in Jenna's voice suggested she felt some guilt.

I was hurting enough to relish it. Then I had to be honest. "I didn't choose you over him. I chose *me* this time."

"What?"

"Rye needs someone to take care of. I don't need that anymore. And if I stayed with him, I might start needing that."

"Are you smoking crack? Where are you coming up with this stuff?"

"Some of it from you. You said it wasn't fair to Rye to step into someone else's life."

"Eddie never had a life, not with you and the girls. Rye wouldn't be stepping into that little prick's shoes."

She didn't know the half of it. "Why are you doing this now? You were against the two of us. What changed your mind?"

Color flushed her thin face. "Okay, Rye isn't talking to me. Told me I interfered for the last time. I think he might even go back into the Marine Corps."

I tossed the menu down, eating was out of the question. "Would he go back in?"

"Hey, he hasn't said anything. He's just working on the house on the hill, but…"

"He won't talk to you." I sighed. "You never listened anyway, Jenna. We told you a million times that you need more than your work."

"So do you."

"I have more." And because I was so ticked off, I told her exactly what. "I have my daughters, my family, and I'm even going back to school."

"What?"

I nodded. "I'm going to take interior design courses."

"Why? You're already doing the work. When you do Rye's house in Heritage Hill and he gets it in the tour, you'll have all kinds of business."

"Jenna." I couldn't think about doing that house with Rye. Pain squeezed my heart over the lost opportunities.

"Okay, we won't talk about Rye. But I heard you got a job lined up redoing Siggy's place. Nobody even knows where he hangs upside down at night. It's a real honor that he'd have you there."

I think he'd had Grandma there, too. Daddy said that she'd been going out at night. "I really enjoy decorating," I said, speaking my dream aloud. "I want to learn more about it."

"So, are you quitting? I heard you got some money in Mrs. Jacques's will."

I'd thought about quitting, about saying goodbye. Doing anything with anyone who had any connection to Rye might hurt too much. But it would hurt more to give up everything to do with him. And it would hurt more than that to give up my renewed friendship with Jenna. I might not have chosen her over Rye, but I still wanted her in my life. I still wanted Rye in my life, if I was honest with myself.

"I'm staying. Probably only chance I'll get to see you is at work, and since it's only part-time, I'll be able to work around my classes."

"Good," Jenna said. "Somebody else might have stopped talking to me. You have a right. I should have stuck by you no matter what decision you made when you married Eddie and when you screwed my brother. That's what friends do. I haven't been a very good friend, Mary Ellen."

I reached across the table, covering her hand with mine. "I shouldn't have let our friendship slip away, either. It meant too much to me, then and now. I'm not a very good friend, either, Jenna."

She linked her fingers with mine and squeezed. "Guess since we're such lousy friends that we're stuck with each other, huh?"

I nodded. "Guess we are. Nobody else would want us."

Somebody snorted nearby, and I glanced up to see Vicki's brother-in-law, Ted, nodding in understanding and disgust. "Hmm, now I'm your lesbian lover," Jenna mocked. "Just when I was thinking about giving in to your badgering and Rye's to get a life and start dating again. Now no man will have me."

I had to say it. "Jenna, no man would have you before they thought you were a lesbian. You scare the crap out of all of them."

"Then they're not man enough for me." She took another swig of her beer.

She was right, as usual. "I'm sure there's somebody out there for you, Jenna. And now that you've agreed to start looking, you'll find him."

"Ditto. But you already found yours. You just have to tell his bitchy big sister to mind her own freakin' business and go for it."

I shook my head and slumped back against the booth. "I'm not ready to go for it yet. I don't want to lose myself again." And Rye was the kind of man in whom a woman could lose herself. She'd enjoy every minute of it, but she'd be lost all the same.

"I can still take him," she offered, "if you want me to beat the crap out of him for you. Then he'll need you to protect him."

I had to laugh at the image of petite Jenna taking on her towering mountain of a brother. "No, thanks. Do me a favor, though?" I asked.

"Anything." It wasn't a flip reply; I knew she meant it.

I drew an envelope out of my purse and slid it next to her beer. "Give this to Rye."

"A love letter?" she asked, hope flickering in her eyes. If she thought it was, she'd read it. There was no privacy with Jenna.

I had to laugh. "No. A deed."

"You're giving him back your house?"

"It was never mine. Tell him I'll be out after Christmas." Maybe I'd have Mrs. Jacques's house cleaned out and redecorated by then. She would have been my first customer; she'd asked me to start on her house, but we'd never gotten around to it. There hadn't been enough time. I ached with missing her. Now living in her house was the right thing to do, for more reasons than just that the cats knew where the litter box was.

"You two had a deal. That house was yours for all the work you've done on the others. He's going to be pissed."

It wasn't the first broken deal between us. The fun-and-games rule had been the first casualty when I'd fallen in love with him instead. "It was too much." All of it.

Enrolling at design school wasn't easy. The admissions office wanted to see a portfolio. I didn't have pictures to represent my work. I had sales of the houses I'd decorated. The school officials didn't understand that and suggested that I might find what I wanted at the community college.

Walking through the halls, passing young girls in floppy hats and thigh-high boots and guys in wool turtlenecks and baggy pants, I surmised that school might not be for me. I might not fit in. But I pretty much hadn't fit in in my own house since birth. Now those drawbacks of clothes and age weren't going to stop me from trying.

Yet age had stopped me from following my heart. How stupid was that? I was still pondering that thought when my new cell phone jangled. I wrestled it from my bulging purse as I slipped and slid down the sidewalk to where I'd parked the Bonneville. As I flipped the phone open, I hoped it was Rye, that somehow he'd found my number. "Hello?"

"Mary Ellen."

I could barely understand my mother after that, sobs choked her voice. But from every other word I picked up, Daddy was in the hospital. She thought he'd had a heart attack.

"Which hospital, Mom? I'll be right there."

"Butterworth."

Thank God, I was close. Rushing to get there I couldn't help but wonder: could Daddy be my third?

The first person I saw as I came through the automatic doors of the emergency room was my grandma. "I did it!" she cried, her face flushed.

"What?"

"I gave your father the heart attack. He walked in on me and Siggy playing strip poker. Keeled over right there in the doorway. Oh my God! I killed him, Mary Ellen!"

"Is he dead?" My heart lurched, and I swayed on my feet, grabbing hold of Grandma's thin shoulders.

She shook her blue head. "Not yet. But it doesn't look good. I did it. It's not right, Mary Ellen. I owe your father so much. He'll never know…"

"Yes, he will. He'll be fine. Calm down." Or she might have a heart attack herself, especially after playing strip poker with Siggy.

"Your father saved the store, the house, or I would have been just like you when your grandfather left. Everything lost to his stupid gambling debts. Never had my luck. Your father's a good man, Mary Ellen. I should have told him that…instead, I killed him!"

I waved a nurse over. "You have to get her something to calm her down. Please." And if Grandma was this bad, how bad was Mom? "And I need to see my dad, Frank Black. Where is he?"

"I'll bring you both back. Follow me." Was that bad? Weren't they supposed to limit the number of relatives brought to see the patient?

"Mary, Mary Ellen," a creaky voice called out from the waiting room. I turned back to see Siggy, juggling two paper cups of coffee. His shirt was misbuttoned and untucked, one suspender dangling from beneath his suit jacket. The last thing either he or my grandmother needed was caffeine. And it had been my bright idea to hook up the two of them.

The nurse stopped and glared at me. "Is he family, too?"

If she thought my grandmother, my mother and me too much family, what would she think when the rest of my family and the neighborhood showed up? I shook my head and called back to Siggy, "We'll be right out."

He settled onto a hard chair. "I'll wait."

I nodded at Siggy and hurried after the nurse who was leading my grandmother by the arm. I couldn't lose her, too. I couldn't lose any of them. And now more than ever, I wanted Rye. I wanted to have one of his mammoth shoulders to lean on.

But I'd dumped him. And now there was only me.

The nurse jerked back a curtain, revealing an area only big enough for the gurney on which my father lay. My mother, squeezed in between the wall, the gurney and a beeping machine, clutched at my father's hand. "Mary Ellen, thank God you're here," she said.

For nearly thirty-one years, I'd hoped she'd have that re-action one day when I walked into a room. But today it didn't make me feel better.

"I'm here, Mom. I'm here, Daddy," I said, squeezing in be-side her to trail my fingers over Daddy's arm.

An IV was sunk into the beefy appendage, pumping flu-id in below his tattoo from the navy. Thin plastic tubes fed oxygen into his nose, and every once in a while, a blood-pres-sure cuff squeezed his arm, reading the level and displaying it on a screen in the corner. Two hundred nine over one hun-dred twenty. Even with my limited medical knowledge, I knew that wasn't good. "How is he?" I asked Mom.

She shook her head. "They hooked him to all these machines when we brought him in, but nobody's told us anything."

I turned back to the nurse, who hovered over Grandma, taking her pulse. "Fast," she mumbled. She didn't know about the strip poker or the guilt.

"You can give her something, right?" I prodded her. The woman had made promises…

"I'll have to check with the doctor, see what meds she's already on."

"She's not on anything."

Daddy groaned. "Damn hag…" His face contorted into a horrible grimace.

"Is he going to be all right?" I asked.

"We're still doing tests. The doctor will talk to you later."

Anger churned in my stomach, threatening to eject the tuna salad I'd had for lunch. "The doctor will talk to us *now*. We need to know what's going on!"

Mom grabbed my arm with her free hand, clutching tight. "Thank you."

The nurse studied me for a minute, no doubt seeing the look I give to the girls when I mean business, the look that says homework better be done, baths taken and pajamas on—it's bedtime because Mom's had enough. God, I'd had enough. I didn't want my father tucked away in a corner behind some curtain, hooked to beeping machines, while no one knew what was going on with him.

The nurse nodded. "I'll get the doctor."

She didn't say when. I should have noticed that. I should have held her to a timetable. Instead, I clutched at Daddy's hand, struck by how old he looked lying back on that small gurney. When had he aged? When had his black hair gone so gray? When had so many lines appeared on his face, skin hanging over his jaw and sagging on his neck? Where had my big, strong daddy gone?

"She's getting a doctor to tell us what's going on," I repeated to Mom, in case she'd missed it. "I'm sure it's nothing. Heartburn. Probably too much spicy jerky, that's all." The blood-pressure reading called me a liar, and so did the fear dampening my palms and throbbing at my temple. I glanced over at Grandma, not liking the gray cast to her skin. "Grandma, he's going to be all right. Don't worry."

"She's worried?" Mom muttered, as shocked as I was. And she probably didn't even know about the strip poker; she must not have been home when it was going on.

"So what happened?" I asked, shaking my head as Grandma started to answer. "Mom?"

Her fingers clenched my arm, then trembled as she loosened her grip. "I don't know…I got home from shopping. And he was kneeling in the doorway, clutching his chest. But he wouldn't let me call for an ambulance. We drove him in. Mr. Ignatius had his car…"

All the color drained from her face. I'd spied another chair on the other side of the curtain. I pulled it into our cramped space and pushed her into it. "Sit down, Mom. He'll be okay." I made that promise despite having no control over the outcome, except praying and harassing doctors. And if one didn't get in here soon, they wouldn't know harassment like I'd give them.

Daddy's fingers squeezed mine. "Jesus—Jesus—"

Grandma vaulted to her feet and clutched at Daddy, activating his blood-pressure cuff. "Oh my God, he's praying. This is it! Don't! Don't walk toward the light!"

"Grandma, he's not dying." Although his blood pressure had gone up a bit more. "Sit down! Calm down!"

"But he hasn't been to confession in years." Mom's voice cracked as she added her comments. "Maybe I should call Father Michael. I better call Father Michael."

Daddy lifted up, rattling the tubes connected to him. "Call Jesus!"

"He sees the light!" Grandma shrieked. "Walk away from it! Come back to us!"

"Shut up," Daddy and I said in unison, my voice louder and stronger than his.

"Do you mean Jesus?" I asked Daddy, pronouncing it the Spanish way.

"Yeah, Jesus. Tell him to close the store tonight…I won't be coming back."

Mom dissolved into wrenching sobs.

Grandma collapsed back into her chair. "He won't be coming back."

"Just tonight. Jesus just needs to close the shop tonight. Daddy will be back there!" I'd make damn sure of it, if I had to clear his arteries myself.

"Call Jesus, Mary Ellen…" Daddy said on a sigh as he slumped back against the gurney.

"I will, Daddy. I'll take care of the store until you get back on your feet, and that'll be soon."

He squeezed my hand. "Good girl…"

If his condition were more serious, wouldn't they have him in surgery now? Wouldn't they have more than that beeping machine monitoring him? I probably had time to call Jesus. "Mom, did you call Bart?"

She shook her head as silent tears rolled down her face. "Just you… I knew you would know what to do."

She did? Had Mom had a stroke when Daddy had the attack? Because something had changed her mind about me, and it would take a medical miracle for that. But her expectation put more pressure on me than her disapproval ever had. Because she expected that I'd know what to do, I had to know.

"Okay, Mom. I think we should let Daddy rest for a while. Why don't you and Grandma go out—"

"Weren't they going to bring her a sedative?" Mom asked.

I doubted that would be anytime soon, but I wasn't about to share that notion with Mom. "She's calmed down now."

And miraculously she had. She sat in her chair in a near stupor. Hell, maybe it was safest to leave her with Daddy and send Mom out to check on Siggy. Or maybe it was safest to do that myself while I made some phone calls. And tracked down that lying nurse. "I'll be right back, Mom. Do you want anything?"

She shook her head. "I'm fine, honey." Honey? Was this my mother? "You better call Father Michael. Your father hasn't been to confession in years…"

Yeah, it was my mother. "Daddy's going to be fine, but I am going to call Bart to let him know what's going on."

"I hope he doesn't drive up. The weatherman said we could get a snowstorm off the lake later today." Always a mother…

I squeezed her shoulder. "I'll tell him to stay there, and I'll call him after we talk to the doctor." If we ever got to talk to a doctor…

I spotted our nurse at the crowded, noisy station in the middle of the E.R. "Miss—"

"A resident will be with you as soon as he can get there," she swore before rushing off to pull another curtain aside and tell more lies to other patients and their families.

I twirled around on a heel, trying to find an exit. I glanced at my watch. The afternoon was wearing on fast, as was my patience. I had to make some phone calls. First, Jesus, because I'd promised Daddy.

I followed another woman who looked as if she had a clue which way was out, and fortunately I wound up in the waiting room.

Siggy jumped up, sloshing coffee over the rims of the paper cups he held in his hands. Fortunately, it had to be tepid coffee by now. "Mary Ellen, how is he? And your grandmother?"

I shrugged. "No news yet. I've gotta make some calls before the resident goes in to see him. And the nurse asked if they can prescribe something for Grandma. She's calmer now, though."

He expelled a shaky sigh. "That's good."

"Thanks for getting my dad here." Although an ambulance probably would have been faster. "But you really don't have to stick around. We'll be fine."

His jaw grew taut. "I want to be here…in case your grandmother needs me." They'd only been going out a couple of weeks, and already they were this serious? They weren't exactly hormone-driven teenagers. But then, the strip poker suggested that hormones were involved.

"That's sweet." And if that nurse had lied about the doctor getting in to see Daddy, I might have to ask Siggy to turn his boys loose on her. "Can you do me a favor?"

He perked up. "Anything."

"Can you get my mom and grandma some tea from the cafeteria? And maybe some crackers." I didn't want either of them passing out from hunger while we waited.

He rushed off—as fast as a hundred-year-old loan shark can rush—toward the sign that pointed toward the cafeteria. How come there weren't such helpful signs in the depths of the E.R.? I hurried outside to use my cell phone. My first call was to Bart, who I promised an update to as soon as I heard.

Concern and frustration vibrated in his voice. "Mary Ellen, call as soon as you hear something. Maybe I should just drive up, anyway…"

"Why?" I asked, answering the question myself. Because I needed him. Daddy needed him. Mom needed him. Because I couldn't handle this on my own despite Mom's newfound faith in me. Instead of those answers, I said, "It might just be heartburn, and then we'll all feel stupid for having you drive all this way."

He blew out a breath that rattled through the phone. "I'm glad you called. Sounds like you got everything under control."

"I'll call you as soon as I hear something." I repeated that promise when I called Jesus about closing the shop tonight.

"Mr. Black was not himself today, Mary Ellen. He kept rubbing his chest. His face was red. I told him to go home to rest awhile." He'd probably thought Daddy had had too much beer and cigarettes. And he was probably right.

"That was wise, Jesus. I'm glad you did. He'll be fine, I'm sure." Yeah, right. I glanced at my watch again as the sun sank lower in the sky. Night came early in December in Michigan. The cold whipped around me, pelting me with flurries that were more ice than snow. I didn't want the girls riding the bus, especially not home to an empty house. And I could call Jenna, but she was probably working.

This wasn't the time to keep my distance from the man I'd just dumped. The girls didn't need their father, not the man who'd never offered them anything in the way of emotional support. They needed Rye. I needed Rye.

My fingers trembled as I dialed his number.

"Hello?" his deep voice rumbled in my ear.

His phone had caller ID, and I could tell from his hello that he knew it was me...and that he questioned why I was calling. But he had still answered.

Despite my dumping him, Rye would still come when I needed him. "Rye, I'm at the hospital."

He sucked in a breath. "You're all right? The girls are all right? Jenna?"

"We're all fine. Daddy's had...a heart attack or something. I'm still waiting to talk to the doctor."

"Do you need me to pick up the girls?" He knew.

"Yes, please. I'd really appreciate—"

"I'll take them home and get them something to eat. Call if you want me to bring them up to the hospital, or if you... need me."

I was calling. I needed him. "Thanks, Rye. I'll be fine. Just take care of the girls until I get home."

"Mary Ellen...take care of you." The connection broke.

"Thank you," I said, but he wasn't listening anymore. I had to be in control again. I didn't have the luxury of leaning on anyone. Because I was the one who people needed to lean on this time. And if this was a test of my newfound resolve, then I could handle it. But when it was all over and Daddy was home again, smoking and drinking in the garage, then I would fall apart.

"I'm scared, Mary Ellen," Daddy confessed to me from his hospital bed.

He'd been admitted after a long, long night in the E.R. where test after test had been run. As I had always feared, some of his arteries were clogged. But I found no comfort in knowing about this problem, not when the only solution was surgery.

I threaded my fingers through his. "You'll be fine, Daddy. You're as strong as a horse."

The doctors agreed. They'd said a weaker man would have died already. And while Daddy's arteries were severely clogged, some over ninety percent, he hadn't really had a heart attack. His heart was strong, even strong enough to withstand walking in on a couple of half-naked senior citizens.

Daddy squeezed his eyes shut, a tear leaking out from one corner and trailing down the side of his face. "You're such a good girl, Mary Ellen."

"Daddy…"

He brought my hand to his mouth, kissing my knuckles. "Such a sweet girl…right from the day we brought you home from the hospital. I never loved anyone the way I loved you, the way you love your girls."

So much it hurt sometimes just to look at them, to watch them sleep, to see them smile or cry... I knew what he meant. "I love you, too, Daddy."

"I've made a lot of mistakes in my life. Did a lot of things I should be sorry for."

Mom had called Father Michael. Where was he? A man of God should be hearing Daddy's confession, not me. I didn't want to learn about all the things my father regretted in his life. From the way Siggy feared him, I imagined there were plenty.

I had always seen Daddy as my big, strong protector, but today I needed to protect him.

"Daddy, shh...it doesn't matter. Forget about the past. Concentrate on the future. That's what's important."

He rolled his head back and forth on the pillow, nearly dislodging the oxygen tubes from his nose. "I don't know if I'll come through this, Mary Ellen."

My stomach lurched. "You will, Daddy. Don't talk like that. Don't think like that."

"I'll lie to your mother. But not to you. You're strong enough to handle the truth. I can see that."

I don't know what he saw, because I didn't feel very strong at that moment. "Daddy..."

"My biggest regret is your marriage to Eddie. I shouldn't have made either of you. You would have been fine without him. You're doing a great job with the girls, Mary Ellen, with your life. I'm proud of you."

I blinked tears from my eyes. "If I hadn't married Eddie, I wouldn't have Shelby, Daddy. I'm happy with my life."

"Always so forgiving. So unselfish," he murmured. "I'm glad you're happy with your life. But you need more. You need to take more…for you."

I shook my head. "I have more than enough." Except Rye. I'd talked to him last night, briefly. I'd thanked him for his help. He'd taken care of the girls the rest of yesterday and all night, no doubt calming their fears more than I had with my call.

I had assured them that their grandpa was going to be fine, and I instructed them to be good for Rye, to do their homework and go to bed early. I even wanted them to go to school the next day. Today. Outside the hospital-room window, the sunrise turned the sky pink behind the thick, wintry clouds. More snow was on the way today.

"All I need is for you to get better, Daddy."

He sighed. "I've done some things, Mary Ellen."

"You saved the shop for Grandma. She told me about it yesterday. You protected your family, always. You're a wonderful man, Daddy. You'll be fine." In this world and the next. But he wasn't going to the next yet. I tightened my grip on his fingers. "You'll be here for Christmas."

"If I'm not…"

"Don't think like that—"

He shook my hand. "Listen, I need to tell you some things. If I don't make it, I need you to take care of the shop. You can run it or sell it, whatever. But you'll need to handle it. Your mother's never had a head for business. Neither has your grandmother."

"Daddy—"

"I put some money away, too." Protecting the future of those he loved, how like Daddy. "I got a couple of accounts, and some cash." Of course. "The cash is taped to the bottom of the fridge in the garage. You'll have to have Rye tip it for you. You'll remember this?"

I nodded. "Yes."

"Morty the lawyer has my will. You're the executor. You'll take care of your mother?"

"Of course, Daddy, but you don't have to do this. You'll be fine." I wasn't going to see Morty the lawyer again this year. I'd seen quite enough of him.

"And if your brother doesn't make it here today…tell him I love him." Daddy squeezed his eyes shut, but more tears leaked out and his voice broke when he continued, "Tell him I'm proud of him. I've always been proud of him."

I nodded. "I know. He knows, too. But you can tell him yourself. He'll be here soon."

And so would Mom and Grandma. I'd had Siggy take them home last night. I'd hoped they'd gotten some sleep because it was going to be a long day. For all of us.

"So where are the girls?" Mom asked as she sat next to me in the waiting room. She loved them so much, maybe having them here would have helped her. But I hadn't wanted them here, worrying, like the rest of us were.

For the tenth time I told her, "School."

"How'd they get there? You never went home last night. Who's been watching them?"

"Rye."

Bart, hearing this for the first time, stopped his pacing and glanced down at me. "So you and him are…"

"Friends. Just friends." Although maybe we weren't even that anymore.

He studied me a while longer. "Just friends? That's kind of a lot to ask of *just* a friend, isn't it?" Little brothers can be such pests.

Barb, who sat nearby at a table playing cards with Grandma, glanced over at us. "My mom could have watched them for you, Mary Ellen. She wouldn't have minded. She wasn't too happy we left her only grandson in Chicago with a neighbor." I don't think Barb was, either.

"I wish you guys wouldn't have risked the icy roads," I said again. "I would have called if—"

Bart shook his head. "I wanted to be here."

I stood up, stretching my muscles, cramped from the long night I'd spent slumped in the chair by Daddy's bed. "I've gotta walk around a bit."

Mom stood, too, apparently reluctant to be parted from me, like yesterday. Bart was her favorite. Why wasn't she turning to him? "You stay here, Mom. Rest."

"But the doctor will want to talk to you, Mary Ellen, when he comes in."

I glanced at my watch. "He'll be a while yet."

A quadruple heart bypass took a while. We had time. "I'll be back in a few minutes. Maybe I should talk to Jesus."

She let me go, probably not even noticing that I hadn't used the Spanish pronunciation. The chapel was empty. Only faint light penetrated the stained glass to splash across the pews. Outside, a storm raged, and inside me as well. Daddy wasn't the only one who was scared. I was scared of losing him, of having Mom lose him. She loved him so much. I dropped to my knees and closed my eyes.

God, I've never been very good at praying. It's probably because you gave me so much without my asking...but I should have thanked you. I just didn't realize what I had and what mattered.

My SUV that had been towed away on the back of the repo truck, that didn't matter. Neither did the expensive house on the outskirts of town. Nor a marriage I hadn't fought very hard to keep, so I'd probably never really wanted it.

What mattered was people, like Mrs. Jacques who had died too soon and my father. They mattered, not possessions, not any of the material things I'd lost or gained, only the people.

My girls, my dad, my mom, my brother and his wife and son, Mrs. Jacques, Grandma, Jenna, even Siggy...and Rye. Rye mattered. Before I'd thought he'd mattered too much. Now I knew it was just enough. And I mattered.

It was all right for me to need people, to need Rye. I had to call him, but when I turned to leave the pew, Mom had slid in beside me.

"I knew you were coming here," she said on a sigh, her rosary wrapped around her hand. "You never call Jesus Jesus. You always know how to pronounce it right...unlike your father."

I laughed softly. "Daddy knows how to say it right. He just refuses."

"He's a stubborn man."

I squeezed her hand. "Yes, he is. That's what's going to get him through this."

"You're so like him. So headstrong, so determined. I admire that about you."

"Mom?" I really didn't know this woman she'd become since Daddy had entered the hospital.

"I know I'm hard on you, too hard. Your father has yelled at me about it. Your grandma has. Even your friend Mrs. Jacques did."

How like her to defend me, even to my own mother. I missed her. "Mom, this isn't the time. We need to concentrate on Daddy right now."

"I wasn't there for you, Mary Ellen, not when you were growing up, not when you went through this nasty divorce with Eddie."

She thought that was nasty? I hadn't threatened him with a meat cleaver. I had packed his bags and let him walk away, no threats of retribution for cheating on me, for treating me like dirt. I just let him wipe his feet on me on his way out the door. And despite a couple shows of temper when he lost our house and wanted me to be for him the woman I was for Rye, I hadn't given him what he deserved.

"He's here, you know…"

"Rye?" I asked, eager to see him, not surprised that he would have come for me, had known I needed him right now more than I ever had.

She shook her head. "Eddie's here."

The vulture was circling. I stood up, finally prepared to shoot that bird out of the sky.

Mom clutched at my arm. "Mary Ellen, I need you to understand."

"What, Mom?"

"I love you."

"Oh, Mom, you make me crazy," I was honest enough to admit, "but I love you, too."

She pulled me back to my knees and into her embrace. She was shaking. "I was so scared."

"Daddy's going to be all right, Mom." Had I finally convinced her of that?

She shook her head. "No, I was so scared that I'd pushed you too far away."

Instead, she held me tighter than she ever had. "Mom..."

She swallowed hard, her throat moving convulsively. But then she spit it out, "I was jealous of you!"

It wasn't the first time I'd heard it, but I still didn't understand it. "Why?"

"Your father loves you so much..."

"He loves you, too, Mom." Why else would he have put up with her nagging?

She shook her head. "Not like he loves you, loved you from the first minute he saw you. Until you came along, I was his special girl."

"Mom..."

"I know it's ridiculous, stupid, petty. I was an only child, Mary Ellen, spoiled. Until you came along, I'd never had to share. I'm not proud of myself. I haven't done anything with my life to be proud of, not like you have."

"Mom, that's crazy."

She shook her head. "I'm not a great mother like you are. God, when you became a mother, you were twelve years younger than I was when I had you. But you were better at it, better at cooking, at keeping a house…"

"It wasn't a contest, Mom."

She nodded. "Not to you. It just came naturally. Loving people just came naturally to you. Not to me. Not after my father died. I've been so scared of losing someone I love again. I love your father so much, Mary Ellen."

"I know you do, Mom."

Tears trailed down her drawn face. "Then why didn't I listen to you? Why did I keep feeding him like I was? I was killing him—"

I squeezed her arms and shook her a bit, hoping to end her fit of hysteria. "Mom, it's not your fault. Dad's got a mind of his own, you know."

She nodded. "I know. I know about the other stuff. The smoking and drinking. He wasn't supposed to be doing those, either. I pretended not to know, but I knew. I should have stopped him."

"Mom, you couldn't have stopped him. You know how stubborn he is. And because of that, he'll be fine."

We'd all be fine. Not that I didn't think she'd have moments of regression. You couldn't just stop a thirty-one-year cycle of criticism. But we were all better than we'd ever been…even with Daddy under the knife.

She smiled through the last of her tears. "You're right. I know you are. You always are, Mary Ellen."

I think I preferred her criticism to her delusions. "Mom…"

Nobody hoped more than me that I was right this time. "So why don't we go back to the waiting room? Gotta make sure Grandma hasn't talked Barb into strip poker."

She actually laughed. "Bart might like that, might get him to stop pacing. You go ahead, honey, keep them all in line like you always do. I'm going to stay here a minute, do some praying, and I'll be back."

"I should stay and say another one, too…"

"But you have to get rid of Eddie."

Just a short while ago, she would have told me to beg him to stay. Finally, she knew I didn't need Eddie. Now only Eddie had to realize it and go away…

She chuckled as she knelt back down.

"What?" I asked, surprised she could find anything humorous right now.

"I was thinking maybe you should have borrowed your daddy's meat cleaver…"

I liked this new Mom.

I hoped Bart hadn't already killed Eddie. I didn't want him doing his usual little-brother trick of stealing my fun. Maybe it was time I had a little fun with Eddie. I didn't have to wonder long if there was carnage in the waiting room. Eddie stood outside, in the corridor between the chapel and my family. I'd once thought he, with his big dreams, was better than them, and I'd left the West Side with him. But I'd left myself, too. I wouldn't have been able to find Mary Ellen Black anywhere but the West Side. My identity was found with my family, my neighborhood, my friends. They'd made me who I was then and who I am now, strong and independent.

"Mary Ellen," Eddie said at my approach. "You should have called me! I shouldn't have had to hear about this from the man who stole my restaurant from me."

"What? Stole it? Siggy made an investment, he's protecting it. God knows you're not very good at keeping things." Funny how the first thing I would take exception to was his remark about Siggy. But then, the old man was nearly family. Eddie wasn't.

"Mary Ellen! Come on. I should have been told your father was here before some old loan shark learned about it. I was Frank's son-in-law for eleven years."

I snorted, a laugh sputtering out, too. "Come on, Eddie. Get off it. The only reason you're here now is because he's under anesthesia and can't kick your ass. And the only reason you married me in the first place was because you were scared to death he'd make good on his threat and grind you into hamburger."

"I never could live up to your daddy, Mary Ellen. That's why I didn't tell you when the debts started piling up. I knew you'd run to him to bail us out. And I knew he'd go ballistic because I hadn't taken care of his little princess. He used to work for Siggy, for crying out loud!" How like Eddie, to come to the hospital when my father was in surgery, and disparage the man. "He's a thug, Mary Ellen!"

Just because Daddy was under anesthesia didn't mean Eddie was safe from an ass kicking. I clenched my fist and swung. And even with my eyes closed, I managed to connect. Tears leaked from my eyes as I waved my hand around, trying to lessen the pain. God, I hoped I hadn't broken anything. I opened my eyes, ignoring Eddie's string of curses, and inspected the swollen and bloody knuckles. "I think I broke it," I muttered, wiggling my fingers.

"You did. You broke it. You broke my nose," Eddie shrieked

as blood spurted from his nostrils. "You crazy bitch! And I was going to take you back."

Despite my injured hand, I shoved him against the wall. "We were over this before, Eddie. *I* don't want *you* back."

"Because of your young stud. Another thug. Should have figured that in the end you'd pick someone just like your *daddy*."

The only thing that saved him from another punch was my throbbing hand. Nothing saved him from my kick that dropped him to his knees. "Eddie, I still can't quite figure out why you're here. You think Daddy's not going to make it, and you can take over the shop to run it into the ground? I don't think you've got the stomach to handle raw meat. Or you think you'd just sell it off to get your restaurant back? Either way, it doesn't matter. I don't want you back."

"The girls…" he groaned, throwing out what had always been his trump card.

I nearly kicked him again. "You've done a really good job of ignoring them."

Maybe like Mom, he'd been jealous of them, jealous of the fact that I loved them so much more than I'd ever loved him. *If* I'd ever loved him. "What's the matter, Eddie? Are you alone now? Did the little waitress leave you for someone else, one of Siggy's thugs, maybe?"

When he winced, I knew I'd struck a nerve. "She did leave you. And you're scared of being alone."

And I realized I wasn't. Even if I'd blown it with Rye, I'd be okay. If any of those things happened that the doctor had warned about, and Daddy had a stroke or worse, I could handle the shop. I could handle Grandma and Siggy. Heck, I could even handle Mom. And as Eddie tucked himself into a fetal position on the floor of the hall, I knew I could handle him, too.

"Mary Ellen, you're upset, irrational…when you calm down, we'll talk again."

I shook my head, surprised at how tenacious he was. "You should have talked to me before, Eddie, before you lost everything. I wouldn't have run to Daddy. I would have helped you. Together we could have saved everything." Probably even our marriage. But it was too late for that now.

He groaned. "Not this again…"

"Exactly. Not this again. Goodbye, Eddie. You're welcome to see the girls whenever you want. I'd like you to be part of their lives…finally. But I don't want you to be part of mine."

Not anymore. And while I wasn't scared of being alone, I did want to share my life with someone, with Rye.

I reached out to help Eddie to his feet, but he flinched and shrank back against the wall. "I'm not going to hurt you," I swore as I used my uninjured hand to help him up.

And he wasn't going to hurt me anymore, either. We were done. And I think it was the first time he realized it, and understood what he'd lost. The woman I'd found with the help of my family and friends. Mary Ellen Black. She was back.

The *ding*, as the elevator doors closed on Eddie's bleeding and swollen face, punctuated my internal announcement.

Broad hands closed over my shoulders, kneading the tense muscles, and Rye's deep voice rumbled close to my ear. "Back to your corner, slugger. Need to spit? Some ice for that hand? You know you shouldn't be swinging without gloves. Usually helps if you actually look where you're swinging, too. But Eddie walked right into that one, the ass."

"Rye…"

"Hypocrite."

"What?" I tried for an offended tone, but his hands felt too good. He felt too good.

"You yelled at me for beating him up, and I didn't even hurt him that bad. I'd certainly never kick him *there*." The flinch of masculine sympathy was in his voice.

I turned in his arms, sliding mine around his broad back. "I didn't yell at you for beating him up. I didn't care about that. It was the reason why you'd done it. To get him to pay me. You were taking care of me."

He dipped forward, leaning his forehead against mine. "I would apologize…"

"You would?"

"If I was sorry. But I'm not. And I would swear to change, but I can't, Mary Ellen. You were right when you said that I need to protect you, but not because I think you need protecting." He lifted my hand from behind his back, bringing it around and to his mouth. His lips pressed soft kisses to my scraped knuckles. "Nobody who saw you beating Eddie just now could think you need protecting."

"Then why do you do so much for me, Rye?"

"Because I love you. And I won't apologize for that, either."

"Being difficult, are you?"

He nodded, a smile starting to spread. The first hint of the dimple teased his cheek. "Yeah. You don't scare me."

I giggled at the idea of my being able to scare a six-foot-three marine. "Really?"

"Actually I'm lying. You do scare me. You can hurt me more than anyone can, Mary Ellen, because I love you."

Rye was such a great guy, handsome, generous, loving... He could find someone closer to his age with less baggage, but I was going to finally take the advice everyone kept giving me. I was going to be selfish. I was going to keep him for myself. "I love you, too, Rye."

And then I knew I'd blown it again. I wasn't being selfish. Because no matter how much younger, or prettier or childless she might be, no other woman could ever love Rye as much as I did. His arms closed tight around me, but I shifted back, keeping some room between us. "And I do need you. I was glad to have you with the girls last night, but I wanted you with me. I wanted you here this morning..."

He pressed a finger over my lips. "School was called off. Snow day. I had to find someone to watch the girls."

"Who?" I hoped he'd thought of Barb's mom.

The dimple flashed as he grinned. "Jenna."

"Jenna?" With my daughters?

He nodded. "I had to arm wrestle her over it. She wanted to come up here and be with you, too. I got here a while ago and Barb told me her mother would be happy to watch them, so I gave her a call. Jenna wanted to be here, too. She's always thought of your dad as a little bit hers. We're all pulling for him, Mary Ellen. Mom's praying hard."

"Your mom could have watched the girls."

His dark eyes widened. "You wouldn't have minded?"

I knew some people were leery of her, that they thought she'd killed her husband and didn't completely trust her. But I'd just beat up my ex, and he'd never laid a hand on me to deserve it. "Of course not. I want her to get to know the girls better."

He ran a hand through my hair. "Is it any wonder I love you?" he asked before kissing me hard and long and deep.

Behind us, someone cleared her throat. "Get a room, you two," my mother advised with a quick laugh.

We followed her back into the waiting room, and I was surprised to see how it had filled. More of Daddy's family had made it, his brother and sisters, and more of the neighbors, including Jesus. This was how the neighborhood rallied, supported and loved each other. *God, thank you for making me a part of this family, this community.*

"I closed the shop, Mary Ellen," Jesus said, rushing up to

me. "I can't be in the shop without your father. It doesn't feel right. The shop is your father."

It wasn't Frank Black's name on the sign, but he'd gotten the blood on his hands to prove it was his. And it would remain his.

"He'll be fine," I assured everyone, and moments later the surgeon walked in and answered all our prayers.

"He did great. He's a very strong man. I'm sure he'll recover quickly," he said before rushing off to scrub for another patient. Assembly-line surgery, and my father had just been one part on the conveyor. But what the doctor lacked in bedside manner, he'd compensated for in skill.

Daddy would be fine. I hoped he would be home in time for Christmas. And maybe that wish would be granted, too.

Bart pried me from the throng of hugging, happy family members and pulled me aside. "I'll stay, help with the shop while he recovers. You don't need to do this on your own," he said.

I gazed at Rye, standing head and shoulders above the rest of the crowd in the waiting room. "No, I don't. And don't worry, little brother. I can handle it. You've got your life in Chicago."

"And you've got your life here." He glanced over at Rye, too. "Not just friends anymore?"

"We're friends...too."

He laughed. "Good for you, Mary Ellen, about Rye and what you did to Eddie in the hall."

My face heated up a bit. "You saw that?"

He nodded. "Long overdue."

"Probably." But my hand still hurt like crazy.

"Who knew, huh?" He laughed.

"What?"

"That even though you're the girl, you take after Dad the most."

"What do you mean? I'll just keep an eye on the shop until he gets back on his feet. I don't want to stay there. I'm signed up to attend classes." Whether the school recognized my "portfolio" or not. And whether or not I fit in with those young students.

"School?"

"Interior design. I already got a job lined up with Siggy." And Rye. I loved working with Rye. "So how am I the most like Daddy?"

He grabbed my hand, admiring my bruised knuckles. "You're a thug, Mary Ellen."

Bart didn't step into my punch but held tight to my fist. "I love you, sis." We hugged tight, then exchanged partners, hugging the next family member or neighbor until everyone had exchanged hugs in celebration of Daddy's successful surgery.

Mom didn't let me go for a while. "You'll teach me how to cook like you do? Light?"

"You mean bland?"

"Yeah."

I nodded. "Sure."

Grandma called her over to where she and Siggy sat on chairs near the window, and I turned to Rye. "Busy later?" I asked.

He shook his head. "Need me to take care of the girls?"

"No." I stepped into his arms, leaning heavily against his muscled chest. "I need you to take care of me."

The center aisle of Saint Adalbert's stretched a mile, or at least it seemed that way when you were trying to balance a heavy dress on stiletto heels. Not to mention that the wrap kept sliding down my shoulders. A strapless dress in January?

But Grandma had insisted. She thought I looked lovely in it. But with her cataracts, what did she know? Enough to win at bingo and poker. In the end, high card had gotten me into this thing. I'd drawn an eight of clovers, and she'd gotten the queen of hearts. When it came to weddings, the queen of hearts would have won no matter if I'd drawn an ace or a joker.

As I neared the next section of pews, I caught sight of Eddie near the back row. Even though his nose had healed, it slanted a little toward the left now. He waved at Amber, who walked ahead of me, her long, thick hair wound into spiral curls that trailed down her back. She lifted her hand from her bouquet, okay, a plastic poinsettia, and offered him a shy wave back.

Shelby had already made it to the altar with her skipping walk. As she stood next to Father Michael, she smiled and waved at the entire congregation gathered for the wedding. When Amber reached the altar, she stepped into place next to Shelby, careful to check for the small piece of masking tape stuck to the marble tile as her mark. Mindful of my heels and the heavy skirt, I slowed down and slid into position next to her.

My gaze skittered across the aisle to where Rye stood behind the groom. God, what the man did to a tuxedo was criminal, as were the thoughts flitting through my head. Rolling around naked on the cold marble floor might not be as hot as I thought...

Lorraine, who doubled as the church organist, struck up the first chords of the wedding march, and I wrestled my mind from the gutter and my attention from Rye to turn to the back of the church.

The bride, in antique white, held tight to Daddy's arm as they began the long trek the girls and I had just taken down the aisle. I hoped it wasn't too much for Daddy. He hadn't been out of the hospital that long, and despite how well he seemed to be doing, we all continued to watch him careful-ly. Despite his gruff objections, I think he loved all the atten-tion. Especially Mom's; she waited for him in the front pew. She'd finally given up doing her own hair and turned herself over to Lorraine's expertise. Her soft brown hair waved around her face. I'd never seen her looking happier. But then she'd probably always been happy, just afraid of losing that happiness; she'd always been where she'd belonged. With my father.

Giving away his mother-in-law brought a huge grin to

Daddy's face and a twinkle to his eyes. Fortunately, Grandma's groom wore the same expression, and like her dress, he was an antique. Siggy eagerly awaited her where he stood next to Rye; he actually leaned a bit on Rye in order to stay upright.

The wedding was sudden. But then they'd *had* to get married... No, not for *that* reason. The only medical miracle was Siggy still being alive at a hundred, or whatever age he really was, and with however many years they had left, they wanted to be together.

Daddy's heart attack had had a profound effect on us all, reminding us of what's most important in life: love.

My gaze strayed from Grandma's slow approach back to Rye. I loved Rye, more and more every day. When we'd gotten back together, I had asked for his patience. Accepting that I loved him had been hard enough for me, had been a big enough risk to my new sense of self. I hadn't wanted to lose Mary Ellen Black again by trying for more than love.

Commitment. Could I be as brave as Grandma and Siggy and try it again? But was their commitment born of courage or senility? Sometimes I wondered. Especially when she'd picked the plastic poinsettias as bouquets.

Now, the green velvet dress she'd chosen for me and the girls, while heavy, was gorgeous. And as Lorraine had sworn when she'd seen them, complemented my new do to perfection. Except it wasn't my new do anymore. It was just me.

And this love between me and Rye wasn't so new anymore. It wasn't just infatuation or based on need and needing to be needed. It was real and built to last, like Rye.

Finally Grandma reached the altar. She and Daddy stopped just before Siggy. Daddy lifted her veil and pressed a kiss to her wrinkled cheek. Despite his sweet gesture, I caught the comment he whispered in her ear, because for Grandma to hear, he had to make his whisper loud. "Good riddance, hag."

"Screw you, too," she rasped back, her smile wide and full of affection. I'd always thought their banter malicious, but now I knew it was just their way. Underneath they cared about each other. The glint in Daddy's eye as he shook hands with Siggy warned the old man to take care of his new bride.

Siggy nodded, then released Daddy's hand to clasp Grandma's. Father Michael came to them, and maybe in deference to their age or because of their previous marriages, he skipped most of the mass and proclaimed them man and wife after they shakily repeated their vows.

Rye held out his arms, one for me, one for the girls to fight over, and we followed the new bride and groom down the aisle. They walked fast now despite their creaky joints, eager to begin their life together. A beginning where other people would be waiting for it to end at their age.

Discounting the senility, I had to give them credit for guts. Because, at my age, thirty-one today, hadn't I just been waiting for my relationship to end? For Rye and I to break up again?

Maybe it was time I thought about this kind of commitment, too. I was brave enough now.

*Turn the page for another exciting NEXT read
that will have all your friends talking.*

If you enjoyed this story, you'll want to pick up
OUT WITH THE OLD, IN WITH THE NEW
by Nancy Robards Thompson, available in September by
Harlequin NEXT.

Confession time. I'm not going on the annual girls' weekend with Alex and Rainey. But how do you tell your best friends you're breaking a ten-year tradition because you don't trust your husband enough to leave him alone for two nights?

It's embarrassing. Humiliating.

Rainey would hate Corbin if she thought he was having an affair. And Alex—she'd kill him. Then they'd both rally around me, like a prizefighter's coaches who were training for the kill.

I'm not ready to deal with it. Saying it out loud makes it so…real.

I can hear Alex now. "Kate, if he's cheating, your staying in town isn't going to stop him. So you can't miss our weekend." And that would inevitably prompt her to add, "If you even *think* he's cheating, why don't you hire a private detective and find out for sure?"

Don't think I haven't considered hiring someone. But for God's sake, it hasn't even been a full twenty-four hours since the bomb dropped. I need time to think, to sort out my options and figure out how to deal with the aftermath, should I discover the man I sleep with every night is being unfaithful.

This ugly jealousy is so new. All I can think of is this time yesterday I trusted my husband. I loved him and was so sure he loved me.

Right now I don't even know my next move. Let me figure that out first. Then I'll sic Alex on him.

So instead of leveling with them, I resort to diversionary tactics. "Palm Beach is too stuffy." I sink into the couch cushions and slant a glance at Rainey. I catch her almost imperceptible eye roll.

"Come on, Kate." Alex scowls at me. "You've managed to pooh-pooh every suggestion we've made tonight. South Beach is too wild. Palm Springs is too boring. Napa's too far." She says this in a singsong voice that makes me want to jump out of my skin. "New York's too... What was wrong with New York?"

I shouldn't have come tonight, but after what happened today, I've been running on autopilot, trying to regain my equilibrium. Quite unsuccessfully, I might add. So I can't blame them for being annoyed. I'd be irritated with me, too. Especially since this girls' getaway is the last one we'll take as *thirtysomethings*.

Yep, the big four-oh looms right down the pike. For each of us, one right after the other. Boom, boom, boom. I'm the first of the three to cross that dubious threshold in May. Alex turns right after me in August—

Turns.

Turns? That's horrible. It sounds like one day we're light and lively and the next we're soured milk. I'd never thought of it that way and wish I hadn't because it gives me yet another reason to dread *turning* forty. Anyhow, Rainey is the baby of the bunch. She *turns* in November.

We started the annual girls' getaway the year of our thirtieth birthdays. So in a sense this year is a double celebration—ten years of annual getaways and our foray into the fabulous forties. I guess that makes me a double party pooper.

"Must we decide this tonight? It's late." I stand up and prepare to leave, ignoring the pair of disapproving looks.

"Palm Beach is perfect. It has spas and shopping. What more could we ask for? All in favor of Palm Beach?"

As I pull my car keys from my bag, the two of them raise their hands, voting yes, looking at me with equal parts exasperation and impatience.

I hitch my Coach bag onto my shoulder. "Okay, fine. Palm Beach. Whatever."

At this point I'll agree to anything; I just want to leave before the walls close in on me. Later, I'll think of a plausible excuse to bow out of the trip. Maybe I'll even tell the truth.

Ha. What a novel idea.

*Here's an exciting sneak peek of Sandra Steffen's
LIFE HAPPENS, available this September from
Harlequin NEXT.*

"Hi, Mom. Long time no see."

Mya moved only enough to force a deep breath.

All three years she'd wondered what her child looked like. Here she was, technically no longer a child. Her pale blond hair was shorter than May's. Brown eyes cold with fury, she was the spitting image of herself at that age, belligerence, bitterness and all.

"Don't tell me you're going to faint."

Still holding perfectly still, Mya said, "I've never fainted in my life."

"Lucky you."

Although she'd tried not to, sometimes Mya had imagined a mother-daughter reunion. Some of the scenarios had been tearful, others awkward. None had depicted a skinny nineteen-year-old girl, glaring at Mya with angry eyes.

Mya glanced at her watch. "It's after midnight."

"So?"

"Happy birthday."

Elle Fletcher clamped her mouth shut. She didn't know

what she'd expected, but it wasn't the emotion burning her eyes and throat. The woman looked pretty normal. It was disturbing how much the brown eyes reminded Ellie of her own, right down to the tears brimming in them.

The hell with that! This woman wanted to cry, let her. Ellie wasn't about to do the same.

Her birth mother's name was Mya Donahue. She was single and thirty-six, and she owned this house, as well as a clothing store called Brynn's over on Market Street. Some of the information had been in the file at the adoption agency. Most of it had required a little digging to uncover. The rest would have to come from Mya, herself, if Elle decided to continue. She didn't want to. She wanted to turn tail and run as far away as she could get.

It was as if Mya knew. Her expression still and serious, she took a backward step, and opened the door farther.

If she'd voiced the invitation, Elle wouldn't have taken it. As it was, she glanced over her shoulder, torn. The night was dark, the street empty except for her rusty Mazda. She'd come this far. Might as well see if any of it had been worth it. Drawing herself up, she went in.

"Would you like to sit down?"

Elle shook her head.

"What's your name?"

"Eleanor. If you want me to answer, call me Elle."

"Hello, Elle. You're shivering."

"That's my problem. You gave up all rights to my problems when you signed on the dotted line, didn't you?"

Mya's smile held a touch of sadness. Glancing away, Elle felt a wretchedness of mind she hadn't planned to feel.

"Could I get you something?"

"I didn't come here to eat."

It must have taken a lot to refrain from asking why she did come, then. Elle stifled the thread of respect trying to worm past her defenses. Mya Donahue hadn't earned any respect. She was nothing to Elle, or almost nothing.

As nonchalantly as possible, Elle glanced out the window toward the street where her car sat, undisturbed. "I have to go." She could feel Mya watching her, could sense the questions she wanted to ask. "What?" Elle asked, and dammit, she couldn't keep her lip from curling.

Mya shook her head. "Do what you have to do, but you're welcome to come back."

Elle took flight before she did something embarrassing, like sink to the sofa and rest her head for a minute, or worse, blurt out the reason she was here. She ran to her car and unlocked it. Mya didn't follow her or call to her. But she stood in the open door in the cold, damp wind. The sight burned the backs of Elle's eyes.

Nobody said this would be easy, but it still ticked her off that it was this hard. The anger was fuel, and she used it to get out of there. She drove carefully, though, for it wasn't anger that had brought her to Maine. She was pretty sure Mya had picked up on that fact. Pulling into a parking space in the cheapest motel she'd found, Elle swallowed hard. When she was certain it was safe, she leaned over the backseat, unfastened the safety belt and took the best thing she'd ever done into her arms. Ten-month-old Kaylie sighed in her sleep, comfortable and secure.

Her daughter's warmth and weight girded Elle's resolve and renewed her courage to do what she had to do. It was possible that all the courage in the world wouldn't be enough.

HARLEQUIN®
Next™

Coming this September

With divorce and the big Four-Oh looming on the horizon, interior designer Kate Hennesy takes a step back to assess her life. Is it time to redecorate?

OUT WITH THE OLD, IN WITH THE NEW

From 2002 Golden Heart winner
Nancy Robards Thomson